PHONE FOR THE FISH KNIVES

DAISY WAUGH

PHONE FOR THE FISH KNIVES

PIATKUS

PIATKUS

First published in Great Britain in 2021 by Piatkus
This paperback edition published in Great Britain in 2021 by Piatkus

1 3 5 7 9 10 8 6 4 2

A CIP catalogue record for this book is
available from the British Library.

ISBN 978-0-349-42250-3

Typeset in Galliard by M Rules
Printed and bound in Great Britain by Clays Ltd, Elcograf S.p.A

Papers used by Piatkus are from well-managed forests and other
responsible sources.

Piatkus
An imprint of
Little, Brown Book Group
Carmelite House
50 Victoria Embankment
London EC4Y 0DZ

An Hachette UK Company
www.hachette.co.uk

www.littlebrown.co.uk

To Selina and Violet

THE TODES OF TODE HALL

THE NORTH LAWN

TUESDAY, 8.41 A.M.

The lawns that stretched around Tode Hall had turned to a drab mustard colour through the summer, making the pale stone of Britain's seventh most recognisable, privately owned stately home appear a tiny bit grubby. But there was nothing to be done. It was mid August and the county of Yorkshire hadn't seen a drop of rain in almost six weeks. On Britain's social media platforms, concern for polar bears and world apocalypse had reached yet more feverish levels. In London, Manchester, Edinburgh – even in York – furious young people were chaining themselves to buses and demanding an end to life as we live it. And in the Old Stables gift shop at the end of the drive, also in the gift shop by the ticket office, and at all three Tode Hall restaurant-cafés, there had been an unprecedented run on individually wrapped frozen lollies. In fact, across the

1

entirety of Tode Hall's retail sector, only lemon-flavoured ice pops remained.

It had been an extraordinary summer: a wonderful summer for almost everyone, and a useful one for the climate-change campaigners. Nevertheless, this being England, everyone was complaining.

Fifty-two-year-old Sir Ecgbert Tode, 12th Baronet, for example, dressed in thick corduroy jacket, polo neck and long trousers, loping across parched lawn, keying security code into private entrance, swatting at imaginary flies, was at that very moment sounding off in a negative way about his body temperature.

'It's only eight-thirty in the morning, Trudy, and I'm already hot,' he moaned. 'I'm literally *boiling*. What is going on? Can you actually believe it?'

He was leaving a voicemail for Alice Liddell, whom he nicknamed 'Trudy' for reasons never entirely clear, also fifty-two years old, and currently employed as Tode Hall's 'Organisational Coordinator', whatever that meant. Nobody seemed to know – least of all Alice, who'd been in the job for almost a year. But it was a nice job. Very low key. It came with a beautiful cottage, set behind a high hedge, in the heart of Tode Hall's ancient Rose Garden, and a small car with broken seat-belts. Alice was a lifelong Londoner, but she'd spent much of her childhood on the estate staying with her late grandmother, the late Lady Tode's lady's maid. So in a way, the Hall felt a bit like home. Sir Ecgbert was calling her this morning because he loved her. But obviously he wasn't going to tell her that.

'By the way I'm at the house,' he said instead. 'And it's like a frying pan, Trudy. An absolutely massive frying pan ...' Ecgbert's voice echoed as he entered the Great Hall. 'In fact

2

the entire country is like one massive frying pan, I've just realised. There's no escape. I'm quite worried about the badgers
in Brendan Wood. God knows how they're coping. Are you
awake? Will you come over for breakfast?'

Alice loved Sir Ecgbert as much as Sir Ecgbert loved Alice.
But she couldn't have told him that, even if she'd wanted to,
because she didn't yet know it herself. In any case, it was far
too early for breakfast, especially after such a strange and disagreeable evening. She reached an arm from beneath her thin
bed sheet and switched off the phone.

Sir Ecgbert, though its natural heir, didn't live at the Hall,
and nor, thankfully, was he responsible for its management.
This was a good thing. The Tode estate constituted not only
one of the grandest and most beautiful houses in the country,
but over 10,000 acres of agricultural land, fifty or sixty small
cottages, the aforementioned gift shops and restaurant-cafés,
a farm shop, a grouse shoot, a luxury campsite, an exhibi-
tion centre, a nursery garden, an archery school, a shooting
range ... the list continues ... It was a very large enterprise
and an important local employer: definitely not something to
be handed over to a man whom, in more than fifty years, had
yet to complete a single day in paid employment. Sir Ecgbert,
nicknamed 'Mad Ecgbert' by friends and family, would not
have made a good manager.

The estate had long been cocooned in family trusts and
clever tax-avoiding wheezes, so no single individual ever really
'owned' it anymore, in any case. But the right to reside in the

3

Hall as king of the castle (not to mention draw an income from its considerable interests) was more fluid. That right would, by tradition, have been Ecgbert's. But shortly before her shocking death, his widowed mother, Lady Tode, had decided to hand the reins to a Tode better suited to the job.

In fact Lady Tode had overlooked all three of her children. She turned instead to Sir Ecgbert's young cousin Egbert (*Mr* Egbert. Also please note the lack of a 'c'). It was generally agreed that Egbert(Mr), together with his beautiful, merry wife, India, were doing a splendid job. There had been a bit of spilled blood in the early months, admittedly, first with Lady Tode herself and then with the other fellow – but luckily no one in the family had been blamed for either death; and better still, ticket sales were up. In the year since young cousin Egbert(Mr) had taken over, visitor numbers to the Hall, already in six figures for the period, were up by 14 per cent. Astonishing. Excellent. Great news all round. Of course, the long hot summer had played its part. Ditto, the newspaper headlines, after all the bloodshed. But therein lies another story (available at all good bookshops).

So.

Ecgbert (*Sir*. Sir Ecgbert has a 'c') wandered around the house a little aimlessly, as was his wont at this time in the morning. He often arrived too early for breakfast. Since the death of his mother, almost ten months ago, he had grown in confidence and stature, and had moved from a luxury boarding house in the local town of Todeister, into a house of his own on the Tode estate. But as this was the first time he had ever lived alone, and it was early days, and he had yet to master the art of keeping food in the fridge, he tended to eat a lot of his meals at the Hall.

4

His good-natured cousin Egbert(Mr) would normally be returning to the house around now, mud-spattered and glowing, post twenty-mile pre-breakfast bike-a-thon. But on this Tuesday morning he had chosen to skip the bike ride and had joined his wife, India, in her luxurious daily lie-in.

Ecgbert(Sir) appeared to have the place to himself. The house was full of guests, as he well knew, having been present at the disagreeable dinner the previous night, but at 8.30 that morning, the place was disconcertingly quiet.

Mrs Carfizzi ought to have been in the kitchen, preparing breakfast for everyone. Ecgbert sniffed the air, hoping for bacon.

Nothing.

He pricked his ears, hoping for sizzling sounds.

Nothing.

He made his way to the kitchen. But there was no sign of life in there. Last night, at the disagreeable dinner, India had mentioned how oddly the Carfizzis were behaving. And it was true, dinner had been an unusually hotchpotch affair. Mrs Carfizzi (the cook) barely put in an appearance all evening and what food she eventually presented definitely wasn't up to scratch. Her husband Mr Carfizzi (the butler) hadn't been much more visible, and he normally adored throwing his weight around when the Hall put on grand dinners.

Uncertainty shimmied and fizzed through the 12th Baronet's long body. What was going on? Had Mrs Carfizzi, born and raised in Calabria, melted in the English heat? It seemed unlikely. But then what had become of her? Ecgbert loved Mrs Carfizzi better than he had loved his own, dead mother. Since he could be bothered to remember, she had always been there, sizzling bacon in the kitchen. Breakfast

5

and Mrs Carfizzi were (or so Sir Ecgbert felt at that instant) the only true constants in his life. And yet . . . here he was. He breathed deeply. His therapist had provided him with techniques for dealing with exactly these types of situations. He tried to remember how they went:

The Being of 'Now': *Six Steps for Feeling OK When Life Deals You Surprises*:

Breathe deeply.

Don't panic!

Remember, you are beautiful.

Bear in mind that Mrs Carfizzi is probably fine.

Perhaps Mrs Carfizzi's alarm clock has broken?

(Something like that.)

Anyway, it occurred to Ecgbert he might need to forage for his own breakfast this morning. And that was fine. An adventure, almost. It reminded him that at the end of the unsatisfactory dinner last night, India had advised guests who were still feeling peckish to help themselves from the large larder beyond the pantry, where there was 'food galore'. Chocolate cake, she said. He didn't feel like chocolate cake for breakfast. He hoped to find Mrs Carfizzi in there, and some bacon sizzling in a pan.

He wandered through the back of the kitchen, past the boot room (for boots), the gun room (for guns), the stick room (for fishing rods, long bows, cricket bats and croquet mallets), the coat room, the overnight safe, the pantry – and so on. He'd not been back here for years, and yet it still smelled the same! He used to spend hours back here as a child, stealing food, swinging off the shelves, making a nuisance of himself. Perhaps he would fry himself an egg? It couldn't be that hard. Or some sausages? God – wouldn't it be marvellous if he found sausages?

6

He was deep in thought as he pulled back the larder door, lost in breakfast imaginings, eyes down, shoulders a little stooped, according to habit. If all else failed it probably wouldn't be the end of the world to eat the cake for breakfast, anyway. Might even be delicious. Seriously. When you thought about it, what was so wrong with eating cake at breakfast?

It was a smallish room. Perhaps fourteen by fourteen feet, with deep shelves from floor to ceiling on every wall, and in the middle of the room, from the ceiling, a line of large metal hooks for hanging game. As he turned on the light, the bulb popped, but he hardly noticed. He knew the room so well.

In the half-light, his head banged softly against something bulky, swinging from the hooks. A massive pheasant, perhaps. A goose. A wild boar. Hanging low. A massive, low-hanging wild boar. Wholly unlikely, of course. But he was hungry and upset about Mrs Carfizzi. His mind was on chocolate cake and sausages, and he thought he might see them both on the shelf behind the ... the bulky object, which swung gently this way and then back, obscuring his view. Irritably, he pushed it aside. The back of his hand brushed against fabric.

He noticed shoes swinging somewhere round his hips. And then he noticed legs, and a torso, and a dark jacket hoiked awkwardly over a drooping head, and between the shoulder blades, embedded deep enough to hold the bodyweight, a rusty meat hook normally used for hanging pheasant.

A horror show.

Ecgbert reacted instinctively. The hook lodged between the shoulder blades looked agonising, and he felt compelled to do something to relieve it. The body was already stiff and cool, but he lifted it with both arms, held it tight, and *jiggled hard*. The hook stayed put – not embedded in flesh, Ecgbert realised, so much as entangled in cloth. He clambered up onto the shelves, just as he had as a child, and tried again. He leaned in, reached for the hook with one arm and yanked. A ripping sound. The hook came free. Ecgbert lost his footing, the body slipped from his grasp and, together, they tumbled to the floor.

This was all very unexpected.

THE NORTH LAWN

MONDAY, 8.41 A.M.

Rewind twenty-four hours and the vibe at Tode Hall had been nothing, if not cheerful.

It was a Monday morning. India didn't normally surface before ten o'clock on weekday mornings, but at 8.41 on that Monday morning, she was up and dressed and smelling of roses, and already en route to the Gardener's House, where fifty-two-year-old Organisational Coordinator, Alice Liddell, was drinking hot chocolate in her dressing gown. Alice didn't tend to start her organisational coordinating until later in the day. But today was an important one, and India (34 yrs) was impatient. She squinted in the morning sunlight as she ambled out across the thirsty lawn, and sighed with merry contentment.

'*I believe I can fly,*' she sang, '*... I believe I can touch the sky...*'

The Estate Offices courtyard and the grounds beyond the East Wing were already a thrilling mass of prop trucks and catering trucks, and Winnebagos and generators. The novelty would wear off soon, no doubt, but for the moment they represented nothing, to India, but excitement and glamour. For the next three weeks Tode Hall was to be taken over by a vast film crew: the house was to be used, once again, as the location for a remake of Frances Piece's famous novel, *Prance to the Music in Time*.

This new screen version was to be even more glamorous and extravagant than the last two screen versions put together: a mega-budget six-part TV series, starring two Oscar winners and, more confusingly, a newcomer spotted by chance while the director, Noah Thistlestrupp, was doing his location recce at the Hall a few months back.

Oliver Mellors, Yorkshire's handsomest gamekeeper, third generation Tode Hall employee, had been spotted on his tractor, and immediately summoned to London for a screen test where, according to Noah Thistlestrupp, he had 'burned the place up with his sex appeal'. Apparently, staff at the production office hadn't been able to sit still for hours afterwards. So – Mellors, much loved estate employee, had been given a month-long sabbatical from his job as head gamekeeper, and he was being paid more for that month of acting than the estate paid him in a year, tending to pheasants. If all went well, Noah Thistlestrupp had informed him, Mellors would never have to tend to pheasants, ever again. And his children, should he ever have any, would be able to attend the sorts of school that taught lacrosse and Mandarin.

But today wasn't about Mellors. Not for India. Today, the two Oscar winners, the series' director (Thistlestrupp), and series' most senior executive producer, Alyster Crowley, were due to stay at Tode Hall as her guests. For complicated, contractual reasons, they were also expecting the ludicrously named Rapunzel Piece, seventy-seven-year-old daughter and

10

copyright heir to Frances Piece, who wrote the famous book, who would be accompanied by her middle-aged son, Norman.

On India's insistence they would all be staying at the house for one night of pre-shoot merrymaking, and she had organised a grand and glamorous dinner to welcome them. The VIPs would be moving into a luxury hotel nearby when filming began the following day. Rapunzel and her son would be returning whence they came, and a few days later, India, Egbert(Mr) and their two young children would be escaping the mayhem for a long holiday on the island of Paxos.

There was much to organise. Or at least, to talk about. Altogether there were to be twelve guests at the dinner tonight, including Mellors, which India's husband Egbert(Mr) worried might be a bit awkward.

Should the men (India worried) be asked to wear dinner jackets? Would Mellors even *have* a dinner jacket? Almost certainly not. And if not, might the film crew costume people be able to lend him one for the night? . . . Also, Mrs Carfizzi didn't understand about offering alternative menus for people with weird dietary habits, and movie stars always had weird dietary habits. Or so India had read. Should they be offering a gluten-free menu to the Oscar winners? And if so, how to explain this to Mrs Carfizzi, whom – despite having worked at Tode Hall since the early 1980s – still seemed incapable of speaking or understanding English?

All this, India needed to discuss with her friend and employee, Organisational Coordinator, Alice Liddell. Alice, India felt certain, would have the answers. Or if she didn't, would at least make the questions go away.

India didn't know the next line of the song. But the sun was still shining.

11

'*I believe I can fly oh why ... I can fly in the sky so high ...*'

At the edge of the parched lawn, by the archway in the wall that led to the Rose Garden, India spotted a shirtless man, chubby, with shoulder-length grey locks, dressed in short running pants and open leather waistcoat. He was peering at the mustard-coloured grass, and something about the angle of his stout, leather-clad trunk made her sense, right away, that he was angry.

House and gardens had been closed to the public since the film crew arrived last week, and would remain closed for the length of the shoot. India assumed therefore, quite rightly, that he was part of the film crew. Even so, it was disconcerting to spot him there. She called out.

'Hello, sir! Hello there – can I help you?'

She noticed he was muttering to himself. She thought that perhaps he was a madman after all, and wondered, briefly, if she ought to keep away. But such caution was never a part of her character. She continued her approach, which was *en route* to the Garden House in any case, and drew up beside him.

'Excuse me – what are you doing?'

He glanced at her, an expression of liverish irritation on his face.

'Oh!' said India. 'Oh, I'm so sorry. It's – it's ...' But then she couldn't remember his name. He was the finance man. Executive Director? Chief Financial Producer? Executive Chief of Finance Production? There were so many titles. In any case, he was American, with Irish connections. She remembered that much. India had met him briefly a week or so ago, when he and a gang of them had turned up with clipboards and spent *hours* roaming around the house and grounds, muttering to each other in boring monotones. This one, she remembered, had seemed to be the one everyone was sucking up to. 'It's you!' she said. 'Sorry! I wondered who it was ... Is everything all right?'

India was easier to place, of course. Not only was she young and blonde and beautiful, she was his hostess: the owner of this outrageously expensive location. Definitely someone he wanted to please. So the liverish scowl was replaced with a broad smile. In his youth, before he got so fat and spoiled and corrupt and unhappy, Alyster Crowley had been an attractive fellow. Charming, too. Not now. Not that he much cared, either way, anymore.

He said: 'Top of the mornin' to you, Mrs Tode!' in an implausible Irish accent. She wasn't sure if it was meant to be funny. 'On this beautiful day.'

Distantly, from the field beyond the nursery garden, where the film people had put what they called their Unit Base, she could hear his helicopter winding down. Was it legal, she wondered, to land a helicopter in someone's field unannounced? In any case it was landed now. Maybe he might let her have a ride in it one day? India had only been in a helicopter once, when she broke her shin, on the mountainside in Zermatt. It had been a source of regret to her ever since, that she'd been in too much pain to look out the window.

'Everything's top-notch,' Alyster Crowley was saying. 'And I thank you for asking. And may I thank you again, dear lady, for being so generous as to allow us into your beautiful home and garden. We are blessed. *Truly* blessed ...'

She didn't say it. But it sat there, between them, and the *tuk-tuk-tuk* of the helicopter winding down, and the bright morning sun: there was nothing generous about the arrangement at all. Egbert(Mr), in his former life a Wandsworth estate agent, had managed to negotiate a phenomenal £400,000 in

13

exchange for allowing the filmmakers into his beautiful home and garden for three weeks. In addition to which his wife got to have dinner with two movie stars. It was a win–win for the Todes and for Tode Hall.

India said: 'Oh my goodness, don't even *think* about that, Brethren ... [No, that wasn't it. What was his name?] It's so exciting for us! Absolutely our pleasure. And I hope you're looking forward to dinner tonight? I know we are! Also, by the way, did I mention? It's black tie. So ... not that it matters really, but I hope you've got a dinner jacket with you! Did you bring a dinner jacket in that amazing helicopter of yours?'

'Ha ha! Mrs Tode! I wouldn't dream of coming to such a gorgeous and stunning mansion as yourself's without bringing the DJ!' He grinned at her. But his attention was really on the grass. He was paying half a million US to shoot a movie in this dung heap and the lawn looked like someone had puked over it.

'Oh I'm so pleased!' India said. 'Clever you! And isn't that lucky! Obviously I should've mentioned it before, but I didn't actually think of it until about three seconds ago. Because we can't *really* have dinner in the Long Gallery without dinner jackets! It wouldn't feel right, would it? Plus poor Mr Carfizzi. He'd have a nervy-b!'

'And we wouldn't want that!' chuckled Alyster. (Who the fuck was Mr Carfizzi?)

'Gotta wear a DJ, Brendan. In the Long Gallery. Golden rule ... It is Brendan, isn't it?'

'Actually it's Alyster,' he said. 'But me, I'll answer to anything!'

'*Alyster*, that's right.' India didn't miss a beat. She never did.

'Well – I'll catch you later, Alyster! And by the way, please, for goodness sake, call me India. Seven o'clock sharp in the Chinese Drawing Room. All right Alyster? Has Mr Carfizzi shown you where you're sleeping?'

'Not yet.'

'Oh … Well, you're a bit early aren't you? … I don't think we were really expecting you until this afternoon. Not to worry. I'm sure he'll show you when the time is right! Any problems, don't hesitate to ask!'

Alyster Crowley's mouth was still smiling. But as India turned to leave he found he couldn't stop the words from bursting out. 'We can't shoot yellow grass,' he barked.

'Hm?'

'I said,' Alyster took an angry breath, 'this is supposed to be a stately home. A perfect English stately mansion. How's anyone going to believe that, when you've got the lawn looking like *a swarm of sick cats have been pissing on it all summer?*'

'A swarm of cats?' India stared at him. Surprised to be spoken to so sharply by someone who, only seconds earlier, had been so comprehensively sucking up. Also amazed that anyone, anywhere, could be so dopey.

'Well, but it hasn't rained for weeks, Alyster. Have you been away? We've got a hosepipe ban.'

Alyster continued to smile. He wished he'd worn a T-shirt now, instead of the leather waistcoat. He could already feel sweat trickling down between his chubby shoulders. Disgusting. He said again: 'How are we supposed to *shoot a movie*, with all the cat piss everywhere?'

India laughed, in shock more than anything else. She said: 'That's not really my area of expertise tbh.' She smiled, but for once, the smile wasn't heartfelt. He was a most unattractive man. Also the leather waistcoat was a curiosity. What had he been thinking when he put it on this morning? *Also*, he was too old for shorts and his thighs were gross. *Also*, had he actually asked anyone before plonking his bloody helicopter in her field? Was that part of the contract?

'Anyway!' she said, edging away. 'I hope you have a fab day! See you later.' But then her good nature won out. 'You know what though, Alyster? You should have a chat with my husband. He might be able to help you.'

'No need for a chat,' Alyster said. 'We just need to get the grass watered.'

'Trouble is we can't do that, obviously,' India pulled a face indicating regret, 'because of the hosepipe ban. But when Eggie was working at Savills in Wandsworth and they were doing the property brochures, if the grass was looking muddy or whatever, they literally used to colour it in on the computer! *Literally!*' She chortled, miming the tiny mouse movements that would have been required. 'It's super-simple. You have to be careful not to overdo it though, or it can look mad. *Over* green, if you know what I mean? But maybe that's an idea for you? Ask him tonight!'

She dazzled him with another big, wide, blue-eyed, pink-cheeked, sweet-natured smile, and hurried on ... Maybe they should use the Yellow Drawing Room this evening, for a change? It was much grander than the Chinese Drawing Room; the two Oscar winners would be impressed ... Except she was planning to wear yellow this evening – she didn't want to fade into the walls ... Red clashed. So red was out. Black – it was too hot for black ... The Chinese Drawing Room or the Yellow? Or come to think of it, had the film people already

16

taken over the Yellow ... Perhaps the Music Room? Was the Imperial Singsong Room out of bounds? ...

By which time she had arrived at the Gardener's House. Alice would know. Probably. They could discuss it over breakfast.

THE GARDENER'S HOUSE

8.47 A.M.

Hearing India's cheerful *rat-a-tat-tat*, Alice Liddell knew at once whom to expect, and sighed, just a little, on the inside. It wasn't yet nine o'clock, after all, and her triplet sons were home, specifically to meet the movie stars – and to see if they could scrum up some work on the film set. They had missed the last direct train from London, as expected, and caught a train that involved changing in Leeds, and which had arrived at York at 2.58 this morning. Brilliantly, they had organised an Uber from the station themselves, which was a major step on their path to maturity (Alice thought). Though that wasn't to suggest there wasn't space for improvement.

Having arrived at the Gardener's House just before 4 a.m., the triplets had decided, mystifyingly, that it still wasn't quite time for bed. They had stayed up for the rest of the night, drinking tinnies and smoking spliffs, and talking in good-natured whispers, so as not to wake anyone up. Only five hours

18

later and the whole house – even, somehow, the rooms they'd not yet been into – looked like a bombsite. It always did when Alice's triplets were at home.

Morman, Jacko and Drez. Twenty-one years old. Third-year students at three separate London-based universities, studying . . . Alice often got their courses muddled up. New-fangled subjects, in any case: Geo-Relocationing. Water Distribution. Confrontation Management.

How she loved them. And how adorable they were. Mild mannered, amenable, modern. Nice looking, too. Lean and athletic and clean featured, beneath the facial hair. Very, very lovely lads, they were, every day and in every way. But right now . . .

Their rucksacks were in the hall, contents spewed across the floor. There were remnants of their 4 a.m. Nutella feast on every surface in the kitchen, and at that moment, just as India knocked on the door, they were getting ready to eat all over again. They were frying bacon, nodding their heads to their chillwave indietronica (music), jiving contentedly over their spitting frying pans.

Also present, as was becoming his habit, there sat Mad Sir Ecgbert, who had tipped up for a second breakfast. Alice liked his company very much under normal circumstances. But the kitchen felt overcrowded this morning.

Along with the triplets and Ecgbert(Sir), there was, perched at the head of the table, resplendent as ever in 1950s satin Balmain kaftan with matching emeralds, Egbert(Mr) and Ecgbert(Sir)'s grandmother, the late Geraldine, Lady Tode (1907–1971). She was a fairly constant guest. She might even take issue with the suggestion that she was a guest at all, bearing in mind she'd been resident in the Gardener's House long before Alice arrived, and would remain there long after Alice left.

In any case, Alice had grown fond of Lady Tode in the year they'd been sharing the house. But she could be difficult. Being old and very grand, and easily offended, she hated to play second fiddle to anyone. Her grandson Ecgbert(Sir) she could tolerate: she was actually quite fond of him. But she never liked it when Alice's triplets came to stay. She'd been making loud, disagreeable comments about them all morning.

'Why doesn't Alice tell those boys to pull their trousers up?' she said.

'Young people often don't pull their trousers up,' Ecgbert replied, 'Isn't that right, Trudy? It's very trendy.'

The triplets couldn't see or hear Lady Tode, but were aware of Ecgbert's eccentricities, so thought nothing of his conversational nonsequiturs. They didn't bother to reply. They were just happy to be in Yorkshire, happy about the bacon, happy about the chillwave indietronica.

In any case, one way or another, there were a lot of personalities in one room.

And there was Alice, still in her dressing gown.

And now, here was India.

Rat-a-tat-tat.

Rat-a-TAT-TAT-TAT-TAT-TAT-TAT-TAT.

(Impatient within seconds.)

'Who the hell's *that*?' asked Sir Ecgbert, lounging in the chair beside his grandmother, his excessively long legs stretching over too much floor space. 'By the way, Dregz'n'Co ... leave me some of that bacon, won't you? If you wouldn't mind. I'm actually still a bit peckish.'

'Hells to the yeppers, bro,' Drez replied. 'You kiffing beans with that, Ecgbert? Mum, have we got beans?'

'I'm kiffing beans,' said Morman.

'Why must they *talk* like that?' moaned Lady Tode (1907–1971). 'Alice, tell them to pull their trousers up.'

Alice ignored them all, and shuffled in her slippers to answer the door.

'TA-DAH!' India beamed up at her. 'Only me! Big day today! Can I come in?' She already had. 'Just met a madman on the lawn, Alice. I think we may be in for a rough few weeks. Or you may be, LOL. We're sugaring off to Paxos ... He was wearing the most appalling get-up.' She shuddered. 'By the way, do you think the costume people would lend Mellors a dinner jacket for tonight? Otherwise he's going to feel like the odd one out ... And he can be tricky enough at the best of—' She stopped. Sniffed the air. 'My goodness! Smell of cannabis *very* strong this morning! It's none of my business of course ... But do you think you might be overdoing it a bit, Alice? It's only nine o—' Again, she stopped. She had arrived at the threshold for the kitchen, spotted Ecgbert(Sir), lounging at the table, and the triplets, wiggling their lean hips in time to the indietronica, looking youthful and handsome, smoking roll-ups and frying bacon. 'ALICE!' she cried. 'What a sight for sore eyes! You didn't tell me the *triplets* were here! When did they arrive? Have they got dinner jackets? Hello boys, how lovely to see you all.'

Hugs all round. The boys loved India and India loved the boys. And then, when all that was over, Ecgbert said, 'Hi India,' and India hugged him, too, because she didn't want him to feel left out.

'Thank God the silly woman can't see *me*,' drawled Lady Tode (1907–1971), who couldn't hug or be hugged anyway, due to being a ghost; and who disapproved of all physical contact except during racy sex which, in her day, she had enjoyed very much indeed.

'Well boys, you'll definitely have to come to the dins tonight. *Definitely!* Won't they, Alice? Do they know?' She turned to the triplets (who were identical, incidentally. Identically delightful in every way). '*Do you know* – who's arriving at the house tonight?'

Of course they did. It was what had brought them to Yorkshire in the first place. But they thought, at this point, it would be more obliging to look a little gormless.

'Only the two most famous film stars literally in the entire world … Did you know they were coming?' India asked.

'Nah!' cried Jacko.

'Negatory!' Morman gasped.

'For definite, we had no idea!' agreed Drez.

India laughed. 'Of course you did! That's why you're here, isn't it?'

Dregz'n'Co, who'd only been trying to be polite, went a bit red and agreed that yes, it was true, they did know. Had known all along. Had come up to Tode, mid never-ending university holiday, in the hope of meeting the stars, and maybe even picking up some work on the set.

India said she had no doubt she could get them some work. She said she was going over to chat with the director, whose name she couldn't remember, directly after this. (She had to tell him about the dinner jackets.) If the boys came along, she could introduce them. 'But,' she said, 'and I don't want to be rude … you have to talk in normal English. You realise that don't you? Otherwise no one will understand you.'

'Damn skippy! Fo'rizzle, we know it!' said Drez. But it was a joke. Everyone laughed, except Lady Tode, who didn't get it.

India said: 'Oh my *God*, they're going to love you! And if they don't, I swear, I'll personally tear up the contract and they

22

can go and find somewhere else to make their TV series ...
Mind you, they're paying us a fortune.'

'I should hope so,' said Geraldine, Lady Tode (1907–1971).
'Of course in my day ...'

India couldn't hear her, and carried on talking. 'On which
subject ... you're going to like this bit of news, boys: Alice, so
will you. Ecgbert ...' She paused to consider it. 'I don't think
you'll mind one way or the other. By the way, what are you
doing here? You seem to be here every time I drop in. *What's
going on?*'

'Nothing!' said Alice, slightly irritably.

'Nothing at all, India. Mind your own business,' snapped
Ecgbert. 'What were you going to say, before your big nose
got in the way?'

'I was going to say,' India said, looking slyly from one to
the other, '... I was going to say ...' For a moment, she
couldn't remember. 'Oh yes! We're getting paid an absolute
fortune by these film guys. And Eggie and I have decided to
divvy it all up, as a sort of midsummer madness bonus for the
people who we actually *like* who help us on the estate. So you
mustn't tell everyone because I'm definitely not giving any
to you-know-who in the office. No one in the office, actually. And I'm not giving any to Mellors either. He's making
enough out of this madness as it is. Plus he's so grumpy these
days ... We're divvying it up ... Actually, tbh Egg and me
are keeping *half.* Because – well, you know. Obviously ... But
Mr and Mrs Carfizzi, Kveta, and you, Alice ... about four
others. Can't remember who, now ... but I've worked out
how much you're getting, Alice. And we're going to give it
to you as soon as filming is over. Shall I say how much it is,
or is it private?'

'Say now!' cried the triplets, waving spatulas, spraying bacon fat.

'There are no secrets here at the Garden House!' boomed Geraldine, Lady Tode (though only Alice and Ecgbert could hear her).

Alice was of course thrilled by this announcement. Nevertheless, being an English woman (of a certain age), she felt vaguely embarrassed to have it discussed in such a breezy manner. She glanced at Ecgbert – not that he would have cared. It was all Monopoly money to him. Even so . . .

India noted Alice's discomfort. 'I'll tell you later,' she said tactfully. 'But anyway, Alice, it's loads . . . At least, I think it is.' For a moment she was unsure. Was £20,000 loads? Or was it nothing? Or was it a medium amount? India had no head for figures, and couldn't remember *for the life of her* how much Alice was paid. So it was hard for her to tell.

THE CATERING TRUCK

10.00 A.M.

On the other side of the long lawn, tucked out of site, hunched over spreadsheets and shovelling vegan hash-browns and sugar-free beetroot smoothies into their mouths, *Prance*'s Master of the Purse Strings (Executive Producer), Alyster Crowley, was holding a breakfast meeting with *Prance*'s director, Noah Thistlestrupp.

They had requisitioned a booth in the unit catering truck and as usual, Alyster Crowley was angry. At that instant, he was focusing his ire on the colour of the grass, but really he was angry about everything: his amazingly uncomfortable waistcoat, his cold mother, his feckless father . . . His first wife, whose name escaped him. His oldest son, who had a drug problem. All the women in the world: who did or who didn't have sex with him. And so on. At that moment, on that sunny August morning, Noah Thistlestrupp was bearing the brunt of Alyster Crowley's lifetime of disillusionment. It was par for the course. Part of the job. It was how Alyster's movies got made.

25

Alyster flew in. Made life as unpleasant as possible for everyone he met. Alyster flew out again.

At that instant, he was threatening to pull a massive slice of the funding – unless somebody did something about the colour of the lawn.

Thistlestrupp was nodding along. He had his iPhone on his lap, under the table. As Alyster ranted, he was sending a text to his pregnant wife Alison (Baby No. 3. Not exciting) about the spare car key, which had gone missing.

Thistlestrupp wrote:

'Don't know sorry x'

'... £400,000 and they can't water the fucking lawn. It's fucking England, isn't it? It's meant to be green.'

'I'm actually very happy with the mustard shade,' Thistlestrupp muttered, putting the phone away. 'I've said so to Dave [Dave Snare, Series Producer]. The mustard represents decay.'

'What? What the fuck are you talking about? American audiences don't want decay. They want lords and ladies with tiaras on. They want bright green fucking lawns.'

The greenness of the lawn had already been discussed at great length, it so happened. David Snare, Series Producer, having been made aware of the situation, had presented Noah Thistlestrupp with an array of options: it would cost half a million to lay fresh green turf on top of the grass that was currently the wrong colour. That had been one option, quickly abandoned. It would cost a little less, approximately £400,000, to 'colour it in', in postproduction, as per India's suggestion earlier. And it would have cost about £200,000 for a fleet of trucks to have been watering the lawns illegally for the past fortnight ... None of these options had been taken up

26

because, by sheer, beautiful luck, Thistlestrupp, whose artistic vision was tantamount, had come to the conclusion that the mustardness of the grass was intrinsic to the message he was trying to deliver. The story he wanted to tell wasn't *Prance to the Music in Time* as per the so-called 'classic novel', which Thistlestrupp hadn't read (he'd read some excellent abbreviated notes, though). Thistlestrupp's interpretation of the book's essential message was about Modernity. To Thistlestrupp, the mustard-coloured lawn represented the decay of capitalism: the ambiguity of place, person, identity and gender; the climate emergency; the end of times.

'England is meant to be green,' Alyster Crowley was saying. 'You want my money? Give me some green fucking lawns.'

Thistlestrupp nodded politely. Crowley would be gone in a day or two, back to LA and his water sprinklers.

'I understand,' Thistlestrupp said. 'You really need to talk about this to Dave.'

'I'm not talking to David. I'm talking to you! Hello?' He rapped the Formica tabletop. 'Hello? Earth to Thistlesfuck. Can you hear me?'

'Like I say,' Thistlestrupp said, 'it's out of my control. You need to talk to Dave ... Is he coming to the dinner tonight? I think he's managed to get out of it, lucky bastard. I presume you're coming?'

'They rent us a dung heap for £400,000 with cat-shit lawns. And all they can talk about is fucking dinner jackets ...'

Thistlestrupp nodded, this time in genuine agreement. Apparently the pre-shoot dinner tonight had been insisted upon by the guy who owned the house. Some sort of anniversary present for his wife: he had ordered in a couple of Oscar-winning court jesters to entertain the lady of the

27

manor. *Talk about decay.* Thistlestrupp despised the British class system, and he wanted to portray that in his work. If that meant donning a dinner jacket and eating off silver in the Long Gallery for one night, then so be it.

Thistlestrupp had Nordic roots, but had spent his adult life in the UK and married a solidly English woman, called Alison. Alison was a partner in a City law firm and without her massive income, his artistic existence would have been impossible. In the meantime, his existence was pretty damn good. Thistlestrupp's Nordic roots weren't obvious: they mostly manifested in his flat blue eyes and neatness of figure. Also in the décor of his £3.75 million semi-detached house in Barnes, south-west London. He preferred the Nordic palette, Danish lighting, rooms without walls or books or anything, really: except inbuilt high-fidelity sound systems and inter-room video connection. Tode Hall, and all it represented, was anathema to him. His version of *Prance to the Music in Time* was going to be brimming with disdain. That was the whole point. It was why, he said, he had 'agreed' to take on the project.

It's worth noting, however, that he had been extremely grateful for the project when it came along. Not to say desperate. Fifteen years ago, Noah Thistlestrupp had been a hot property: the new boy on the block. He'd had a hit with a movie called *Teardrop Sundae*, now long forgotten. It wasn't very good, but it caught the wind, briefly, and somebody in it – not Thistlestrupp – was nominated for a BAFTA. After the success of *Teardrop* there came a flurry of promising offers … And from among them all, he picked a turkey … Then he picked another turkey. And then, inevitably, there came a new, new boy on the block, and everyone lost interest in Thistlestrupp, and the promising offers dwindled, and then they stopped. But the Thistlestrupp sprogs kept on coming, and so did their school fees ... Thank heavens for Alison and her outlandishly high salary. Thistlestrupp ought to have been more grateful. In fact, her success was one of the many reasons he resented her.

More to the point, thank heavens for his agent. Somehow, after a string of humiliatingly low-level directing jobs, she'd pulled this one out of the hat. A six-part series. Big budget. Big stars. It was his chance to redeem himself both on the world stage and at the Nordic breakfast island.

In the meantime ... there was no question that the Long Gallery dinner was going to be a drag. Thistlestrupp didn't enjoy making polite conversation. Also it would mean spending the evening away from thirty-four-year-old Wardrobe Assistant, KitKat, with whom he was currently enjoying one of his madhot extra-maritals. Thistlestrupp enjoyed a madhot extra-marital on every film set he worked on, these days. It was one of the (ever diminishing) perks of the job, and he was infuriated that KitKat wouldn't be coming with him to the dinner tonight.

He decided to send her a text.

'You can tell Dave Snare,' ranted Alyster, 'to tell those toffee-nose fuckmonkeys if they want my money, they'd better get their lawn green, or we're pulling out ... '

'I WANT YOU', wrote Thistlestrupp, in caps.

KitKat texted back at once. But Thistlestrupp didn't get a chance to look at the message because, as it pinged through, who should stroll into the truck and slide into the little booth beside Alyster ...

... Drum roll please ...

None other than ...

Oscar's Best Actress in a Leading Role for 2007 or thereabouts ... Actor and Humanitarian, the Blessed, the Centred, the Happily Self-Partnered, one and only Ms Livvie Kellet! Preferred pronouns she/her.

TA-DAH!

Livvie was very sexy. More so on screen than in the flesh. In the flesh, there was just too much of her. Not literally of course. She was tiny: elfin and wiry. She had short dark hair and enormous grey eyes. Tiny bones. Big bosoms. And she was beautiful, almost inhumanly so. But the way she moved, the way she pawed and shimmied and eyeballed – a lot of people found it disconcerting. Her minuscule, perfectly formed presence hummed with a sort of air-sucking sexual neediness which translated into magic on screen, but which, day by day on the living earth, as a superstar, had made Livvie Kellet increasingly insecure and impossible to deal with.

TA-DAH, indeed.

Like Thistlestrupp, Livvie's career had been on a slow downward spiral over recent years. She had further to fall, mind. And no solid Alison figure to pick up the pieces when she landed. Livvie was as neurotic as it is possible to be without being hospitalised. She was convinced she didn't get offered the best roles anymore because she was losing her looks. But at forty-one years old, and with all the magicians of the Californian beauty industry at her disposal, of course she wasn't losing her looks. It was simply that she, like Thistlestrupp, had lent her talent to a few too many turkeys. Plus, she was a nightmare. Nobody denied she was a good actress. She was one of the best. It was just that nobody wanted to work with her.

And then along came this: a perfect role. And an opportunity to spend a few months back home in Ol' Blighty. Livvie had been more determined to land this role than any role since leaving RADA. And the things she'd done to achieve it would make most women quail. Which is why most women would never be Livvie Kellet. She was a wreck, poor love. Almost entirely made of hot air and nonsense. And yet there was something magnificent about her, too. Ta-dah.

In any case, Alyster Crowley thought she was hot stuff.

She shimmied and pawed onto the banquette beside him, waving her tight buttocks in his face just long enough for his sweaty hand to give them a little pinch.

She didn't appear to notice.

'Hey, *baby*,' she said to him. 'Good to see you! I heard the 'copter ... Thought it must be you.' They pecked, lip on lip.

'Hey,' said Thistlestrupp.

'Hey *Noah*!' she said, leaning right over the Formica table-top to lay a lip-to-lip on him, too. 'How's it going?' Livvie fancied Noah. Those flat, blue, unreadable eyes did something for her. She couldn't resist them. But she noticed he hardly ever used them to look at her. Maybe that was part of the allure. He didn't fancy her back.

Livvie had grown up in Kingston upon Thames, the daughter of two teachers. She'd spent most of her adult life in Los Angeles and spoke – it was a lovely husky voice – with the hint of a Californian drawl.

Noah said briskly: 'Yeah, it's going good, Livvie.' He shuffled as far back from her as he could. 'All good.' He looked at his beetroot smoothie and tried to ignore the feeling of her eyes, boring into the top of his head. *What did she want from him?* 'How's your trailer?' he asked. 'Is it all OK?'

Livvie's agent had insisted that her trailer be 'demonstrably'

31

larger than her co-star's, the Oscar-winning Teddy MacIntosh. This had caused quite a lot of difficulty. Or it would do as soon as her co-star noticed. In the meantime, the trailers had been parked at angles that made the sizes hard to compare, also with Oliver Mellors's far smaller one parked in between.

'Oh it's perfect!' said Livvie. 'Thanks so much! It's heaven! And the beautiful flowers! I was *so so* touched by the flowers! How did you know? Thank you!'

The flowers had been stipulated in the contract, too. Fresh flowers every day. Narcissus (daffodils) and hyacinth. Because of the Greek myths, apparently, and Livvie currently being inspired by myths. The flowers needed to be flown in each morning.

'You must come and visit me, Noah . . . Come and see for yourself.'

'Will do,' snapped Thistlestrupp.

'*I'll* come and visit you, darling,' said Alyster Crowley, squeezing her high upper thigh, tightly, so it pinched. 'We don't want our most beautiful star getting lonesome.' She sent him a smile, blew him a kiss.

He smirked, and a low noise bubbled from somewhere within his chest – it was a mix of despair, desire, contempt . . . Livvie settled him down with a little wink, and they moved on.

'I haven't seen Teddy today,' she said, turning back to Thistlestrupp. She dipped a finger into his beetroot smoothie, and licked. 'Has he got here yet?' The actors had been rehearsing in London all week. This afternoon and tomorrow they would be rehearsing at the location, and filming was due to begin in earnest early midweek.

'Sure, Teddy's here,' Thistlestrupp said. 'He got here yesterday, same as you. Why don't you go and say hi to him? See if he's noticed you've got a better trailer than him?'

Livvie opened her eyes. 'Have I really? That's so awful!'

Alyster snorted.

'That shouldn't be happening!' Livvie said. 'Noah, Teddy's one of our greatest living performers – we are blessed to have him with us on this show. If he finds out his trailer is smaller than mine, he's going to be mortified . . .'

Alyster said: 'Well you shouldn't have demanded it then, should you darling?'

Livvie ignored him. 'Why would anyone want to insult Teddy in that way? Literally for no reason? Teddy is such a great actor. I swear, if anything, he should have a larger trailer than me. Not smaller. I find it—' She stopped. Shook her head. Lost for words momentarily. But not for long. 'I find it genuinely disgusting and incomprehensible.'

Thistlestrupp was saved a response by the merry arrival, at that instant . . .

Coo-eee!

. . . of their hostess, India Tode, who'd climbed the steps into the catering truck and was standing at the end of the walkway, the triplets forming a semicircle behind her.

THE CATERING TRUCK

10.25 A.M.

ndia said: 'Oh my God! As I live and breathe. *Livvie Kellet!* We meet at last.'

Livvie didn't know this woman. She had no idea who India was, or why they would be meeting at all, let alone at last. But she smiled her big movie-star smile – because when she wasn't being a nightmare, she had good manners. She'd been famous for long enough to know it was her duty to put people at their ease around her. Plus – she liked it. She needed it. People being star-struck around her made her feel valuable, and nothing much else did anymore – except sex. Obviously.

Livvie noticed the triplets – an extraordinary vision, by any standards. 'Hello lads!' she said. 'And oh *wow*! What a sight to see! Am I dreaming? *How great to meet you all!*'

India continued her advance, sashaying through the drab catering truck towards them with her usual exuberance. 'I'm India Tode. You probably know. Or maybe you don't. Alyster and I are old chums, aren't we Alyster?' She grinned at him. He

34

had no choice but to smile back. 'And you're the director, aren't you?' she said, looking at Noah Thistlestrupp. 'Very important! We've already met. Plus I spotted you earlier, actually. Chatting away, very animatedly! Didn't want to interrupt ... Anyway ...' India turned back to Livvie. 'I am India Tode, as you probably know. I actually live here, if you can believe it. In this insane house! And *these* ...' she turned to the triplets, grinning like nincompoops (handsome ones) behind her, 'these triplets are ...' India paused. 'Actually, you know, I'm not going to tell you which is which, because you're never going to remember. No offence, boys. Basically, one's Morman, one's Drez and the other is Jacko. And they are all wonderful in different ways. But I mean ...'

'Mostly we just get called Dregz'n'Co,' said Morman, with a goofy, happy grin. 'High confuzilings otherwise.'

'That's right,' India said. She nudged the nearest one. 'They do also speak English. When they concentrate. You'll meet their mother at dinner this evening. She's a great friend. You're going to love her. In fact you'll meet them all. Oh – which reminds me. I meant to ask ...' She looked at Thistlestrupp, but still couldn't remember his name, because India had no head for names (or figures). '*Have you got a dinner jacket?* Dinner's in the Long Gallery. And Mr Carfizzi, our butler, goes a bit c-r-a-z-y if the men don't wear dinner jackets in the Long Gallery. Is that OK? Will you be able to sort one out?'

'Yes, yes,' said Thistlestrupp. 'I've been told.'

'... I was wondering if maybe you had any spare ones. For the triplets.' India added. 'Seeing as the show is a costume drama. And everyone's always wearing dinner jackets in the book ... Might you have a bunch of spare ones in the costume cupboard or whatever? Also, I was worried about Mellors.

Oliver [India corrected herself]. Seriously! They all need dinner jackets. Poor Carfizzi takes it very seriously. We don't want to rub him up the wrong way by looking scruffy!'

But Livvie was more interested in the triplets. 'No, but seriously,' she said to one of them, as if she really, really wanted to know: 'which of you is which?'

Morman shook his head. 'It's no bother,' he replied. 'You need knowledgeability to get into the, like, individual details.'

Thistlestrupp and Alyster Crowley would have sent India and the triplets packing at that point, but Livvie was so excited by the sight of them neither dared to suggest it. She was clapping her hands with delight, eyes flicking from one triplet to the next. Were they *really* working on the set? What fun! What would they be doing? More to the point, what wouldn't they be doing?! They were so *hilarious*. She just wanted to *gobble them up.*

'... Not exactly sure ...' muttered one of them, his cheeks burning.

They all giggled.

In any case it was agreed, in the face of so much enthusiasm from the star, that all three boys would have to be found work on the set. Thistlestrupp said he knew for a fact that Wardrobe could benefit from an extra pair of hands, and he put in a quick call to KitKat (he couldn't resist) demanding her presence in the catering truck so she could take her pick. Livvie said she needed someone to help her with her lines, which was absurd, but no one was going to argue. And then she said it wouldn't be fair if she had a triplet, and her co-star, Teddy, didn't. Especially after the trailer debacle. He wouldn't tolerate the injustice, Livvie declared, and nor 'in good conscience' could she.

So Livvie, India and two of the Dregz'n'Co triplets headed

out to the trailers to deliver Teddy his prize, leaving one of them (Jacko) for KitKat to take with her back to Wardrobe. They passed KitKat en route, and India stopped and gawked, and said:

'Oooh!'

Livvie was leading the way, chatting joyfully to the boys, asking them questions about their lives and absolutely not listening to the answers. India lagged behind. Never having been on a film set before, she was amazed by it all. There were so many young people, just standing around! So many trucks and cables and lights and noises and peculiar-looking machines. She ran to catch up with Livvie.

'Who's that girl?' she asked Livvie.

Livvie, slightly irritated, said: 'Which girl?' She wasn't even sure why India was still tagging along.

India pointed to KitKat, just then climbing the steps to the catering truck. '*That* one. I think she's doing costumes . . . Did you hear him – your director? I've forgotten his name again. Did you hear him, when he was phoning her to come over? I smelled a rat, then . . . Plus I saw them together, earlier.' India beamed at the movie star, not star-struck any longer, too swept up in the joy of her own gossip. She tapped her nose. 'I have a sense for these things, Livvie. Trust me. And if those guys aren't . . .' she ground her fists together, 'I'll eat my own head!'

Livvie didn't like this. She felt the blood flow into her cheeks. She felt her eyes stinging. *What the fuck?* Just like that, the movie-star bonhomie vanished. She stopped still, glowered at India, who noticed the change in mood, and dropped her fists at once.

'Sorry!' India said, crestfallen. 'Have I spoken out of turn? Is that taboo?'

Livvie said: 'Noah Thistlestrupp happens to be a happily married man. His wife is expecting their third child at any minute. They are blissfully happily married. And I don't really think, under those circumstances, what you're saying is appropriate or supportive to women.'

'... God ...' said India.

'This isn't about Noah Thistlestrupp, in any case,' Livvie continued. 'This is about women supporting women. I'm actually quite personally offended. And that's aside from the *fact* that Noah Thistlestrupp isn't that sort of a guy, you know? The film industry has moved on from all that kind of shit. *It doesn't happen anymore, OK*? I also happen to have a lot of respect for him as an artist.'

'OK. Sorry,' India said again. 'Crikey.'

Livvie nodded. She felt like crying. Or kicking someone. Instead, she breathed. *Gathered*. 'Let's forget it, shall we? ... I'll take the boys from here. And we'll see you at dinner. All right?' Livvie recovered her smile, and bestowed it on India one more time.

India backed away. So ... Livvie Kellet was insane! Clearly. India couldn't wait to hit the phone and share this hilarious new piece of info with her friends. 'Great stuff,' India said. 'So sorry I upset you .... See you later then. Chinese Drawing Room. Black tie. Seven o'clock sharp.' She glanced at the boys, who had witnessed Livvie's temper tantrum. They were standing behind the star, looking a little disconcerted. India sent them a wink. 'Good luck!' she whispered. The boys giggled, thoroughly embarrassed. Livvie didn't seem to notice.

THE CARETAKER'S FLAT

11.00 A.M.

M r Carfizzi was in two minds about the film-crew invasion. He had fond memories of previous filmmakers' visits to Tode Hall over the years. Most specifically from the early eighties, not long after he and Mrs Carfizzi had started work at the Hall, when Laurence Olivier himself had graced them all with his presence. That had been for the last but one remake of *Prance to the Music in Time*. Lord Olivier had played the dying Marquis, and Carfizzi would never forget how kindly the great actor had treated him during the filming.

In Mr Carfizzi's opinion, Lord Olivier's performance as the dying Marquis had been one of the greatest moments of his Lordship's career. Just as waiting on his Lordship, while his Lordship graced the Hall with his Lordship's remarkable presence, had been a career high for Mr Carfizzi. Nothing would ever match it.

Nevertheless, this was exciting. Mr Carfizzi was particularly delighted to be welcoming the Oscar winner, Teddy

MacIntosh, to the Hall. As he fussed about inside the silver pantry, polishing candlesticks for the Long Gallery table this evening, he wondered what Teddy's favourite pudding was, and whether it was worth discussing the matter with his wife.

He thought, on this occasion, that it might be worth a try. So he laid down the candlestick, which was already quite shiny anyway, locked the silver pantry, and headed towards the flat in the basement where he and his wife lived. She was a woman of deeply entrenched habit (so far as he knew) and she generally slipped back to the flat at this time for a cup of coffee, brewed in her own particular way, from her own, particular coffee pot.

He rarely intruded. Why would he? But the more he thought about Teddy MacIntosh's possible taste in puddings, the more urgently he realised he needed to discuss the matter with his wife.

It was a funny thing about Mrs Carfizzi. In forty-two years she had never contradicted her husband. She waited on him. She fitted herself around his small, neat life as meekly as any wife in history, and in return, he hardly noticed her. He never thanked or complimented her. In fact, in forty-two years he'd never felt moved, even, to make love to her. She never argued, never asked for anything, never complained. He had long ago stopped wondering why – if, that is, he'd ever started. Mrs Carfizzi (as he called her) was, to Mr Carfizzi, perhaps to a greater degree than any unappreciated spouse in the history of unappreciated spouses, simply a handy piece of furniture – with a human smell.

But there was one area where she simply would not be commanded, and that was in her cooking. She cooked all day, every day, so far as he could tell: exquisite Calabrian dishes for the two of them, and the worst of grey, English nursery food for

40

the Todes, because that was what Sir Ecgbert 11th (deceased) had liked best.

Over the years Emma Tode, deceased wife of the deceased Ecgbert 11th, had asked Mrs Carfizzi to change the menu a hundred times, with no success. India and her husband Egbert(Mr) had tried it too. But no matter how often or how politely the Todes requested it, Mrs Carfizzi would not change the menus. Mr Carfizzi knew this. And yet – for Teddy MacIntosh – it didn't stop him giving it a try.

He skipped down the stairs and let himself into their sitting room, which opened directly from a basement lobby in the main house.

The room's proportions were small and mean. Its only window looked out onto the wheelhubs of cars parked in the Estate Offices courtyard. But the Carfizzis had stamped their mark on the place, nonetheless. In fact, over the years, they had lavished the place with funds and love, and transformed it into a mini wonderland of leather and glittering crystal. (How, on their miserable estate salaries, remained a mystery. But that's another story.)

Mrs Carfizzi had clearly not been expecting him.

She was sitting at the gilt and glass coffee table in the middle of the sitting room, her back to the door, with a laptop open in front of her, and a strange man's face staring out from the screen. She was speaking very quickly in a language that Mr Carfizzi thought might have been Russian, or Portuguese. Or possibly Dutch.

This is just an approximation of the words that were tumbling so fluently from her mouth:

Вячеслав, уверяю вас, я не ношу никаких трусов. Вы хотите, чтобы я показал вам?

She sounded earnest, and a little angry.

And from the tone of her interlocutor's wheedling reply ...

Я бы очень этого хотел. Однако я думаю, что у нас есть компания

... it seemed that he was feeling the same way.

Mr Carfizzi stood behind her, frozen in time. Was this the woman he had married over forty years ago, and with whom he had only come to discuss profiteroles? Or was he dreaming? And who was the weasel she was addressing? He had a moustache, and a mean face, and a woolly brimmed hat, a bit like Doctor Zhivago. It was too much! On such a day. With Teddy MacIntosh in need of a pudding. Mr Carfizzi felt tears springing. Never, in his long life, had he ever felt so deceived.

'... *Amore*? ...' he queried. '*Cara mia*? ...' Never before. Always, before: 'Mrs Carfizzi.'

She slammed down the laptop lid and turned her slow bulk to look at him. And for a moment, he could hardly recognise her soft, pillowy face. She was a different woman. Tough, angry, confident .... *Kinda sexy* ... Terrifying.

'*What*?' she snapped. And then, she seemed to focus. Before his eyes, her normal face slid back into place. Deadpan, bored, obedient. In a normal voice, and in her mother tongue, she asked him what he wanted. But he honestly couldn't remember.

'Nothing,' he said (*niente* in Italian). 'I think I must be dreaming.' He started backing out of the room. He might have continued backing out of the room, buried the experience deep inside himself, persuaded himself that, yes, it really had been a dream, and never mentioned it again. But then, who should turn up, knock-knocking, popping her head round the sitting-room door ...

... A drum roll please ...

'Coo-ee!'

... but India Tode. Fresh from her unhappy exchange with Livvie Kellet – and still, unbelievably, obsessing over dinner jackets. She wanted to warn Carfizzi of the possibility that some of the guests – the triplets, to be specific – might have to attend the dinner in just shirt and tie. Since nobody had made it clear whether KitKat in the Wardrobe department would be able to help them out, India felt she should prepare the ground for disappointment. She didn't want Mr Carfizzi insulting the triplets over dinner. Also, more importantly, she didn't want him getting upset or taking offence. Things between them had not been easy at the start, when India first came to Tode Hall. There had been some terrible clashes. But they had made peace since, and it was a great relief to both of them. Nowadays they were exceptionally careful of each other's feelings.

India glanced at Mrs Carfizzi, who looked normal again, and then back at Mr Carfizzi, who looked as if he'd seen a ghost. She asked him if everything was all right. He meant to say yes, of course it was. Everything was fine. He was hoping to encourage his wife to make profiteroles for pudding. But different words came out of his mouth. He said:

'*Mrs Carfizzi is speaking Russian!*'

'Really?' said India. Not very interested. 'That's peculiar. She's not even very good at English ...' She turned to Mrs Carfizzi. 'Can you speak Russian now, Mrs Carfizzi? That's amazing.'

Mr Carfizzi had noticed something else, too. The laptop on the table in front of her – was something he had never seen before. They shared a big, square computer, which squatted on a table in the corner of the room, which Mr Carfizzi barely touched, but which his wife used – constantly, so far as he could tell, to Skype her relations in Calabria. And there it still squatted now. So what was this new machine? Where had it come from?

He pointed to the laptop. 'What is that thing?' he demanded. 'Why have I never seen it before?'

Mrs Carfizzi didn't reply. Like a surly teenager, she dragged it towards her, pulled open a drawer in the kitchen dresser – a drawer which Mr Carfizzi had never opened, barely been aware existed – and, sliding aside a pistol which was clearly visible to everyone in the room, she laid the laptop away.

'Mrs Carfizzi!' India cried. 'Oh my goodness! *Is that a gun?*'

Mr Carfizzi, in his alarm, broke his strict professional code and began to gabble at her in Italian.

His wife looked impassively on. She watched his lips moving up and down. When they stopped, she said, in perfect English:

'Forget what you saw. It's none of your business.'

'Excuse *me*,' spluttered India. 'I think it is! If you're harbouring ... whatever it's called ... illegal contraband or whatever ... in this house. I mean seriously, it could lead to all sorts of trouble. For goodness sake, Mrs Carfizzi! Get a grip! I should probably fire you! I mean, literally. On the spot. Except ...' Poor Mad Ecgbert(Sir) would be heartbroken if Mrs Carfizzi left. It would be awful for him. Also, India didn't much believe in telling people how they ought to live. Why shouldn't Mrs Carfizzi speak Russian and keep a pistol in her kitchen drawer if that was what she wanted? Why not? ... Also, above all, there were fourteen people for dinner, two of them Oscar winners. This was not a good time.

'Why were you talking in Russian?' Mr Carfizzi asked. 'Was it Russian?'

Mrs Carfizzi said: 'Because it's the only language he speaks. We had something urgent we needed to communicate.'

Her husband could only stare. Who was this woman? Tears rolled down his cheeks. *He thought of all the times he'd told himself he was dreaming* ...

India forced a little grin, despite not much appreciating the weird, unfriendly expression on Mrs Carfizzi's face and finding the whole situation quite disturbing – 'Anyway! Look! I'm sure there's an explanation ... Let's have a good long chat about it, shall we – I mean, after this wretched dinner. Maybe when Eggie and me and the kids have got back from our hols. Don't you think? You, me, Mr Carfizzi, Eggie ... I'm sure we can sort it all out. I'm sure there's a terribly simple explanation ...'

Mrs Carfizzi shrugged. 'Fine,' she said. And then, to both of them: 'Why are you here, anyway? What do you want?'

A conversation about puddings and dinner jackets followed, but nobody put much of their heart into it. India said she had to dash. Mr Carfizzi seemed to be less concerned than India had feared, vis-à-vis the dinner-jacket situation. And Mrs Carfizzi, on this occasion, had been intending to make profiteroles anyway.

India wanted to ask Mr Carfizzi to fetch Rapunzel Piece and her middle-aged son from Todeister train station later. But under the circumstances, she thought better of it. He wasn't himself. She suggested, instead, that he take a few hours off.

'It's going to be a long night tonight,' India said. She smiled. 'You're not a young man anymore, you know! Why don't you have a quick nap?'

Meekly, he nodded, and padded off to his room.

THE OSCAR WINNER'S TRAILER

11.15 A.M.

Teddy MacIntosh's trailer may have been demonstrably smaller than Livvie Kellet's but he was hardly roughing it in there. The theme was olive green – elegant, but masculine. The interior, according to its brochure, which currently lay unread on a shelf above the lavatory, was divided into a #jus'hangin' zone, a #munching pod and a 'bathroomette', which had a power shower, many mirrors, and a long row of unopened masculine-themed beauty lotions. There was a bowl of lychees on the table in #jus'hangin' (as stipulated in his contract), and two TVs: one in the #munching pod, and one – somewhat pointlessly, Teddy thought – hanging by the door to the lavatory. When Livvie dropped in with her gift of a triplet, he was stretched out on one of the olive-green sofas, shoes off, on the phone to his agent. He was slightly irritated by the interruption.

However, Livvie was his co-star. It was important to his own performance that the two of them connected on a mutually respectful basis for the length of the shoot so he said to his agent:

'I've got to go. I'm just putting it out there, yeah? I'm angry, and I'm disappointed, and I feel it's going to be very hard for me to grow when the essence of who I am and what I feel I represent is being undermined at this point in time. I feel *very* undermined. And I do feel this is going to impact on my performance, which is basically what we're talking about here. Because how can I trust?' There was a pause. The agent was saying something lovely to him. Teddy stood up, nodding, almost listening, and made his way to the trailer door to welcome his co-star in. She was getting impatient. 'Sure,' Teddy said, 'I hear you. Just – I'm very unhappy about this. So if you could have a quiet word ... All right? OK. Super! Love you. Big kiss. Yeah. Talk later.'

He hung up. Opened the door.

Teddy MacIntosh had been blessed in so many ways. Yet he was probably the unhappiest man alive. Or so it sometimes felt to him. Considered by many to be one of the most talented actors of his generation, he was also beautiful, and much loved. He was the third son of a kindly and successful investment banker (not that Teddy needed his father's money anymore) and of an elegant mother who worshipped the air her boys breathed, the ground they walked on, and every word they uttered. She played a lot of bridge.

And yet. Something was missing. For all the talent and beauty and money and love, Teddy MacIntosh could barely conjure a moment from his adult life that hadn't been riddled with personal anxiety. He spent a lot of time and money with shrinks. But even that caused him anxiety. He worried they might iron out that magical ingredient inside him, which made him such a remarkable actor. And without that he would be lost. If Teddy couldn't act, he didn't imagine he would know how to live. And this, by the way, wasn't Teddy MacIntosh being pretentious. This was just Teddy being Teddy. He was self-obsessed, ungrateful, disingenuous, untrusting, spoilt, jealous, resentful, vain ... Teddy was an artist. There was nothing to Teddy, except for that.

And here stood Livvie, standing in the mustard-coloured grass outside his trailer, grinning neurotically up at him.

'Surprise!' she said.

He looked at the boys. Lovely looking boys, he thought. Identical.

'And guess what,' Livvie said, giggling, '*there's even another one!*'

Teddy invited them in. Hugs and handshakes. And a bit of joshing about which Dregz'n'Co should be allocated to which actor. Livvie and Teddy both objected quite strongly to the suggestion that they call the triplets all by the same name.

'It's dehumanising,' said the actor and humanitarian, Livvie Kellet.

'Trouble being,' said Morman, 'we look the same, so you'll be confuslings. And then you'll be ginchy, like, as if you know which is which, and that's just going to be pressure.' He shrugged. 'Why put yourself through it?'

'He's right,' nodded Drez. 'Trust us. We know.'

'How about,' suggested Teddy, 'you identify yourselves and then, to save our blushes – if you wouldn't find it insulting,

48

and please forgive me if you do because I swear I'm stumbling in the dark here. Because I can't imagine what it must be like, you know, to have *two* human beings who look exactly like you, walking the earth surface . . . '

'Dank,' Morman said.

Jacko said: 'Dookie fresh.'

They both giggled.

'Hm?' Teddy paused. 'What's that?'

'Boys, you've gotta talk in *English*,' Livvie reminded them. 'I mean, I'm digging it, I really am. But you gotta remember we're *old*. OK? We Won't Understand What You Are Saying . . . All right?'

Teddy said: 'I think we need to organise some name tags.'

After that, the actors slightly lost interest. They had nothing much for the boys to do, and it was a little awkward, having them hanging around without their name tags. Livvie said she felt a sudden and powerful yen for an overripe banana.

'My body must be craving potassium,' she said, as if it was interesting. 'I don't know *why* . . . ' Teddy suggested the boys hunt down some overripe bananas, and since rehearsals weren't due to start for another hour or two, he invited Livvie to join him for a cuppa.

She took off her shoes and folded her limber body onto the other olive sofa, and they discussed the thing they always discussed when together and alone in the room.

Oliver bloody Mellors.

Oliver Mellors, as previously mentioned, was head game-keeper at Tode Hall, and (not that he much cared) one of the best-looking men in Yorkshire, if not the world. He hadn't been offered just any part, either. It was – without going into unnecessary details – the third most important role in the show.

Some people might even suggest it was the most important role of all. Mellors had been hired to play Lord Greystoke, who is lover to both Teddy's character (Lord Tintin) and to Livvie's (Lady Steph). A big part, then. For a man who'd just stepped down from his tractor.

Teddy and Livvie did not want to be snobbish. They weren't snobbish, actually. They believed in equal opportunities for everyone; not just for old Harrovians and the children of Kingston upon Thames-based teachers. *Of course they did*. They believed in nurturing and encouraging raw talent wherever it was found. But they also believed in the value of training. And – yes – Mellors looked the part. There was no question about that. And – yes – it so happened he wasn't a bad actor, either. But he was no match for them. And it was, they felt, an insult to their craft that they should be put on screen with someone who had no training, and who – as became increasingly clear during the last few days of rehearsals – had absolutely no respect for those who did. Mellors didn't take the work seriously. Worse than that, he seemed to disdain those who did.

Teddy called his agent every day to voice his outrage and sense of hurt. He was doing it when Livvie and the two triplets came knocking. Livvie sympathised. She didn't like Mellors. She didn't like his haughty attitude. But she hadn't taken the situation as badly as Teddy for the simple reason that Mellors, being male (preferred pronouns he/him), did not pose a direct threat.

'If our art, as Actor, is reduced to nothing more than screen sex appeal, then I ask you, what's the point?' That's what Teddy was saying, while peeling a lychee. He, like Livvie, actually had a lot of screen sex appeal himself. But it wasn't innate, it was down to his skill as an actor. There was nothing especially sexually appealing about Teddy MacIntosh in real life. In real life, Teddy was too neurotic, too self-centred, too unhappy, too fragile to have any energy left for sex, and it showed. Only last week, his chief shrink had suggested he had an 'abnormally low sex drive'. It had made him slightly tearful. But then a lot of things did.

'I think we should go on strike,' Teddy said. 'For our art, Livvie. Seriously, it's a fucking insult. Mellors is an arse. I hate him. I think we should go on strike now, before we start shooting, and I think we should stay on strike until they get someone in Greystoke's role who actually knows how to act. Who has a proper respect for his art and the art form . . . The man doesn't even watch movies! He told me yesterday he had *never been to a play in his entire life*!' Teddy swallowed the lychee, spat out the pip. Watched it flying across the room and landing on the coffee table between them. 'We should insist they get someone to play Greystoke who isn't a fucking arse. What do you think, Livvie? Are you in?'

Livvie was not in. Most definitely not. But she had to find a way of saying so that made it sound like she would have been, if the situation had been different. If things were in her control.

'Yes,' she said. 'You bet.'

'What?' Teddy had not been expecting that. He wasn't sure he was ready for it, either.

'I mean I *am*. Obviously . . . But I think we should have a chat with our agents. Before we do anything. Don't you think? Plus, you know – I don't want to do something that's going to piss anyone off as long as Alyster Crowley is on set . . . He'll kill us. Literally. I think he would, you know.'

They fell silent, thinking about that.

51

THE GAMEKEEPER'S COTTAGE

12.00 P.M.

Unlike Teddy MacIntosh, Oliver Mellors, the handsomest gamekeeper in Yorkshire, if not the world, did have quite a high sex drive, and due to his newly unhappy circumstances, was at a bit of a loss as to what to do with it – aside from the very thing he was doing at the moment KitKat from Wardrobe came knocking at his cottage door. He'd been in London rehearsing for a week, and had come home last night to the house he thought he shared with his wife, only to find she'd packed up and left while he was away. He'd been half expecting it; she'd been ignoring his messages for several days. But even so. The reality was a shock.

He'd hated the rehearsal week. He hated acting, didn't like actors – didn't like London, hadn't liked anyone he met. Didn't like the endless chatter, the eternal hurry, the stink of petrol, the selfish, self-important faces. He'd been longing to come home. If his wife had been there, waiting for him, he would have been the happiest man alive.

52

But she wasn't. And it was his fault, and he knew it. He was never the easiest man to live with. Add to that, he was a faithless dog; and Todeister was a small community, and she just kept on catching him out with other women. He supposed the thought of him alone all week, making hay in the Big Smoke, had been more than she could stand. And now here he was on his own, with his laptop, and his flies undone, and somebody knocking at the door.

When he opened the door she smiled at him. 'Sorry,' she said. 'Are you busy?'

'What do you want?' he asked (ignoring the question). 'I'm not due on set for a few hours yet.'

She was bearing dinner jackets. Obviously. She asked if she could come in.

Mellors would have said no. After the week he'd had, he longed for some time on his own. On the other hand, she was smiling. And he was lonely. And she was pretty. And, he thought – *you never know* ... bloody hell, why not?

It was very pleasant, the process of trying on the jackets with her. Very pleasant indeed. She stood close to him while she checked the fit: Not too tight here? And what about here?

He said it felt OK.

She wanted to know, was he enjoying the experience of being a soon-to-be movie star?

He said it was OK.

Was he looking forward to the dinner tonight?

He said, not specially. And then, because she smelled good and he liked her golden stripy hair, he confided to her that it was going to be awkward, sitting in the Long Gallery, being waited on by Mr Carfizzi, who normally tended to think he was a cut above staff who worked outside. Also, he wasn't looking forward to standing around in the Chinese Drawing Room in a dinner jacket, sipping champagne, which he disliked, and listening to people talk rubbish. His father, he said, would be laughing at him, up in heaven.

KitKat didn't see why it followed that people would be talking rubbish. And then, weirdly, perhaps, but she was standing very close and she smelled lovely, and she was smiling – he kissed her. KitKat kissed him back.

... Noah Thistlestrupp's flat blue eyes and cool caresses vanished – pop! – into a bloodless past. She felt a smidgen of guilt for abandoning him so quickly. But then again (she reminded herself) he was the one who was married – and with Baby No. 3 on the way, for heaven's sake. He was the bastard who was cheating on his pregnant wife. He was the one who ought to have been feeling guilty. Not KitKat.

Mellors said: 'Are you coming to the dinner tonight?'

She said not. 'Unfortunately I'm not important enough.'

Mellors didn't reply. Without consulting her – she would have told him not to – he texted India. Could he bring a plus one to the dinner tonight? He put his phone back in his pocket, and returned his attention to KitKat. Things were looking up. In a way. Which isn't to say he wasn't still heartbroken, because he was. If his wife had walked into the cottage kitchen at that instant, he would have thrown KitKat out of the nearest window. But his wife wasn't going to do that. She was probably staying with her sister in Buxton.

Standing in the kitchen, his wife's letter lying open on the table still, beside the residues of the milkless breakfast cereal he'd eaten last night, and of the milkless cereal he'd eaten this morning, they kissed again.

A successful kiss for both of them.

THE PINEAPPLE ROOM

2.00 P.M.

SECTION THREE: 'KISSING': A FORM OF ABUSE

Nicola Tode, fifty-four, older sister of Ecgbert(Sir), recently heartbroken, currently recuperating in her childhood bedroom at Tode Hall, underlined the words KISSING and ABUSE and sat back to consider what to write next.

When people asked Nicola what she was working on, which they didn't often, because they weren't interested, she would explain that it was 'a cross between a very personal memoir and self-help book for everyone, basically posing the question what is wrong with people? And also, basically, questioning how we can help them, so they can learn to behave normally again.'

There was a lot wrong with people, as far as Nicola was concerned. In fact, the more words she wrote, the more obvious it would have been to anyone who bothered to read them, that Nicola really didn't like people at all. Section Three was about kissing, but it was the tip of the iceberg. Nicola hoped her book (working title: *What is Wrong with People?*) would help others in similar situations to her own. By sharing her own sense of disgust, misery, isolation, disappointment and rage, she hoped ... *what*? There was nobody in Nicola's life that cared enough to press her for an answer on it. Which was fortunate, because she didn't have one. The main aim of writing *What is Wrong with People?*, if there was any aim at all, was to keep writing it until she found something better to do. Currently there was nothing better on the horizon.

Nicola's return to Tode Hall had come as quite a surprise to her cousins (and hosts). She had never been anything but hostile towards them until the morning, a week ago, when she and her large suitcase arrived at the breakfast table where Egbert(Mr) and Ecgbert(Sir) were enjoying some companionable bacon and scrambled egg.

'How long are you here for?' Ecgbert(Sir) had demanded, when he noticed the size of her suitcase.

She said she didn't know.

'Well you can't stay here for ever, you know,' he said. 'Especially if you're just going to keep banging on about Trotsky.'

She hadn't mentioned Trotsky.

'What's wrong with your own place?'

She'd replied, enigmatically, that she 'just couldn't be there at the moment. Because of the memories.' Also the flat was currently being repainted. Nicola had come home to regenerate, she said. And above all, to write.

'*Write?*' cried Ecgbert(Sir). 'Don't be ridiculous, Nicola. You can't even write your own name without getting in a tangle. You hardly know your alphabet ... What have you got to write about anyway?'

She would have told him, but Egbert(Mr) had finished his breakfast and he needed to crack on. Before she had a chance to answer the question, Egbert(Mr) was on his feet, kissing her cheek and assuring her that she would always be welcome at Tode Hall, and that she should stay as long as she wanted.

Ecgbert(Sir) snorted. 'You won't be saying that in a week.'

India and Egbert tried their dutiful best to be welcoming, but Nicola was hard work. Nobody liked her much: not her brother Ecgbert(Sir), nor Mr and Mrs Carfizzi, nor Oliver Mellors, nor Kveta the housekeeper. No one. She was 'a bristly, disagreeable kind of a person' as mild-mannered Egbert(Mr) observed to his wife: always offended about something and always picking fights. Nevertheless, *she was family*. And clearly, she was in a bad way. This was her childhood home, and apparently she had nowhere else to go.

Nicola was a socialist. At the age of fifty-four, politics was her 'little thing' (as her mother used to put it), and for the last twenty years she'd worn a red beret like Che Guevara, to highlight the point. Over the years she'd given away a lot of her wealth, often to contradictory causes. But there was always more where it came from, tied up in trusts specifically to stop her from ever running out. Nicola had never needed to work for a living, and never would, and that was part of the reason why she had never really found herself much of a place in the world.

Around the time her mother died, Nicola had been involved in a community project offering beauty-care counselling at a youth support centre in Leith, Edinburgh. Nicola didn't know anything about beauty care. She, herself, looked like a gangly rat, just up from the sewers: dirty and ragged and watchful and furtive. So it was hard to know what beauty tips she might have been sharing. But maybe that was the point. In any case, her involvement with the centre didn't last long. Either she was fired (her family never did get to the bottom of it) or the project was withdrawn due to lack of funding, or both. Nicola was devastated.

The situation was made all the more painful for Nicola because she had formed a relationship while working at the youth centre, with a fellow volunteer named Bone. After the community project ended, Bone, who worked for a tool hire company during the day, quickly found herself another voluntary placement elsewhere. Nicola didn't. Couldn't. Nobody seemed to want her, even as a volunteer. Nicola had no other friends, and no job to keep her busy. She had nothing to focus on but Bone. She made Bone's life a misery.

And then, shortly after Bone ended the relationship, a story reached the press. Bone had reported Nicola for pestering, or peeping – or something sufficiently creepy that an injunction had been laid, forbidding Nicola to make contact with her, or to be anywhere within 100 metres of where she lived or worked.

This was harsh. And humiliating. And now here she was, back at Tode Hall, reeling from the knocks, trying to soothe a broken heart by writing things down as they came to her.

SECTION THREE: 'KISSING': A FORM OF ABUSE?

Nicola wanted to break taboos. Write the unwritable. She wanted to help people, by breaking taboos and writing the unwritable. She chewed on her pen. It smelled of spit and

58

plastic. Really, she ought to be using her computer, but – it was too fiddly. Nicola wasn't great with computers. Also, there was the security issue. A computer could be hacked. Her ideas might be stolen.

Nicola's desk looked out over the park, and the wide acres of mustard-coloured lawn. It looked out past the Atlas Fountain, towards the huge eighteenth-century mausoleum where her mother, father and eleven generations of ancestors lay buried. She was familiar with the view: it was exceptional, but it didn't inspire her much. To the south, if she chose to glance that way, she could glimpse the roof of the Gardener's House, and to the east, peeping from behind the edge of East Wing courtyard, a hint of the film crew's Unit Base, where Livvie and Teddy (and Mellors) had their variously sized trailers. Nicola would never admit it, but secretly she was very excited about meeting the Oscar stars tonight. Especially the actor and activist Livvie Kellet, who was such a great role model for young women today. Nicola hoped that the two of them, being equally passionate about the issues that really mattered, would form a very real connection over and above the absurdity of their palatial surroundings. Nicola was actually feeling quite nervous. She had high hopes. So much so, though it was only two o'clock, she had already changed for dinner.

Right now, however, she wanted to concentrate on the memoir. Kissing and Abuse. Kissing and Abuse. With the stinking pen, she patted out a rhythm on her teeth . . .

It had been many years since Nicola had tried to write anything longer than a text or a shopping list. But this didn't seem to inhibit her. On the contrary, she felt inspired. As if something marvellous and powerful had been untapped at last.

*Kissing, as in the intermingling of lips and tungues
between human mouths, has been a quasi-mandatory
aspect of intersex as well as opposite sex intamacy
situations for sum time. Probably millenniums. This
needs consideration in 21st century as it is now conciderd
a form of penetratally-centric abuse, whereby one
person's space is imposed upon within another's space,
and this is unacceptable to meny people of gender, in the
currant climate.*

Brilliant. She felt she was getting into her stride. But then who should come knocking at the door ...

India Tode, healthy, smiling, and golden-haired, without waiting for the call to proceed, popped her beautiful head round Nicola's massive mahogany door.

'Hi-yaaa!' she beamed, to Nicola's great annoyance. 'Just checking in! ... You know about the big dinner tonight, don't you?'

Nicola scowled at her. 'Yes, I'm aware of it, thank you ... I do actually happen to be *working* at the moment though, India.'

'Sorry! Didn't mean to interrupt.' India came in anyway. At her heels were her two young children, Ludo (4 yrs) and Passion (3 yrs). India had bumped into them in the kitchen, where they and the au pair had been making jam tarts together. They were being extra cute, so she'd scooped them up and brought them along.

'What is it you're working on again? I know you said ...' India did not understand Nicola. Nothing about her made any sense. After all, there was nothing *intrinsically* wrong about her – but the way she dressed! Her dirty hair, her hideous clothes, her pale face, which was always covered in a mysterious film of grease, as if she'd just woken from a dreadful nightmare. India believed, and quite firmly, that if Nicola could only be persuaded to have a bath and a spruce up, and to lose that silly beret, she would be a whole lot happier for it. She realised Nicola didn't like her much. Nicola didn't like anyone very much, so far as India could see. India didn't take it personally. In fact she felt sorry for her. She felt sure that if only Nicola would allow her to provide a little guidance, give her a few style hints, and so on, maybe even persuade her to take up biking, Nicola's life would be transformed. And perhaps she was right. But no matter how often India tried to help, and she did try, Nicola remained stolidly hostile.

She was 'checking in' this afternoon because she thought Nicola might benefit from a girl chat about *what to wear* for the glamorous evening ahead.

Nicola said: 'It's a self-help book. For people who find it difficult to self-identify in an environment which is hostile to personal belief systems with regard to cultural identity, cis gender and—'

White noise.

'What?' India hadn't listened. She hadn't even started to listen. She was not one iota wiser. She said: 'You know it's black tie this evening, don't you?' She pulled a face. 'Mr Carfizzi would have an eppie otherwise, wouldn't he? ... By the way, Mrs Carfizzi's behaving very oddly atm. Have you noticed? She's suddenly started speaking brilliant English ... Also *Russian*, apparently ...' Ludo had jumped onto Nicola's unmade, two-hundred-and-fifty-year-old, four-poster bed. He was pulling on the damask hangings.

Nicola said: 'Ludo, could you stop that, please?'

Ludo ignored her. Passion wanted to join him on the bed,

but she was just too small to climb up on her own. She started whimpering. Ludo, inheritor of his parents' good nature, paused at once to haul her up.

Bounce, bounce, bounce.

'Actually, darlings,' said India. 'You need to be a bit careful. It's a very precious bed. Could you be sweet and get down?'

Passion had spotted an entertaining lotion by Nicola's bedside. A pump-action bottle of something medical. She picked it up.

'Could you not?' Nicola said. ' . . . Passion. Could you not, please. That's my HRT gel. It happens to be very important to me.'

'Yes, don't do that Pashie,' India said, but Passion ignored her. India sat down in an armchair by the window. 'So. Do you know what you're going to wear? I'm in two minds . . . But it's going to be green or blue, I think, if we're in the Chinese Drawing Room. And there are only fourteen of us, so it seems a bit pointless to open up another room. Plus the film people have taken over the Yellow Drawing Room, *and* the Imperial Singsong Room – which I hadn't realised they were planning – *and* the Emerald Room, can you believe it? What do they *need* all those rooms for? So our options are a bit limited . . . '

'Sorry India. I'm actually trying to write . . . ' Nicola said.

It was rude. But Nicola was always rude. It didn't count.

'You know, you and I are more or less the same size,' India said. 'OK I'm a bit taller than you. But we're both slim . . . So – if you want to *borrow* anything . . . ' There was something about Nicola: a smell, to be brutal, that came off her and the things she touched: a mix of old clothes and disinfectant, and the thought of her bare skin against anything India might one day wear again herself was not especially thrilling to her. Also,

62

Nicola smoked roll-ups, and a lot of her clothes had burn marks in them. So it was a generous offer. India did not like Nicola. But here she was, living under India's roof. India sensed her cousin-in-law's misery, and wanted to help in the best way she could. She offered up her wardrobe.

'No thanks,' Nicola said.

'Really? But I've got so much stuff! I just *bet* we could find something you liked in there. If you wanted. Why don't you come with me now? I could help you pick something out. It might be fun!'

'No thanks,' Nicola said again. If India asked her one more time, she might just burst into tears. Couldn't India see? *She was already changed for dinner!* In her best fleece and leggings. She'd even taken a shower. Why couldn't India understand that not everybody wanted to look like a supermodel all the time? Why couldn't she leave her alone? Nicola forced herself to smile. 'Thank you for the offer,' she said. 'But I'm fine ... If you don't mind. I was in the middle of writing something quite important. So ... thanks, though. For the offer. I just really would prefer it if you left me alone.'

India considered this. And then, with a shrug of defeat, she stood up. 'Please yourself,' she said. It sounded huffy. 'Come on children, let's go. Nicola's got important work to do.'

THE LONG GALLERY

4.00 P.M.

Somebody needed to fetch Rapunzel Piece and her middle-aged son, Norman, off the 4.47 p.m. London train.

By 4 p.m. Mr Carfizzi had yet to emerge from his midday nap, so India and Kveta, the housekeeper, were laying up dinner in the Long Gallery without him. Oliver Mellors, who'd used, sometimes, to lend a hand with emergency chauffeuring, was busy in rehearsals with the Oscar winners. Mrs Carfizzi, back to playing the monoglot, was busy in the kitchen cooking grey beef for dinner, and anyway couldn't drive. And Egbert(Mr) had disappeared for a meeting in York. India was faintly annoyed with him for having arranged it on this afternoon of all afternoons. But it was too bad. She sent him a text.

'Babe, what time does your meeting end? Mrs Carfizzi's gone nuts. Mr Carfizzi's gone to bed in a huff :(Mellors is in "rehearsals" (!!!) SOMEBODY'S got to pick up the Pieces lol. Train gets in 4.47 p.m. – can you?'

Egbert(Mr) texted back.

'Ha ha ha! Very funny, Munch!! Pick up the Pieces!!! Clever thing! I'm wrapping up now but I don't think I'll make it to Todeister on time. Sooo sorry not to be able to help. Back as soon as I can XXX'

She sent back a love heart, which pulsated, which she thought was quite cool, and went over to the Gardener's House, to see if Alice could pick up the Pieces instead.

Alice had a desk in the Hall, but she didn't tend to use it very much. She preferred to work from her own home – so much so, that when the *Prance* production team had begged for extra office space, she'd quite happily agreed to let them use hers. She rather regretted it now. With the triplets back, dropping in and out, and Ecgbert(Sir) and Lady Tode (1907–1971) semi-permanently ensconced at the kitchen table, she was finding it quite hard to concentrate. As Organisational Coordinator, it was Alice's job to pick up pieces. She was quite pleased to get out of the house.

'By the way,' India said, 'Oliver Mellors asked if he could bring a plus one. I said he couldn't. Do you think that was mean?'

Alice thought about it. 'Depends who he wanted to bring. You know his wife's just left him?'

'Yes, I heard that … Serves him right, *a bit* though. Don't you think?' said India.

'A bit,' Alice agreed.

'Anyway that was sort of my point. God knows who he was planning to bring … Some old strumpet he picked up in the pub last night, if his record's anything to go by … I just didn't think we could risk it. Anyway, so I said no, and he's going to be extra surly this evening. If that's possible. Just giving you the heads-up.'

'Do you think,' asked Ecgbert(Sir), settling himself into the passenger seat of Alice Liddell's estate-owned Fiat Panda, with the broken seatbelt, 'that there is such a thing as true love? I mean, in middle age? Do you think it's possible to fall in love, in middle age, Trudy?'

'No,' replied Alice, without a second thought, and started the engine.

'Oh.'

They drove in silence for a while. Alice was a bad driver. Also she'd taken ages to remember where she left the car keys, so they were late for the train. Ecgbert(Sir) throwing her love-related curve balls was the last thing she needed.

After a while Ecgbert said, a little sadly: 'Are you sure?'

'What a ridiculous question, Ecgbert,' piped up Lady Tode from the back seat. She was wearing sable, a matching hat and coat, and she'd snuck into the car without either of them noticing. She did it often. In the early days, Alice had needed to summon her from the old sugar pot she called home. But she'd learned to exit the pot at will, fairly quickly, and now only ever seemed to return either to sulk, or to change clothes. It meant there was no knowing when or where she might appear.

They jumped. 'Of course middle-aged people can fall in love!' she said. 'In fact – in my experience it's probably the peak time.'

This wasn't something Alice wanted to hear. She was quite annoyed that Lady Tode had come along in the first place. Nobody invited her. Ever. Once in a while it would be nice if she and Ecgbert could spend a bit of time together without her.

66

'Granny!' snapped Ecgbert. 'Who said you could come along?'

Lady Tode bristled at that. She was offended, as she often was, and though she didn't say anything, they knew it at once in the front seat, because her emotions tended to manifest in noxious-smelling seepages: the stronger the emotion the thicker, greener and more offensive the gas. This time it was only mild. A wisp of green smog floating by the rear-view mirror: a soft smell of methane. It was enough to get the message across.

'Sorry,' Ecgbert mumbled. 'Just ... you know. You can't come everywhere with us. It's weird for us. Isn't it, Trudy? Don't you think?'

Alice took her time to reply. She slowed down for a pheasant, and then to wave at Ben Weatherstaff, who worked in the Rose Garden.

'Well it is a *bit* odd,' Alice said at last. 'But never mind. You're here now.'

She was there now. It was a twenty-minute drive to the station, so long as they didn't get caught behind a tractor. Lady Tode held forth for most of the journey. She had a lot of opinions about the guests they were en route to pick up, and she was keen to share them.

Norman Wright, the middle-aged son, was in fact 'only a nephew', she informed them, incorrectly.

He was a professor 'of something pointless', she couldn't remember what (Chinese history), a confirmed bachelor, 'and a most unprepossessing gentleman, if he's still travelling around the country with his aunt ... Pathetic, really.' So that was Norman, according to Lady Tode. When pushed by Ecgbert, she admitted she'd never met him, and moved seamlessly

67

on, to offer her impressions of the seventy-seven-year-old Rapunzel Piece.

'Have you actually met her, Granny? Otherwise it's not that interesting.'

'I most certainly have. And she, my dears,' declared Lady Tode, 'is an *absolute pill.*'

In this, Lady Tode was not wrong.

The famous author Frances Piece (1903–1989) may have been a fine novelist, but, as has been gleefully noted since by her many biographers, she was not a kind or loving mother. She had two children – with her customary cleverness, both at the same time. Rapunzel was a twin. The other one, Rapunzel's brother, died when he was only eight years old: and there were plenty of rumours as to the cause. Neglect certainly played a part. Frances Piece was too busy, writing masterpieces and gadding about in smart houses like Tode Hall, to concentrate on employing quality childcare. (Ditto the father, although, to be fair, at that point he was already dead.)

What had started as maternal indifference turned, after the boy's death, to a most vicious, guilt-driven revulsion, and from then on, Frances Piece hated her surviving daughter. Sixty-nine years later, Rapunzel bore the scars of her miserable childhood in almost every choice she made and word she spoke.

However.

On the bright side, unlike her twin, she had at least survived to adulthood, and indeed for the past thirty years had outlived her hateful mother. Rapunzel Piece was sole heir to the Piece writing fortune, which made her a rich woman. Also, in this particular situation, a powerful one. The big-budget, star-spangled six-part TV series about to get underway at Tode Hall could never have gone ahead without her say-so.

And then there was Norman Wright. Lady Tode assumed he was a nephew because it explained their different surnames, but the reason was more interesting, and much sadder, than that. Norman had been conceived while Rapunzel was in her last year at school and about to head up to Oxford University. Which, for a woman, in 1963, was quite a thing.

Norman was the product of a fling with a school porter, recently arrived from Poland. When the pregnancy was discovered, the porter was fired and Rapunzel was expelled. She was forbidden from finishing school, let alone taking her place at university. Though there would have been nothing to prevent her from studying, since her mother also made her give up the baby for adoption. Farewell, Norman.

... Until twenty-seven years later, in 1990, less than a year after Rapunzel buried her own mother, Norman came knocking at her door. At first, she refused to believe it was him. She kept him on the doorstep, made him present his documents: made him wait outside while she fetched her reading glasses. But then – there he was. Hello Norman. Small and bald and chubby – the same white hair and pink eyes she remembered when they took him from her. Her beloved albino boy. This was the happiest day of Rapunzel's life. She clung to him, she wept all the tears that she had kept unshed, for all those years.

'You're so ugly,' she sobbed. 'I can hardly believe how ugly you are.'

He was ugly too, poor fellow: less for his unfortunate colouring, more for the small, sad, shrunken way he carried himself after a lifetime of people staring and recoiling.

'I am ugly,' he said. 'I'm very sorry.'

She said, 'My baby boy, my Norman, it doesn't matter!'

But after that first, delirious day of reunion, things quickly deteriorated. Family relationships tend to follow a pattern, no matter even the best intentions, and Rapunzel didn't have it within her to love her ugly, middle-aged son in any healthy way. He had witnessed her, at her weakest moment, clinging to him and sobbing – the two things she most despised – and he'd been paying for it ever since. Why did he put up with her? It was a question anyone who saw them together would ask.

He liked the money his mother promised him: that was certainly a part of it. But it wasn't the only reason. There was also pity – because he would never forget how she clung to him on that one and only day. And there was a sort of lingering, hopeless hopefulness, too, that she might one day be kind to him again. In the meantime, they were constantly in contact. She rang him day and night, always with a new and more devious way to make herself disagreeable. Unsettling him had become her life sport. Which was why, at the last sweltering minute, under the guise of saving money, she had insisted on their travelling to Todeister by coach instead of train. The journey took an hour-and-a-half longer, and saved £7. It meant Norman had to take the afternoon off work.

Norman, unmarried, shy, always an outsider, could never quite bring himself to abandon her. Mostly, though, he wished he'd never tracked her down. He would have been a far happier man without her.

The train pulled in and pulled out of Todeister station, and sure enough, nobody fitting the guests' description disembarked. It was a small station. Nobody disembarked at all.

There followed frantic telephone calls between Alice and India, India and Egbert(Mr), Egbert(Mr) and Norman, until finally the confusion was cleared. There had been a breakdown in communication. Rapunzel was meant to have told the Todes about their altered travel arrangements, but she never did. She claimed she thought Norman was going to do it, but she was lying. She knew very well that he hadn't, because she had assured him that she would do it herself. In the car, on the way to the Hall, Norman apologised profusely, to everyone, even though it wasn't his fault.

Rapunzel, sitting in the front, beside Alice, said: 'Silly Norman! I ask you. It's all very well being a world expert in Shang Dynasty warcraft, dear. Or whatever. But it doesn't get you very far when you're stuck at a coach station in Todeister.'

Alice said: 'Not to worry. We've found each other now.'

And in the back of the car, squeezed, or hovering, between Ecgbert(Sir) and Norman, Geraldine Tode said: 'Pah! I'm telling you, she's a dreadful woman. She did it on purpose.'

Ecgbert and Alice heard her, loud and clear. They suspected Lady Tode was right.

THE GREAT HALL

6.30 P.M.

And there we have it. At last. The full party. By 6.30 p.m. on that sweltering Monday evening in August, those who were staying at the Hall for the night were upstairs changing for dinner. By morning, one of them would be a killer and one of them would be dead.

While they arrange themselves in their finery, their borrowed dinner jackets or, in Nicola Tode's case, agonise between pairs of dirty jeggings, let's run through the cast again. Readers might like to put a fold in the page, the better to refer back to it later.

HOUSEHOLD

TODE, Ecgbert (Sir) 52 yrs. Oldest son and rightful heir to Tode Hall. Disinherited by his late mother for being unreliable. Lives on the estate. First cousin to busy Egbert(Mr). Brother to hopeless Nicola, also to Esmé, currently absent in Australia.

CARFIZZI (Mr) 73 yrs. Butler and caretaker at Tode Hall since 1982. Lives with Mrs Carfizzi in a basement flat below the kitchen. Calabrian. Prefers men.

CARFIZZI (Mrs) 71 yrs. Cook. Married to Mr Carfizzi since beginning of time. Also Calabrian. Very mysterious.

LIDDELL, Alice (Mrs) 52 yrs. Divorced mother to triplets, Morman, Drez and Jacko. Employed at Tode Hall since 2018 as its 'Organisational Coordinator'. Friend, confidante and Picker-Up-of-Pieces to all the Todes, especially India.

LIDDELL, Dregz'n'Co 21 yrs. London-based triplets, Morman, Jacko and Drez. Staying at the Gardener's House with their mother Alice during their university holidays.

MELLORS, Oliver (Mr) 36 yrs. Tode Hall's head gamekeeper. Recently abandoned by his wife. Spotted by film director Noah Thistlestrupp and now co-starring in the remake of *Prance to the Music in Time*. Hot.

TODE, Egbert (Mr) 35 yrs. Former estate agent. Master of Tode Hall. Adoring husband to India. First cousin to Nicola and Ecgbert Tode(Sir). Father to Ludo and Passion. Decent.

TODE, Geraldine (Lady Tode) 1907–1971. Most elegant former mistress of Tode Hall. Grandmother to Ecgbert(Sir), Egbert(Mr) and Nicola. Dead.

TODE, India (Mrs) 34 yrs. Blonde and breezy mistress of the house. Wife to Egbert(Mr). Mother to Ludo and Passion.

TODE, Ludo (Master) 4 yrs. Son to India and Egbert(Mr).

TODE, Nicola (Ms) 54 yrs. Socialist. Lesbian. Staying at the Hall to nurse a broken heart but resident in Edinburgh.

TODE, Passion (Miss) 3 yrs. Daughter to India and Egbert(Mr).

GUESTS

CROWLEY, Alyster (Mr) 67 yrs. Hollywood-based bigwig film producer. Executive Producer, *Prance to the Music in Time*.

KELLET, Livvie (Ms) 41 yrs. Oscar winner. Actor-activist-humanitarian. Preferred pronouns she/her.

MACINTOSH, Teddy (Mr) 39 yrs. Oscar winner. Old Harrovian. Mostly gay.

PIECE, Rapunzel (Miss) 77 yrs. Spinster daughter of world-renowned novelist Frances Piece, author of *Prance to the Music in Time*. Sole heir and owner of Piece copyright.

SMITH, KitKat (Miss) 30 yrs. *Prance to the Music in Time* Wardrobe Design Assistant. Trying to make her way in the world.

THISTLESTRUPP, Noah, 47 yrs. London-based film director with Nordic roots. Married to a high-earning City solicitor, with a third child on the way.

WRIGHT, Norman (Mr) 60 yrs. Biological son of Rapunzel Piece. Professor of Chinese History, Middlesex University. Bachelor.

THE CHINESE DRAWING ROOM

7.10 P.M.

Oliver Mellors decided to ignore India's message, and brought a plus one with him anyway. He sidled into the Chinese Drawing Room, wearing a dark red velvet dinner jacket, looking *smoking hot*, and holding KitKat loosely by the hand. India spotted them at once, but a few other guests had already congregated, so she felt she couldn't make a fuss. She dispatched her husband to go and 'deal with it' instead.

So Egbert(Mr) pulled Mellors to one side and said:

'Now look here. Poor old India's been working *like mad*, getting all this stuff together. It's not as easy as it looks ... with the *placement* and so on ... You can't just tip up with an unaccounted-for bird. It's not really on ... India's terribly upset ...' Egbert(Mr) glanced across at KitKat, chatting politely, in a dress from Whistles. 'Who is she, anyway?' Egbert(Mr) couldn't help note the lovely ankles; the overall gorgeousness, the luscious long blonde hair. A bit like India, only not.

Mellors said to Egbert, whom he would never address by his first name, no matter how many times Egbert asked: 'My wife's left me, Mr Tode. What were I supposed to do?'

Egbert was always the last to hear the gossip. At the news, his firm jaw dropped, albeit briefly. 'Gosh, that's terrible news, Mr Mellors. Terrible. I'm really sorry.'

'I'm wretched,' stated Mellors. 'There's those might say I deserve it. But I love her, Mr Tode. I do.'

After that, Egbert couldn't wait to bring an end to the conversation. 'Look. I'll have a word with India,' he said, backing away. 'Not to worry. No problem at all ... What's her name again? We'll get a place laid up for her right away.' Egbert hovered in agony. He and Mellors had always had a good, professional relationship. But they had never discussed anything, really, that wasn't pheasant or grouse related. This was very awkward for him. Everything about it was awkward. Mellors in a borrowed dinner jacket, drinking champagne in the Chinese Drawing Room was awkward enough. Mellors in a dinner jacket with a broken heart, drinking champagne in the Chinese Drawing Room – was making Egbert sweat even more than he would have been anyway, in his dinner jacket, in this mad, sultry heat. He patted Mellors on the shoulder. Just the once. 'Sorry, mate,' he said. 'Awfully sorry. I'll see what I can do,' and quickly stepped away.

Most of the guests were still in their bedrooms at that point. But Ecgbert(Sir) and Nicola were milling around, helping themselves to Mrs Carfizzi's disgusting canapés. Ditto the Dregz'n'Co trio. They'd found a plate of cocktail sausages and were hovering round it like vultures, shoving three in their mouths at a time.

Alice had just arrived, looking unusually smart – looking

lovely, in fact, in a shimmering summer dress; green and blue and swishy, and maybe a little frayed at the edges. Despite having the three boys in the house, she had even managed to get into the bathroom to wash her wild, mostly yellow hair.

Rapunzel, dressed like a French peasant in thick black tights and Dr Martens, was already manspreading on the sofa, slurping balefully on a glass of champagne. Her unhappy son, Norman, stood beside her, looking more like a dog on a chain than a middle-aged Professor of History. He was being chatted at by KitKat, who was updating him, in detail, about her career.

KitKat's lover, at least until this morning, Noah Thistlestrupp, hadn't yet surfaced. As India hissed to her husband when he reported back on his failed mission regarding the plus one, Thistlestrupp was 'probably going to go apeshit' when he saw KitKat on Mellors's smoking-hot arm. 'This is much worse than if Mellors had brought some old strumpet from the Tode Arms,' she told him. 'If my instincts are correct, and as you know Eggie, they usually are, we'll have fireworks about this. Do you think poor Mellors knows she and Thistlestrupp have been having it off?'

Egbert(Mr) was shocked. '*Have* they?'

'I saw them snogging behind one of the caravan thingies this morning. Well not snogging, but sort of. Groping. Whatever. It was pretty obvious.'

'Well, I must say that's a bit awkward.'

'But d'you think Mellors knows?'

'Well *I don't know*, Munch! How am I supposed to know?'

India gave up on him. She went over to discuss it with Mellors herself.

She said: 'Bit cheeky!'

Mellors smiled. A nice, rueful smile. 'I know. Sorry.'

India, not blind to his hotness but still annoyed, said: 'I told you, you couldn't bring anyone. I don't know why you bothered to ask if you were going to bring her anyway.'

'Katie left me.'

'Yeah, I know that. Horrible for you. But let's face it, it's not like ... Anyway, I'm sorry about it. But the problem is ...' She hesitated, suddenly uncertain. She prided herself on her romance-related hunches which, since her early teens, had proved time and again to be spot on. Even so, she needed to be careful. 'I'm pretty certain that your friend, Pussy Galore, whatever she calls herself—'

'KitKat.'

'KitKat ... I'm almost certain she and Noah Thistlestrupp – I'm pretty sure ...' she dropped her voice and leaned in, 'that – you know. I'm pretty sure they're—'

'Not anymore,' said Mellors.

'What? Not since this morning?'

Mellors nodded: 'She's going to say something to him during dinner.'

'Oh, for God's sake!'

Mellors shrugged. 'He's a married man. He should know better.'

'Oh! That is *rich*, coming from you!' India took a breath to tell him that KitKat needed to leave; but then Carfizzi shimmied up, looking only slightly better since his afternoon rest. Word had reached him, he said to India, that there was an extra guest for dinner. Was this correct and should he lay an extra place?

'No!' snapped India. 'You shouldn't.'

'Yes,' replied Mellors. 'You should.'

Carfizzi surprised them both. He turned to Mellors, whom

78

he generally didn't deign to speak to at all. Gave him a glittery smile. 'May I say, Mr Mellors, how well you look in the dinner jacket. You should wear the colour more often.'

'Thank you,' said Mellors. 'That's nice of you to say.'

'Not at all,' murmured Mr Carfizzi. 'The pleasure is mine.'

'Mrs Tode and me were just talking about my friend over there, who's very keen to come to the dinner tonight. I were saying to Mrs Tode that if my friend isn't able to join us, then I'm not either.'

'Oh come *on*,' said India. 'You're just being stupid now.'

Mellors smiled. '*You* come on,' he said.

India wasn't accustomed to having her wishes overruled. She might have continued to fight – it would have been better if she had, considering what came next. But just then, there arrived in the room the Oscar winners, walking arm in arm, like a royal couple. It was too exciting.

'Fuck it,' she said, with a flick of her golden hair. 'Fine. She can stay. Just – please. Don't have a fisticuffs with the director in the middle of dinner?'

Mellors smirked. A brave smirk. Not really a reflection of how he felt, which was miserable. He wished the TV series had never come to Tode Hall. He wished he'd never gone to the screen test. He wished he'd never signed the contract. He wished his wife would come home, and everything could go back to normal.

In the meantime, here he was. Dressed like an idiot in a room the size of his house. And there was KitKat, all dolled up in her finest, leaping at life. He had asked her if Thistlestrupp might try to get her fired when he saw the two of them together, but she'd been confident he wouldn't. Not with a pregnant wife in the background – especially one who earned most of the money. She said he wouldn't dare.

Livvie and Teddy glided over. Livvie, all bosom and shoulders and astonishing red velvet, ignored Mellors (with whom she'd spent all afternoon in rehearsals), clasped India's hands in both of hers, and greeted her as if their unhappy meeting earlier in the day had never happened; as if India was the only woman in the world Livvie wanted to talk to. She gazed into India's bright blue eyes and asked: 'How can you even *stand* to *exist* amid this kind of ... *supernatural* ... beauty?'

For a moment India thought Livvie was referring to her own, Livvie's, supernatural beauty, which she thought was a bit off. But then she realised she was talking about the house. 'Oh you mean the *house*?' she said carelessly. 'You get used to it pretty quick.'

'Do you? *Do you*? I don't believe I would,' declared Livvie. 'I would breathe it in, every morning. The unearthly beauty ...' She breathed, preparing to expand. Luckily, at that point, Teddy, standing beside her, interrupted.

'Teddy MacIntosh,' he said. 'We haven't met.'

India giggled, extracting her hand from Livvie's as she spoke. 'I know who you are!' she said. '*Big* fan! Especially in that Nazi movie. What was it called? My goodness, I literally sobbed my guts out!'

Teddy said he thought he might have been in the same house at Harrow as India's cousin, Toby.

'OMG,' she said. 'That's amazing! What house were you in? I'll ask him.'

So that was nice.

A brief lull before the storm.

Noah Thistlestrupp ambled in, having taken many wrong turns down many dark corridors. *How*, he asked himself, *could one family live in a house this large while others lived on the streets*? Oh, he was angry about the injustice of the world by the time he found the Chinese Drawing Room. Mr Carfizzi handed him a glass of champagne.

Slurp One. And he spotted KitKat, talking to a small, fat, middle-aged albino. Yuk. Slurp. *What the hell was she doing here*? He spotted Oliver Mellors making his way over to join her ... Did he imagine it? SLURP-SLURP. Oliver Mellors was running his hand over her arse!

Thistlestrupp moved towards them – and was intercepted by Alice. Picker-Up-of-Pieces. Organisational Coordinator. Very good at sensing the vibe and keeping things mellow.

'Hello there, I'm Alice Liddell. We haven't met – I work on the estate. You've very kindly employed my three sons today and I just wanted to say *thank you*.'

'What's that?' he said, looking over her head. 'Excuse me ...' He tried to sidestep her, but Alice – never an athlete, but always a good dancer – did something tiny and brilliant with her feet. Her skirt swayed; and somehow, it made his progress impossible. She said: 'India tells me you're upset about the colour of the grass. It *is* rather grey ...'

Thistlestrupp kept his eyes on Mellors, who must have felt it, because he turned, glanced across at Thistlestrupp and smiled.

'What the fuck?' muttered Thistlestrupp. 'Excuse me ...'

This time it was India who blocked his path. She swept towards him, husband in tow. '*Here* he is!' she cried. 'Eggie, you remember Noah Thistlestrupp, the amazing, brilliant, fantastic film director ...' she smiled. 'Eggie, you have to talk to Mr Thistlestrupp about the lawns. Everyone's terribly upset about the lawns, apparently, but don't you remember how you used to colour them in when they weren't green enough, when you were doing the brochures at Savills?'

Thistlestrupp shook his head. 'I don't actually care about the grass. I keep telling everyone. Would you excuse me?'

Again he tried to slip away. But it was not to be.

'Well *I* care about the grass, Thistlestrupp.' As if from nowhere, up stepped Alyster Crowley. Slurping and sweating. Dressed in shirtsleeves. 'I care very much.'

'Ohhh!' cried India. 'Hello again Alyster! Did you decide against the dinner jacket in the end?'

'Too hot,' he said. He looked and sounded even fatter and more American than he usually did, in this fine English drawing room. He stood out like a sore thumb. Not that he cared. 'Haven't you guys heard of AC in this country?'

'To be honest with you, Alyster,' said Egbert(Mr), 'we don't often need it. This is very unusual weather for Yorkshire. The farms are really suffering ...'

'So is your lawn,' boomed Alyster. 'I've had my people look again at the contract. You're gonna need to do something with the lawn, Egbert my friend, or we'll run into trouble, you and me.' Slurp.

Mr Carfizzi refilled everyone's glass.

Mellors whispered something into KitKat's ear.

Noah Thistlestrupp said: 'Would you excuse me?'

But Alyster Crowley put a hand on his shoulder.

Ecgbert(Sir) didn't feel much inspired by the company so far. He had never heard of either Oscar winner; and after the short journey from Todeister coach station, didn't want to spend another moment with the dreaded Rapunzel. The only person he wanted to talk to was Alice, but she was busy being organisational, floating around the room stopping arguments, so he wandered over to the next best thing: the triplets had set themselves up in a corner, and were giggling shyly among themselves.

'Can I join you?' he said.

'For sure, Ecgbert!' they said warmly.

'Thank you.' He joined them, thereby forming a smart but aimless quadrant. Hands in pockets.

A silence fell.

'What shall we talk about?' Ecgbert said.

They didn't know what to suggest.

'You know, I knew your ma when we were fourteen. Did you know that? We were great friends.'

They nodded understandingly.

Ecgbert continued to gaze at her. She looked, he thought, like the most scrumptious sort of a hippy. Curvaceous and colourful, with all the beads and everything. And the amazing yellow hair. He thought she probably dyed it. He thought quite right. It was very yellow. She dyed it herself, once a month, over the bathtub, usually while a little stoned. 'She's very beautiful, you know,' he said.

'Fo'rizzle, I think she used to be,' nodded one of them, agreeably. 'There are pictures, aren't there?' He turned to his brothers for confirmation.

'She still is,' Ecgbert said.

And then – there was Lady Tode again. Hair swept in its usual chignon, dressed in suede Balenciaga toga-dress (pale pink) with rose diamonds in her ears. 'Darling,' she said, amid little puffs of methane. 'These wretched boys don't want to talk to you *at all*. Stop mooning about in the corner and go and talk to the adults. For goodness sake. Seize the moment! Why don't you go and talk to that sensational-looking little actress over there? Do ask her who made her dress.'

'But I want to talk to *Alice*,' he replied.

'For sure!' said the boys. 'Why not?'

THE CHINESE DRAWING ROOM

7.30 P.M.

I t would be another half hour before Carfizzi announced
dinner was ready, but it was already clear that the evening
was unlikely to be a success. The temperature didn't help.
Even now, at 7.30 p.m., the women's feet were swelling in their
evening shoes, and the men were sweating in their jackets. The
heat made everyone snappy.

–There was Noah Thistlestrupp, itching for a fight
with Mellors, and Mellors wanting to walk off the film
altogether. And there was KitKat, boring everyone
about her career.

–There was Teddy MacIntosh, who had decided to
put Oliver Mellors into Coventry for arriving late to
afternoon rehearsals (tousled and smoking hot, thanks
to KitKat's embraces), without explanation or apology.
Teddy wasn't someone who stood on his dignity – as
he explained to Thistlestrupp, and Livvie, and his agent

whom he'd called three times today; and to anyone within earshot, in fact – apart from Alyster Crowley, who was scary, or, indeed, Oliver Mellors himself. But he could not tolerate such lack of respect. He had decided he would not be speaking one word to his co-star until his co-star came to his trailer and apologised.

–There was Alyster Crowley, being even more disagreeable than usual because he was accustomed to being the most important presence in any gathering, and he felt outshone by the aristocrats, lording it over him in their dogshit house. Alyster's ancestors were Irish immigrants – or they had been, a hundred and fifty years ago. It wasn't something he thought about often: but here, in this house, he felt prickly on his ancestors' behalf: this family, who were half a million dollars richer, thanks to him, had been living it up *in these very rooms* while his own family had been starving to death for lack of potatoes. He couldn't get it out of his head. One way or another he was going to make them pay for it. Starting with the lawn.

–And there was Rapunzel, giving off stink vibes indiscriminately. She possessed an uncanny sense for sniffing out the people who disliked her most, and then making a beeline for them. In fact she had just then risen from her sofa – as Lady Tode was ordering her grandson Ecgbert(Sir) to talk to Livvie. She was hobbling across the room to insult him.

Ecgbert(Sir) spotted her coming. He shuffled sideways to block her, and found himself confronted by his sister Nicola. She was looking unusually lively.

Nicola said to Ecgbert(Sir): 'Come with me, Ecgbert.'

He said no, automatically.

She grabbed his arm. 'Be a sport. Come over with me. We can introduce ourselves to Livvie Kellet.'

'But I don't want to.'

'Just *be nice*. For once. Won't you? I can't do it on my own.'

So he tagged along. Nicola tapped Livvie on her shimmering shoulder. Livvie turned: saw the plain woman in the silly beret gazing up at her in adoration, and did the thing she did best. She glowed. She beamed. She was very gracious. She was sweet, actually. While a blushing, spluttering Nicola stumbled out a garbled recitation of her entire life story, Livvie looked very much as if she was listening. She said:

'That's amazing Nicola … *Amazing* …'

Nicola told her about the self-help book.

'Brave *you*,' Livvie said. Nicola felt, at that moment, as if she was the only woman in the world. Her feet (sweltering in trainers) lifted a couple of inches off the ground, and before her eyes, Livvie Kellet grew wings.

'I think you're such an inspiration to young women,' Nicola said.

'Not *me*,' smiled Livvie. 'Yes, I do the best I can, but it's people like *you*, working on the ground with youngsters. Doing …' Livvie drew a blank, '… the truly amazing things that you do …' Livvie held her chest: hot hands to red velvet bosom. 'Honest to God – not that I believe in "God" per se: as in the all-powerful white male. When I say "God" I mean earth-divinity. Woman-spirit. *Gaia*. Anyway, honest to my divinity, Gaia, I feel humbled in your presence, Nicola Tode. I really do.'

'Thank you,' said Nicola, burning with love. 'I am humbled, and blessed. I feel blessed …'

Lady Tode, never far off, had joined the merry throng.

'Tell her to stop, Ecgbert,' she drawled. 'Tell Nicola to *stop* ... Right now. *Order* her to stop.'

'I can't,' said Ecgbert. 'She's having fun.'

Nicola turned on him. 'It's not really about "fun", Ecgbert,' she said. 'I don't expect you to understand this, as a man living in a "man's" body, as it were. But I feel gratitude, as a woman, from seeing others feel valued. And if my work enables this, as such ... ' she glanced at Livvie to check she was listening. Livvie nodded, just as if she had been: 'Then that is my job done. "Fun" is a very diminishing way of putting it.'

'Goddit!' Ecgbert said.

'Tell her to stop!' his grandmother cried.

Ecgbert pulled at his woolly grey hair. 'I can't, Granny. I wish I could.'

'What?' said Nicola.

Luckily, Rapunzel's slow, determined hobble had brought her to its point. At that moment she, too, joined the group.

'This must be Nicola, is it?' she said, peering at Nicola as if at a piece of bad fruit. 'I haven't set eyes on you since you were a baby. You weren't a very attractive baby. Do you know who I am?'

Nicola said to Ecgbert: 'Who's Granny?'

Livvie said to Rapunzel: 'I know who you are, Miss Piece! Your mother was the greatest novelist to have ever lived! I've read every word she ever wrote! Literally! I finish one book, and I can't stop myself starting it all over again! And then I read another one. Her way with words ... I can't get enough of it!' Livvie sighed. 'An amazing woman! Such an inspiration to women. It's an honour to meet you, Miss Piece! I'm Livvie ... '

Rapunzel glanced briefly at Livvie, clocked her neediness

(for possible future sport), and returned her laser attention to Nicola. 'I don't really know anything about you,' she said. 'Your mother was a great beauty ... Well. I thought she was *hideous*. Since you ask.'

'No one did,' observed Ecgbert.

'I couldn't see what all the fuss was about. I always assumed it was snobbery. Because she looked perfectly ordinary to me. But people get dazzled by the Hall. You've probably noticed. People suck up, don't they? Pretend to like you, when – I mean, why *would* they? ... But that's *people* for you, isn't it? They used to say she was a great beauty ...' Rapunzel looked Nicola up and then down; let her eyes linger on the unfortunate jeggings, and Nicola's favourite trainers. 'I don't suppose anyone says it about you ...'

'My sister *is* beautiful,' cried Ecgbert, incensed. 'She's ravishing! I don't suppose anyone ever says it about *you*, Rapunzel Piece. I should think that's what you mean.'

'Bravo!' cried Lady Tode. 'Good for you, Ecgbert!'

'Thank you,' he replied. He looked at his sister, worried she might be about to cry or something, but she looked the same as normal.

Livvie said: 'Every woman is beautiful. It doesn't matter what she looks like. As woman, we are beautiful. And I say this, as woman. I call it womanbeauty, like it's one word. It's my new word! I love it so much. I believe in womanbeauty with every fibre of my being ...'

A pause. Nicola was nodding, feverishly, and her chin was trembling.

Ecgbert(Sir) and Lady Tode started giggling.

'Well you would say that, wouldn't you?' Rapunzel said at last. 'You're an actress.' She waved a wizened arm to encompass

Livvie's luscious shoulders, cleavage, the red velvet dress, the unearthly womanbeauty. 'You've built your career on – well, I won't say *whoring* yourself, but we all know it's what I mean ...'

Mr Carfizzi stood by the door and cleared his throat. Dinner was served.

THE LONG GALLERY (EAST END)

8.00 P.M.

'Have you talked to Rapunzel yet?' India whispered to Egbert(Mr), as they led the guests from the Chinese Drawing Room, through the Imperial Singsong Room, the Music Room, the Great Hall, the Turquoise Drawing Room ... to the Long Gallery, which ran the full length of the West Wing ... 'Is she as absolutely ghastly as I think she is? I don't think I've ever met anyone so horrible in my life!'

Egbert was a bit shocked: 'Oh, I'm sure she's a sweet old thing, when you get to know her,' he said. 'But I must admit ...' Mr Carfizzi heard them coming and pulled open the Long Gallery doors, and at that moment, Egbert's eye fell upon the tiny, glittering table in the middle of the massive room, and he gasped. 'Gosh Munch! It looks terrific! *Well done!*'

India pulled a face.

There were now sixteen people for dinner. But the Long Gallery was long indeed – 150-feet long, in fact, and the table in the middle, when it was fully extended, could seat two hundred. Looking at it now, with so much silverware in so much space, twinkling in the candlelight, India vaguely wished she'd opted for one of the smaller dining rooms. The Red Dining Room, where they generally ate, had two Reynolds on the walls, among other treasures, and seated twenty people with comfort and ease. Or there was the Knights' Parlour, also quite large, with two Gainsboroughs, a Titian and a Stubbs. It would have worked equally well. She realised she'd been showing off: trying to impress the Oscar winners with the size of her dining room. It seemed a bit silly now. With the table reduced to its shortest length, and only sixteen places laid, and with no welcoming fire burning in the grate on such a sweltering night, it looked worse than silly. It looked a bit tragic.

'You don't think we should have used one of the smaller dining rooms?' India asked.

Adamantly, Egbert(Mr) shook his head. 'Munch,' he said, '*you* are amazing. *This* is amazing. I don't know how you do it! Everything looks marvellous. Absolutely amazing and terrific.'

'Thank you, Eggie,' she said, and kissed him on the cheek.

India had agonised over the *placement*. But with so many broken and swollen egos, and in such a small party, it would have been impossible to get it absolutely right. She didn't, in any case.

She put herself between Teddy MacIntosh, who was famous, and Noah Thistlestrupp, who was reasonably young, and had a decent figure. This, she knew, might cause offence to Alyster Crowley, whose finance everybody was depending on, and who was therefore the most important person in the party. But after their meeting on the lawn this morning, she'd been unable to get the image of his sweaty, leather-clad torso out of her head. Also she'd been shocked by his bad manners, and when it came to the crux, placement-decision-making moment, she realised she couldn't face an evening watching him eat. She put him between Ecgbert(Sir) and Rapunzel Piece. On every count, this was a mistake.

She had taken care, at least, not to put KitKat beside either Mellors or Thistlestrupp. But it wasn't enough. The table was slim, and they were easily within each other's earshot. This too was a mistake.

The Placement Went Like This

(EAST END)
INDIA TODE

TEDDY MACINTOSH		NOAH THISTLESTRUPP
MORMAN		NICOLA TODE
KITKAT SMITH		OLIVER MELLORS
ALICE LIDDELL		DREZ
JACKO		ECGBERT TODE (SIR)
NORMAN WRIGHT		ALYSTER CROWLEY
LIVVIE KELLET		RAPUNZEL PIECE

EGBERT TODE (MR)
(WEST END)

The guests filed in, and India directed them to their badly considered places.

Thistlestrupp still hadn't managed to pull KitKat aside.

Every time he approached, no matter how slyly, she seemed to sense it and slither away. And the more she slithered, the more desperate he became, the more he longed to drag Oliver Mellors out of the room and punch him; which he knew he couldn't do, partly for professional reasons, partly because he knew Mellors would punch him back, much harder.

Thus far, Thistlestrupp contained his temper. He took his seat beside his hostess and the rather tragic-looking sister, whose name he couldn't remember and who looked like she needed a bath, and tried, in vain, to catch KitKat's eye across the table.

Oliver Mellors, meanwhile, whose family had worked for the Todes for a century or maybe even two, took his seat on Nicola Tode's other side. Their heads were barely a metre apart. In all the years of knowing one another, they had never been in such close proximity. He looked at her, with his smoky-green eyes, and smiled.

'Bit weird, in't it?'

Nicola blushed. Such was the power of Mellors. Then, being more or less incapable of giving an honest response to anyone, about anything, she said: 'Bit weird, in what way?'

Mellors lost interest. He turned to Alice Liddell, sitting beside KitKat, just across the table from him (see diagram). He said to her – because he felt a little responsible for KitKat, having brought her along:

'You've met KitKat then, have you?'

Noah Thistlestrupp's ears pricked up.

Alice said to Mellors: 'We've already introduced ourselves, thanks ... KitKat's been telling me about her career.'

'Aye,' said Mellors. 'She does that.'

His smoky-green attention meandered further up the table,

94

towards his co-star Teddy, who was looking even more tense and sorrowful than usual.

'That young lady has a *very* promising career ahead of her,' Noah Thistlestrupp yelled to Alice, across KitKat, across the table. 'Mark my words. She's a very, very talented individual ... Gorgeous too!'

'That's nice,' said Alice, feeling embarrassed for him.

KitKat, through coquettishly pursed lips, replied : 'I don't think my *gorgeousness* is super-relevant to my professional skill set and capabilities, thanks very much, Noah.'

Thistlestrupp said: 'No, of course not. I was just saying ...'

'People wouldn't say that about you, would they?' she said, getting the wind behind her. She was nervous: already a bit drunk. 'You wouldn't hear people say: "a very talented director. Gorgeous too." Would you?'

Mellors sniggered. 'He is, though, in't he? Don't you think so, Teddy? In't Thistlestrupp gorgeous?'

Teddy, who was having a tense and sorrowful conversation with Morman (or possibly Drez?) about the pros and cons of legalising cannabis, shot them both an evil look. He hadn't been planning to respond, as per the rules of Coventry, but then Oliver Mellors looked so damn *complacent*, in his gorgeous smoking jacket; and Thistlestrupp had been so *arsey* this afternoon, when Teddy had complained about the Mellors punctuality issue. So he said: 'Not gorgeous to me, Oliver, no. Just because I'm gay, I don't have to fancy every man I ever meet ... On the other hand, you and Thistlestrupp obviously have a thing you need to do together. Perhaps you two should get a room.'

'Whaaat?' said Mellors. He was still laughing.

India said: 'Crikey.' She looked at Alice. Pulled a face. 'Am I missing something?'

Alice shrugged. 'Maybe.'

Teddy said: 'Laugh, by all means. Laugh away! I'm so happy you find it funny. The way you find it funny, turning up to rehearsals forty-five minutes late.'

Mellors's laughter died, but he was still semi-smiling. He said: 'Want to know *why* I were late, Teddy?'

'I think we'd all like to know that,' snapped Thistlestrupp. 'Eh, KitKat?'

'Not really,' said KitKat, blushing. It was beginning to occur to her that she might have bitten off more than she could chew. Thistlestrupp was so uptight. Mellors was so smoking hot and dangerous. And here they all were, stuck at the same end of the table. Maybe, this wasn't going to work out so well for her after all? Maybe she shouldn't have agreed to come to the dinner?

'I were stuck on'phone with your agent,' Mellors was saying to Teddy. 'Couldn't get him off. He said I wasn't to tell you. But you're not a baby, are you, Teddy?'

Teddy looked uncertain. Was he a baby? *Surely not.* On the other hand, he could feel his heart thumping.

He could always feel his heart thumping when he was stressed. It was a thing. He'd discussed the issue with his cardiologist, his therapist, his dermatologist, his personal trainer, immunologist, nutritionist, oncologist, chiropodist, voice coach, cleaner, spiritualist and even his dentist. Nobody seemed able to help. Mellors's remark had his heart beating so hard, he could feel it beating even as far as his fingertips. He could feel his hands shake. But – the thing about Teddy that must never be forgotten – he may have been a baby, but he knew how to act. So he gave a brilliant little chuckle. Extra-light. 'Been chatting to Steve, have you? Don't tell me he's trying to poach you?'

'Steven. That's right. I told him I had no interest,' Mellors said. '. . . He seemed unwilling to believe it. God knows why.'

Even Teddy couldn't act his way through the impact of that. Teddy had been on the phone to Steven three times since the end of the late-running rehearsal: *three times*. And Steven hadn't said a word. Not a single word. Teddy held on to his heart, and stared at Mellors, dumbstruck.

Carfizzi appeared to fill the wine glasses.

Somehow his tailcoat had become caught in the waistband of his trousers. Also, what little hair he had, usually slick and smoothed with rich-smelling unctions, was poking off his head at multiple angles.

Alice said, to break the Teddy–Mellors tension: 'Ah! Mr Carfizzi has come offering refills!' And then, noting Carfizzi's uncharacteristically dishevelled appearance, 'Is everything OK?'

'Everything is perfectly fine thank you, Mrs Liddell,' he replied stiffly. 'Mrs Carfizzi is just preparing the dinner.'

'Oh good,' said Alice, slightly confused. 'Well, that's good . . .'

'I certainly *hope* she's preparing dinner!' said India. 'That is, I hope she's already prepared it by now, Mr Carfizzi! We're all starving, ha ha!'

But nobody laughed. Mr Carfizzi, who was Italian, looked as though he might be about to cry.

Alice said brightly: 'Mmm. I wonder what Mrs Carfizzi is preparing for us.' Which she didn't wonder at all.

'The same as always,' Carfizzi said. It sounded defensive.

'How *lovely*!' Alice cried. Which it wouldn't be, because it never was.

Meanwhile the stare-off between Teddy MacIntosh and Oliver Mellors continued, until it became impossible for the others to ignore. Thistlestrupp, with his professional hat on, realised the situation needed to be rescued, or there was a risk that one or other of his actors might walk off the show. If Teddy walked – so would the finance. If Mellors walked – and this was the truth: it was what was killing Teddy, because he knew it too – if *Mellors* walked, they would lose the star of the show.

Thistlestrupp offered an unconvincing, Nordic-style *ho ho*. 'Take it easy, guys,' he said. 'Teddy, be cool, my friend. I think Oliver is trying to wind us up. Steven would have told you, I'm sure ...'

Mellors smiled. Very smoky. Also a little menacing. 'Are you calling me a liar?' he asked.

Teddy said: 'Yes. I don't believe you. What did he say?'

Cue, Alice, chief vibe manager and keeper of the peace. 'Nicola! How's the book going? Why don't you tell everyone about the book. It's a self-help book, isn't it?'

'I would,' Nicola said, 'but I'm still reeling from Mr Thistlestrupp's comments regarding KitKat's gorgeousness, to be frank with you. I actually thought that kind of comment had gone out with the dinosaurs.'

At this point most of the guests were still reasonably sober. Things could only get worse.

THE LONG GALLERY (WEST END)

8.59 P.M.

At 8.59 p.m. the guests had been sitting at that small table in that very large room for over three-quarters of an hour, their voices bouncing off the domed ceiling above – a gathering of argumentative ants stranded in the middle of a deep, dark ocean – and still no food had materialised.

First Alice, then Egbert(Mr), and finally India had trotted off to the kitchen to discover the cause of the delay, only to be shoo-ed away, one by one. Mrs Carfizzi *looked* the same. The food smelled the same. Everything looked more or less normal, and Mr Carfizzi assured them, one by one, that everything was under control. Once, twice, three times, he came in to refill the guests' glasses.

When, at last, the first course was presented – cold prawns in Thousand Island dressing, with pepper on top – Egbert(Mr), who rarely drank, was the only sober person left at the table.

Livvie Kellet looked down in horror at the plate Carfizzi laid in front of her. She was hungry, her fork was poised. And then the food came into focus. She turned to Egbert(Mr) and said: 'But it's—' With great care, she laid the fork back down again. Dropped her chin, the better to collect herself. 'I think there's been a mistake ...'

'Hm?' Egbert looked attentive. 'What's that? ... Do dig in, Livvie! You must be famished. Crikey, I know I am! I was actually seriously beginning to give up hope!'

'Did no one on my side inform your people? Did they not discuss my dietary desideratum?'

'Errr, what's that?' said Egbert(Mr). Frozen with awkwardness. Longing to eat. 'I must admit – I haven't got the foggiest ...' He turned to his wife, at the far end of the table. 'India! I say, *India* ...' But she didn't hear him. She had enough to cope with on her end.

Livvie said: 'I've been vegan since April, Egbert. I would have thought you would have known.'

'God. Sorry. Are you? Have you? I'm so sorry. I really am. Nobody said. I say, India – I'll be honest with you, Livvie. I'm not even sure we've got anything ... rice? We've probably got some rice. God. This is awfully embarrassing. I really can't apologise enough ...' He laid down his own fork, so tantalisingly loaded with prawn and pepper. Christ, he was hungry. 'INDIA! Darling – can you call Mr Carfizzi? *Poor Livvie*. Unfortunately she can't eat the prawns ... She's a *vegan*!' He laughed, out of embarrassment mostly. Also because he did not take veganism seriously. He turned back to Livvie. Her chin was still down, the better to collect herself. She was very angry.

'I would have thought,' she said again, 'that you might have been aware. I've been very active, via my social media platforms, really ... *trying* ... to raise awareness. It just seems so strange that you didn't know about it.' She sounded suspicious, as if the Todes, knowing her vegan stance, had fed her prawns with pepper specifically to torment her.

'It does seem awfully strange,' agreed Egbert(Mr) politely. Although he'd never heard of Livvie Kellet until a month ago, let alone been aware of her active social media platforms. In fact, even now, he wasn't 100 per cent certain what veganism really meant. They couldn't eat eggs. He was pretty clear on that. But could they eat prawns? Apparently not. It wasn't a question he'd ever needed to trouble himself with, until this moment.

Norman Wright, sitting on Livvie's other side, was so thrilled by her proximity that his voice had been bouncing, like a teenage boy, ever since they sat down. He gazed greedily at the full plate of food in front of her and wondered if he dared to suggest she slide it over. He kept on and on staring at it, rubbing his hands up and down his short thighs, licking his lips, trying to summon the courage to put in a request. She assumed he was looking at her cleavage.

'Norman, would you mind?' she snapped.

'What? Mind *what*?' Norman burned with shame. 'Sorry? *Sorry*. I'm so sorry. What have I done?'

At the other side of the table Norman's mother, busy antagonising Alyster Crowley about being American (not that he cared), noticed Norman's social discomfort and broke off to enjoy the moment. 'What have you done now, Norman?' she crowed. 'Are you harassing that poor young lady?'

'Not at all,' he said. 'I was just—' he pointed a short, tentative finger at her plate.

'She's out of your league, dear. I shouldn't bother,' shouted his mother.

'But I wasn't—'

Livvie was always tetchy when peckish, and doubly tetchy when she felt her standing as an actress was in any way being challenged (as it had been by the shrimp). She said: 'I think you were. Actually, Norman. No offence. But as a woman, I'd really rather you didn't.'

'But I *wasn't*,' he said.

'Are you saying she imagined it?' Rapunzel asked. 'HA HA HA! In your dreams, Norman dear. *In your dreams!*'

Egbert(Mr) said: 'Actually I think you're being a *bit* harsh, Rapunzel. If you don't mind me saying . . .'

'I do mind, as it happens,' said Livvie.

Alyster joined in. 'Oh *come ON Egbert*,' he cried, smacking the table so the silver shook. 'Are you telling me Mr Norman over there *wouldn't* like to get a handful of the beautiful Ms Kellet?' He laughed heartily, but quite alone. Not that he cared. 'There's not a red-blooded man in this room who wouldn't want a piece of Livvie Kellet,' he said. He did something with his meaty hands: a double cupping motion, which was absolutely uncalled-for, and he knew it.

Livvie pretended, brilliantly, not to notice.

'Bit much,' muttered Egbert(Mr). Because, as it happened, he did not want a piece of Livvie Kellet. He was finding her very hard work. Almost as disagreeable, in her own way, as Rapunzel, on his other side. More than anything, he longed to grab a piece of toast from the kitchen, and slip away to bed. Anything would be better than this.

He glanced at Norman, who looked quite blank. Shell-shocked, perhaps. He wondered why Norman put up with his awful mother. *Must be the money*, he concluded. Same reason any one of them put up with the old bag. He and India certainly wouldn't have invited her here if there hadn't been a lot of pressure applied from the TV people. Apparently she and/or her mother insisted on staying at the Hall in the run-up to the filming of every *Prance* adaptation yet made at the house. And since nothing could happen without her signature – here she was.

As always, when confronted by difficult individuals, Egbert was very polite.

He turned to her: 'Rapunzel,' he said, 'I imagine you've probably read the script for this exciting new adaptation, have you? Gone through it with a fine-tooth comb, I should think! Guarding your mama's legacy ... Brilliant of you, I must say. India and I *had a go* but you know ...' He turned to loop in Alyster and Norman, '*Personally speaking* I find it ruddy hard, with a script, working out what on earth is going on. Sort of – one doesn't quite know if one is coming or going ... Somebody's speaking, or somebody *isn't* speaking. It sort of jumps about. Do you find? ...'

Nobody answered, so he ploughed on.

'I must say, it had India and me absolutely defeated!' he continued. 'Page somethingorother. I think I made it to page fifteen! India did a *bit* better ...'

Livvie had by then been delivered a plate of apple and carrot, some bread and some olive oil. Carfizzi assured her that the bread was vegan, which almost certainly wasn't the case, but she seemed happy to believe it, and that was the important thing. Livvie, back to her better self, clutched Carfizzi's serving arm, and thanked him for the apple and carrot, as if he'd pulled her from a burning building. Her mood now fractionally restored, she decided to be nice.

She said: 'The fabulous thing about this new adaptation, Egbert, is its amazing emphasis on the issues that are relevant to all of us today ...'

'Too right!' agreed Egbert.

'. . . in the modern world, as we live it at this moment in time,' Livvie continued. '*Prance to the Music* is such an amazing book, as you know, but people can sometimes get confused into believing it's super elitist—'

'Ugh!' said Egbert, rolling his eyes in solid agreement.

'—due to its hetero-normative attitudes, and the characters being, quote-unquote, "upper class". But that's the thing. That's what Noah is really highlighting in this adaptation. These people aren't really "upper class". What they are is *people*. And no, they're not hetero-normal, they're *homo-normal*! Because that's what we all are, when you think about it. That's what's so modern about the book. It speaks to all of us, no matter our sexuality, ethnicity and attitudes towards climate change. It speaks for *now*.' She grinned, ready to be agreed with. She hadn't read the novel.

As per tradition, Alyster, Egbert(Mr) and Norman hadn't been listening. They were mostly watching her lips moving, and nodding. Thinking about:

Alyster: green lawns – potato famine as movie – Livvie's underwear – money.

Egbert: bed – toasted cheese – Bradley Wiggins.

Norman: life without his mother – toasted cheese – money – Livvie's underwear.

'Couldn't agree more,' Egbert said amiably. 'By the way, how is your carrot and apple? Looks a bit grim, I must admit . . . I do hope we can sort out something a bit more exciting for your main course. I really am so sorry.'

. . . But Rapunzel had been listening. With her little bat ears. She may have done nothing more with her life than pick arguments and make life unpleasant for people. But her

104

mind was sharp. All the sharper, perhaps, for it never having needed to be used for anything, except proving others wrong. Rapunzel knew and understood her mother's work better than anyone in the world. Too well, perhaps, considering how many other books there are in the world, and how few other novels Rapunzel had ever read. But she had studied her mother's books to an obsessive degree (psychologists might draw some obvious conclusions). Only someone very foolhardy – or stupid – would attempt to lecture her on their meaning.

Rapunzel leaned across the table, her laser-beam eyes fixed on Livvie (who was still smiling like a superstar, nibbling on her dismal carrot).

'I'm sorry dear,' she murmured, 'I only caught a snatch of that. Could you repeat?'

THE LONG GALLERY (WEST END)

9.47 P.M.

Livvie Kellet couldn't remember what she'd said.

She would have been happy to come up with some fresh drivel, but it turned out Rapunzel didn't want to hear it anyway. 'The thing about me,' Livvie began (always a good way to start), 'is I have a very special relationship with literature.'

Rapunzel cut her off. She turned to Alyster Crowley. 'Are you going to educate your actress, Mr Crowley?' she asked him. 'Or shall I?'

Alyster Crowley waved a hand, as if to dismiss whatever it was Livvie had said, which he hadn't been listening to.

The gesture inflamed Rapunzel. 'I'm not sure this woman is fit to play any part in my mother's novel. She clearly doesn't have the faintest idea what it's about.'

'Sure she does,' said Alyster Crowley. 'She's one of the greatest actors of her generation. Don't you worry. Are we going to get any more food, Egbert, or is this another of these potato-famine situations you Brits are so fond of?'

Little Rapunzel tapped the table – the sort of gentle tap that Norman knew well: a sign of bad things to come. She cleared her throat and said, in a quiet voice that bounced off the ceiling and carried the length of the table. 'Perhaps you haven't studied your contract as closely as I have, Mr Crowley. It is not I who needs to worry.'

Such was the power of her tiny voice that for one small beat, the room fell silent.

And then Carfizzi arrived holding a messy plate of sandwiches. He looked terrible. He'd lost the jacket altogether now, and there were black smears on his face and white shirt, as if he'd been rolling around in a coal shed.

He said: 'Ladies and gentlemen, I am truly so sorry. Unfortunately my wife has been taken sick, and has had to retire for the evening. Dinner ... The dinner ... is not ... It's not what was planned. But I have made some sandwiches. From vegetarian vegan bread,' he added quickly. 'So I hope you will forgive ...' He bowed his head, unable to continue with whatever speech he had prepared, and quietly, with all the dignity that was left to him, laid the sandwiches onto the table. 'Excuse me,' he said. 'I will go and fetch more wine.'

More silence. It became clear that Mr Carfizzi was crying.

India jumped to her feet, ran around the table and wrapped him in an unwanted hug. 'Oh my goodness, don't worry one teeny tiny *bit*, Mr Carfizzi,' she cried. 'We don't care, do we?' she said to her guests. 'I bet the sandwiches are delicious!' Over the butler's shoulder, as she led him towards the door (such a very long walk) she said to her Organisational Manager: 'D'you mind taking over?'

Alice said: 'Absolutely. Everyone – help yourselves to some of these delicious-looking sandwiches ... I'm going to nip off to the kitchen and see if there's anything more I can rustle up.'

Things never really recovered from there. It was a bad evening. By 10.30 p.m. the sandwiches had all been eaten, and it was time for bed. India returned to the Long Gallery, full of apologies, but far from crushed. Mr and Mrs Carfizzi, she assured everyone (not that they much cared), were 'absolutely fine, just a bit overtired.' She cracked a few good-natured jokes about the lack of a decent dinner.

'Tbh the food was never the big selling point at Tode Hall. But I hope you've all had *fun*, eating your dins in this amazing room! I know I have! And – really ...' she glanced across at her husband, who looked weary but loving and as proud as ever of his irrepressible wife, '... Egbert and I just want to welcome you all to the house, and *thank you* for setting your fabulous TV series here, and giving us all so much lovely money ... It's such an honour to have these absolutely world-class actors here with us tonight—'

'Here here!' said Egbert(Mr).

'Don't forget the triplets,' Ecgbert(Sir) shouted. 'Just because they're not famous doesn't mean they're not welcome. The triplets are always welcome.'

'You bet!' said India, slightly confused.

Alice chuckled happily. 'Thank you,' she said.

'We mean it!' said Ecgbert(Sir) to the triplets. 'You're welcome anytime.'

'Anyway the point is,' India continued, 'I've just got two things to say and then I, for one, am definitely going to bed. Number one ...' She frowned. What was point number one again? Everyone had drunk far too much this evening, including India. 'Point number one ... Good luck with the filming. I think I've already said that?'

'Here here!' said Egbert(Mr).

'Point number two ... was also very important.' Again, she had to rummage through her brain to find it. 'Sorry! Point number two ... is a bit boring. But you need to be aware that, not surprisingly, we've got some pretty serious, state-of-the-art alarm systems going on here at the Hall, which Egbert and I *still* haven't really got to grips with. Have we Eggie?'

'Well—' said Eggie(Mr), who had got to grips with them ages ago.

'Basically they go off, you know, if a bloody butterfly goes ... anywhere it's not supposed to. Unless Carfizzi stays up, and let's face it, that looks very unlikely, they're going to sort of switch on automatically at 2.30 a.m. – that's right, isn't it Eggie?'

'That's correct,' said Eggie.

'So – I'm just saying, it's probably best not to sleepwalk! If you can help it, hahaha ... Go to the lavatory by all means,' she added. 'But don't go wandering downstairs, or anything mad like that. You'll have the entire North Yorkshire constabulary weighing down on you. With truncheons. So – be warned! External doors, ditto. If you feel the sudden urge for a *promenade de nuit* (as Mummy used to call them), you need to take the exit *beneath the chapel*, which is ... Well it's at the far end of the East Wing, beyond this room ... It's quite complicated ... Those of you who aren't staying the night – Mellors, Alice, Ecgbert ... you obviously know all this. KitKat ... I don't think you're staying with us tonight ... Errmm ... Anyway, look. I'm just going to leave that with you. And FINALLY ...'

'Well done, Munch! You're doing brilliantly!'

'I just want to say, I'm really sorry about the lack of food. There's actually a lot of food – biscuits, cakes, breakfast cereal, you name it – you'll find it in the larder, behind the kitchen. If anyone wants to come with me now, I'll show you exactly where to find the larder. And then – sorry guys, but I've run out of steam. Please, please – help yourselves to all the food and drink you want, only please do it before you go to bed . . . I don't want *anyone* to go to bed feeling hungry. But also – obviously we don't want the North Yorks police whizzing up the drive at 3 a.m. because somebody's looking for a sausage roll.'

She took two volunteers with her to show them the route to the larder, and then, having explained to them how to find their way back to the Long Gallery, she slipped gratefully to her bed.

THE CARETAKER'S FLAT

11.59 P.M.

BANG.
   One gunshot.
   One big hole in the wall.
   But Tode Hall is a very large house – the size of a small town; and the Carfizzi's flat was tucked away in the basement. Whoever was still up and about didn't hear the noise. And everyone else, drunk when they went to bed, slept right on through.

THE LARDER

TUESDAY, 9 A.M.

Sir Ecgbert had landed on top of the body, his nose pressed up against its cold cheek. He recoiled, disentangled himself, and tried to remember *not to panic*.

Breathe deeply.

Don't panic!

Remember, you are beautiful.

It wasn't working. Also, thank goodness, the body did not belong to Mrs Carfizzi. Which meant, presumably, that her alarm clock was broken. In the meantime – *Here was a bad situation. What to do?*

He should call his cousin, of course. Egbert(Mr) was good in a crisis. He was always good. He was a strong and reliable man in every respect. He would call his younger cousin Egbert. In a moment. But first—

Actually, first, he needed to get out of the larder. It was disgusting to be in this confined place, under the circumstances. He needed to talk to Alice. He dialled her again, but

112

of course – she'd switched off the phone. He left a voicemail. It didn't make much sense. But he couldn't take his eyes off the body. Or the face, actually. Gruesome. There was blood on the old red-tiled floor. He lifted his feet. There were puddles that were still sticky.

'Trudy,' he said. 'This is serious. We have a guest down. Repeat, a guest down. Urgent action required. Over and out.' He hung up then, and wondered why he'd said it like that: as if he was in a war movie. 'It's because I'm in shock,' he said, out loud, and redialled. His hands were shaking, so it took a while.

'Trudy. Wake up. I need you. Something awful's happened, and I think I'm the only one who's awake. I don't want to call the police, obviously. If I can help it. Especially after all the fuss last time. But it's not looking good. I mean – look I really don't see why you can't pick up. *Pick up*, for goodness sake.' He hung up then, and immediately regretted his flash of impatience. She wouldn't be impressed.

'It's because I'm in shock,' he said again; was about to redial, when he noticed in the corner of his vision, a wisp of green gas floating by.

'Granny! Thank God!' he said, looking up. But he couldn't see her. 'Where are you?'

'Out here. Come out, Ecgbert. You shouldn't be in there. It's too grisly, darling. Come out and tell me what you're thinking, and whom you are telephoning on that little machine of yours. Not the police, I presume?'

'Of course not, Granny,' he said, putting the phone away. 'I was trying to get hold of Alice.'

His grandmother, wearing plus fours, brimmed cap and tailored jacket in the Tode family tweed, and with a shotgun strapped over her shoulder, looked incongruous, standing in the boot room on that August morning. Nevertheless, as always, with the smell of methane there came a cool breeze, as if she had just stepped out of a refrigerator. If she hadn't been a ghost, he might have hugged her.

'Alice is already on her way,' she said. 'She was absolutely asleep, but I got through to her eventually ... I think she may have smoked rather too much cannabis last night, after the dinner. Anyway, I've woken her, *finally*. As I say, she's on her way.'

Ecgbert(Sir) indicated the larder door, now closed. 'Granny, I think we have to call the police.'

'Nonsense!'

'We can't just leave it lying there ...'

Geraldine said, hopefully: 'Do you think it's a suicide?'

Ecgbert thought about that for a moment. 'Very unlikely, Granny. Much as we would love that. Why would anyone top themselves in a larder when they're probably looking for chocolate cake?'

Geraldine nodded: 'You're quite right. I think we should get rid of the cake.'

And then along came Alice, to talk some sense.

She looked a bit wild this morning: bottle-blonde hair unusually tousled, and last night's mascara still very much on show. But her skin was brown, after the long summer, and there was something about her movements that made Ecgbert's heart miss a beat. She looked healthy and calm – Ecgbert thought she looked beautiful. He said:

'*There* you are! There's a dead body in the larder, Trudy. It was hanging off one of the meat hooks when I went in to get cake ... I unhooked it and I think I may have pulled something in my back. What do we do now?'

'Who is it?' asked Alice.

'Granny thinks we should clear out the chocolate cake and try and pass it off as a suicide. But I don't think that's going to work . . .'

'Who is it?' Alice asked again.

'There's a bloody great knife sticking out the back.'

'Ecgbert, who is it?' Alice asked again.

'Hmm?' he said, still thinking about the knife. 'Oh, don't worry, it's only Rapunzel. So. No harm done.'

Lady Tode nodded approvingly: 'I told you she was dreadful.'

Alice said, 'I'm not sure she deserved to be *murdered* . . . Poor old thing.'

'I didn't *say* she deserved to be murdered,' replied Lady Tode. 'But it had to be someone, so it's just as well it was her . . . That's all I was saying.'

'OK,' said Alice.

But Lady Tode was not quite mollified, 'You shouldn't be such a prig, Alice. It's very tiresome.'

'I don't think I was being priggish . . .'

'In any case after the way she behaved last night, I don't suppose there was a person in the house who didn't *want* to kill her.'

A pause. So it was Rapunzel. As Alice walked across the lawn to the house, she'd wondered. It might have been Mellors. Except he wasn't a guest, and in the voicemail Ecgbert had said there was a 'guest' down. Or Alyster Crowley, perhaps. No one seemed to much like him. But no, Rapunzel made the most sense. Of course. She'd alienated, threatened or insulted pretty much everyone at dinner last night. And in this heat . . .

Alice was not a stranger to dead bodies. Aged fourteen, she'd come home from school and found her mother dead from an

115

overdose. Since when, nothing much shook her. She'd helped out when Carfizzi discovered Lady Tode (Emma, Ecgbert's mother) dead as a doornail in the family mausoleum, less than a year ago. And here she was again. 'Right,' she said, bracing herself. 'First things first ... I should probably have a quick look. And then – you do realise, Ecgbert, that when you took the body down, you completely wrecked the crime scene?'

'I wasn't thinking straight,' he said.

She nodded. 'No,' she said. 'Of course not. Who would be? ... I'm going to pop my head round the door, and have a quick look. I probably should. And then we'll work out what to do.'

'I warn you,' said Ecgbert, 'it's not very nice. Also – watch where you put your feet. There's blood everywhere. Some of it's still a bit sticky.'

The electric light wasn't working but there was sunlight coming in from the boot-room window next door, and it didn't take long for Alice's eyes to adjust.

Rapunzel lay on the ground where Ecgbert(Sir) had left her, face twisted towards the door, and a knife with an ivory handle sticking out of her back. Blood was, indeed, everywhere. It seemed astonishing that such a small (and bloodless) old woman could ever have contained quite so much of it. Alice remembered thinking the same when she found Lady Tode in the mausoleum. But Lady Tode had been dead for a fortnight when they found her. Rapunzel couldn't have been dead for more than a few hours. There were pools of her blood here and

116

there, where there were troughs and dips in the old larder tiling floor, and they still glistened, very slightly. Her black velvet jacket had ripped at the collar where it had caught on the meat hook. Ecgbert had ripped it further when he unhooked her, revealing a surprisingly cheerful canary yellow satin lining: a hint, after her death, of a hidden playfulness. Too late.

Splattered and squashed beneath one of her black-stockinged legs, coated in blood, there lay a large slice of chocolate cake. Rapunzel must have been eating it when the killer struck, Alice deduced, because there were chocolate smudges around her mouth and hands.

In the corner of the larder a small stepladder lay on its side. Alice thought that perhaps Rapunzel had been standing on it, because the plate that held the rest of the chocolate cake was on a high shelf above their heads. Rapunzel wouldn't have been able to reach it without standing on something, or climbing onto the shelves (which seemed unlikely).

And then there was the knife, sticking out of her back. It had an ivory and silver handle and it, like so much else, was smeared with dried blood and chocolate.

Alice shouted behind her to Ecgbert(Sir): 'Did you notice the knife, Ecgbert? Looks to me like it was the same one that was used to cut the cake.'

Lady Tode called back: 'You're quite right, dear. It's a very beautiful cake knife. I bought it in 1932, in a sweet little shop in Venice, of all places. Who would have thought it would end up ... where it has ... What a funny old world!' she chortled.

'Granny,' said Ecgbert. 'This is quite serious.'

Alice said: 'So if she's standing on the ladder, with her back to the door ... and she's eating the cake ... She's gobbling it, maybe – hence all the chocolate round her face. Maybe she had

117

the knife in her hand, ready to cut some more ... She gets her jacket caught on the hook, and she's hanging there – maybe? Someone comes in ... Someone she's already insulted. Maybe she insults them again, even as she's hanging there, asking for help ... I mean ...'

Lady Tode said: 'One wouldn't have been able to resist simply *grabbing* the knife off her and *plunging it in* ...'

'Speak for yourself, Granny,' said Ecgbert.

'Don't be a prig, darling,' said Lady Tode, giving off a slight smell. 'You're worse than Alice. In any case I'm the only person in the house who couldn't have done it, even if I'd wanted to ...'

Alice took one last look at the room, shuddered at the blood-shed – and closed the door. She turned back to the others.

'We'll have to break it to Norman,' she said.

'Assuming he doesn't already know,' said Lady Tode. 'He would be one's prime suspect.'

'Possibly,' said Alice. 'Even so ... I mean ... If he *didn't* do it I'm not sure he's going to want to see her like this. It is his mother, after all.'

Alice felt a rush of mother-related memories in-coming. For one brief moment, a great wave of misery rose up and threatened to engulf her. It wasn't something she wanted to deal with at the moment. Or ever, actually.

Ecgbert whacked her on the nearest shoulder: too hard. It was meant to be a comforting pat. 'Poor Trudy,' he said while she recovered her balance. 'Probably stirs things up a bit, does it? The dead mother aspect.'

'Not at all,' replied Alice, briskly. 'Not for me. Perhaps for you ...' She smiled at him, but it was quite a sad smile. 'Neither of our mothers died in the best of circumstances ...'

Ecgbert, to change the conversation, said: 'How did *your* mother die, Granny? I'm sure I've been told. It was something quite funny wasn't it?'

'She was run over by an omnibus,' replied Lady Tode, 'in the village of Piddletrenthide. She was sixty-three.'

Ecgbert nodded. 'Yes, of course.'

Another pause.

Alice said: 'Piddletrenthide is a funny name.'

'It's a village in Dorset,' said Lady Tode. 'Very pretty . . . Or it was. Now then what are we to do with this ghastly woman?'

'Is it worth removing the fish knife,' Ecgbert suggested. 'And trying to . . . I don't know . . . After all, she had plenty of reasons to kill herself, I'm sure.'

'I think that's a bad idea,' said Alice.

Lady Tode said, 'Ecgbert, darling, it's not a fish knife. Don't be silly.'

'Sorry. I mean – the knife you got in Florence or whatever.'

'It most certainly wasn't a fish knife.'

'In any case,' said Alice, 'I don't think we should remove it.'

Lady Tode nodded. 'She's right you know. I don't think we'd fool anyone.'

'Probably not,' Ecgbert agreed.

'Definitely not,' said Alice. 'We need to call the police. The poor woman's been stabbed in the back. She's been murdered. I'm going to fetch Egbert. – And India,' she added as an afterthought, though at first she wasn't sure how India might help. 'And where are the Carfizzis? They're usually up at this time. In fact – Ecgbert, why were you ever in the larder in the first place?'

It was decided that Ecgbert(Sir) should go in search of the Carfizzis, who'd been behaving so oddly the previous evening, and that Alice should update the young Todes. None of the guests had yet surfaced, but even so, they didn't want to risk anyone wandering into the crime scene in search of breakfast, so Ecgbert fetched a chair from the kitchen and put it in front of the larder door. He wrote a sign:

VERY SERIOUS WARNING – DO NOT ENTER

And stuck it on the chair.

'I do wonder who did it, don't you?' said Ecgbert(Sir). 'It could have been anyone. She was vile to Nicola last night. Nicola was quite upset … At least, I presume she was. She didn't show it. A bit grim if Nicola did it …'

'Don't be silly,' said Lady Tode. 'Rapunzel was vile to everyone. I would have thought it was fairly obvious who did it … After all, who gets the money when she dies? And my goodness, he must have hated her. Don't you think? *The way she spoke to him!*'

120

THE CARETAKER'S FLAT

Ecgbert(Sir) located the Carfizzis, as expected, at home in their inexplicably luxurious basement flat. Rather, Mr Carfizzi came to the door when Ecgbert knocked, and swore that Mrs Carfizzi was at home, but sick in bed. Carfizzi was already up and about. He looked more himself. His thinning hair was once again smoothed with expensive unctions, and – because the house was full of important guests – he was dressed not in his everyday Italian slacks and bright cashmere sweater, but in formal butler wear, clean and ironed and appropriately tucked in.

He held the flat's connecting door so that Ecgbert couldn't step beyond it. Behind him, there lingered a slight smell of gunpowder. Carfizzi had needed to move his wife's image of the Madonna to cover the hole in the wall. But other than that, the room was in order, and even if it hadn't been, what with everything else that was going on, Ecgbert probably wouldn't have noticed anyway.

Carfizzi was full of remorse for what had happened the

previous evening, and for their late arrival to work this morning. His wife had been up half the night, he said, sobbing over the recent death of a sister. Perhaps, suggested Mr Carfizzi, when all the filming was done, he and his wife could have a holiday back in Calabria. In the meantime ... Mr Carfizzi would be upstairs within moments.

'Breakfast,' Carfizzi said, 'will be served in the Red Dining Room, as usual. It may be a little slower than normal. But Mrs Carfizzi tells me she has already prepared the kedgeree. And of course I can make eggs and sausages and so on ...'

Ecgbert(Sir) said, 'Oh smashing,' and prepared to wander back upstairs. 'By the way – slightly grim news, I'm afraid. I found Rapunzel Piece dead in the larder this morning.'

'You did?'

'So – don't go in the larder. If you don't want to get a nasty fright. We don't want to involve the police ...'

'Of course not,' said Mr Carfizzi, wearing his Inscrutable Butler face.

'But it might be rather difficult not to.' Ecgbert grimaced. 'Someone put a fish knife in her back, Carfizzi.'

'My goodness,' muttered Carfizzi.

'Yup. Pretty nasty ...' Ecgbert nodded thoughtfully. He sighed. 'Anyway,' he said, 'I'll leave you to crack on, shall I? Trudy is fetching Egbert and India. And then I imagine we'll be having a confab in the Red Dining Room ... about what to do next. So, as I say. Coffee whenever you're ready. And tell Mrs Carfizzi – you know ...' he looked embarrassed ' ... that I'm really sorry about the sister and everything. Tell her we miss her upstairs.'

'I certainly shall, Sir Ecgbert,' said Mr Carfizzi, with a stately bow, and he closed the door.

THE RED DINING ROOM

Egbert(Mr) and India came downstairs in their pyjamas. This was something India did often and Egbert(Mr) had never done before. Egbert(Mr), having been apprised of the fundaments, cleverly suggested that the guests, who'd not yet surfaced, be directed to a separate breakfast in the Knights' Parlour, at the other end of the house. This would keep them at bay until the household was more, as he put it, 'on top of things'.

While Carfizzi, Ecgbert(Sir) and Alice put the parallel breakfast arrangements into motion, the young Todes had gone together to the larder, to examine the scene of the crime. Egbert(Mr) told his wife he would have preferred to do it alone.

'Munchie, it'll upset you,' he said.

She said, 'Of course it won't!'

But then of course it did.

There was blood on the ground, which had seeped under the larder door and into the boot room beyond. India accidentally touched it with her toe, which freaked her out. But she forged on. Put her head around the larder door and, having looked at the body and the shelves of food above it, and retreated asap to confer with her friends in the Red Dining Room, she actually came up with some very useful observations.

India could see, for example, that there must have been quite a run on the food during the night.

When she and Carfizzi had left the larder at the guests' disposal, and she had managed to escape to her bed, there had been a second tray of messy sandwiches on the shelf, two whole chocolate cakes and five or six packets of ready-made jam tarts. Now, although most of the sandwiches remained, all the jam tarts were gone, and so had one-and-a-half of the chocolate cakes. It was evidence, India suggested, that the larder may have seen quite a few visitors during the night.

'Either that or a couple of exceptionally greedy individuals,' she added. 'But even somebody really greedy – Alyster Crowley, say, or Norman – even those two together would have needed help to make a hole like that in the food.' She asked Ecgbert(Sir) and Alice if they had eaten anything from the larder last night, but neither had. Alice said she couldn't speak for the triplets, however, whose appetites were prodigious.

'Rapunzel didn't eat a thing during supper,' Alice observed.

'Well there wasn't much to eat, Trudy,' said Ecgbert(Sir). 'Except for the prawns – and the sandwiches of course.' Carfizzi had just come in with another pot of coffee. Ecgbert didn't want to offend him. 'Which were delicious, Carfizzi. Obviously.'

Carfizzi, standing at the side table brushing crumbs from a toast rack, acknowledged the comment with a butler-style demi-smile, put the coffee beside the crumb-free toast rack and lingered to fuss over the teaspoons.

Alice said: 'I think Rapunzel may have been a bit peculiar

around food ... The piece of cake that's lying under her knee at the moment ... Have you seen the size of it? Plus, there was chocolate all over her face, as if she'd been ...'

'Really troughing it down,' India finished for her. 'Yes, I noticed that. There must be about a third of the cake on the floor with her.'

Egbert(Mr) said to Ecgbert(Sir): 'Ah, the details the ladies notice! Amazing, isn't it, Coz?' He held his palms aloft and offered up a light genuflection. 'I am in awe,' he said.

The ladies ignored him.

Everybody slurped on their coffee and wondered how long they could hold out before finally telephoning the police.

'At some point,' said Egbert(Mr), 'we're going to have to let the guests know what's happened. And I'm just thinking aloud at this point, but – vis-à-vis insurance, I'm pretty sure we're not actually covered, as it were, for *murder*. And what we don't want is these wretched film people withholding funds, simply because – you know – of this very unfortunate situation ... Honestly I don't see why filming can't continue absolutely as planned. The larder end of the house is a reasonably separate entity, as it were, from the state rooms, so there's really no need for too much disruption. And I don't want to be ...' he cast around for the appropriate word, '*horrid*,' he said, 'but, erm, as Mr Crowley was attempting to imply vis-à-vis the ruddy lawns, I fear that if we don't present the house in a way that is useful to the film crew, they may not be obliged to pay us a bean ...'

'That's outrageous!' said India.

'Which, of course, in face of this terrible tragedy is not the chief concern,' he added pointlessly. 'On the other hand, I have a nasty feeling Mr Crowley will leap on any excuse to screw us over. Excuse my horrid language. So – net-net. What we need to do is concentrate on *really minimising disruption*. Are we agreed?'

'Do you mean we'll have gone to all this trouble and they're not even going to cough up?' India said. 'That's ridiculous.'

'What I'm saying is, perhaps we should have a little chat with Mr Crowley *before* we bring in the police. If we all know what we're saying before the police get here, we can really minimise disruption all round . . .'

'I do think it's outrageous,' India said again. 'It's hardly *our* fault Rapunzel got murdered. For goodness sake! Why should *we* have to pay for it?'

Egbert(Mr) continued: 'One thing we can be very grateful for,' he said, 'is the absence of tourists. Heaven only knows . . . Imagine if we had tourists roaming around at this point . . . Not that they'd be allowed in the larder, obviously. But they'd certainly want to know what the police were doing here. In their plastic body suits and everything.' He sighed. Was there no end to the dramas? He felt as if they'd only just shaken off the last murder at Tode Hall. 'It really is a bit much,' he said. 'Don't you think?'

'It certainly is!' agreed India. But she looked quite cheerful about it. 'And there was me, thinking life in the country would be boring!'

'I really think,' said Alice, 'we shouldn't wait any longer. We should call the police.'

'Trudy's absolutely right,' agreed Ecgbert(Sir). 'It's a hot day. She's going to start stinking soon. Also – somebody's got to tell Norman.'

'If he doesn't know it already,' said Lady Tode, sitting at the end of the table, still with the shotgun strapped to her back. As usual, only Alice and Ecgbert(Sir) could hear her.

126

'Right then,' said Egbert(Mr). He stood up. It was time for action.

India and Alice, he suggested, should find Norman and break the news to him that his mother was dead. He, meanwhile, would 'just jolly well bite the bullet, as it were,' and call the police. He suggested they all meet back here in the Red Dining Room in twenty minutes or so.

'What about me?' asked Ecgbert(Sir). 'You silly ass, you forgot about me!'

Egbert(Mr) looked nonplussed. 'Well – I ...'

'Not to worry. I'll head over to the Knights' Parlour and see if any of the guests are up. Find out what info I can glean.'

'No!' cried his cousin. 'God no. Absolutely not!'

Ecgbert(Sir) sent him a look: not entirely agreeable. He was already on his feet. Being exceedingly tall, it didn't take him many strides to reach the fine mahogany door. He pulled it back with some force. It was large and heavy, and caused a pleasant rush of air to come into the warm room. He paused, turned first to Egbert(Mr), grinned and winked at him. 'You think I'll muck everything up?'

'No! Of course not,' lied his cousin. 'I do *not* think that ...'

Ecgbert turned to Alice: 'Trudy, I don't suppose you want to come with me? I'm not sure it'll take both of you to break the news to Norman. Especially, as Granny so rightly says, he probably already knows ... What do you think?'

Alice said: 'Good idea. I'll come with you.'

'Excellent!' said the E-berts, together.

THE KNIGHTS' PARLOUR

Alyster Crowley was the only guest to have surfaced when Alice and Ecgbert arrived in the Knights' Parlour. They found him alone at the far end of a long dining table, the dead eyes of painted Todes gazing at him from every wall, and from each corner, the empty helmets of standing armour. He seemed oblivious to them all: a mountain of hot, unhealthy flesh, answering emails on his iPad, munching and squelching on his breakfast with such greedy relish that Alice could have sworn she saw the portraits wince. Mr Carfizzi had piled Crowley's plate high with bacon and eggs (both taken from the death-scene larder, not that anyone needed to know). Crowley seemed remarkably contented.

'Uh-huh,' he said when they walked in, still munching, not really looking up.

Alice said: 'Good morning, Mr Crowley!'

'Alyster,' he said, still looking at his iPad. 'For chrissakes call me Alyster.'

'I hope you slept well, Alyster?' she continued.

But Ecgbert was never one for pleasantries. He sat down in the seat opposite Crowley's and he went straight to point. 'I'll tell you who *didn't* sleep well,' he said. 'Sadly ... Tragically ... Gosh, did you get bacon? We didn't, did we Trudy?'

Alyster Crowley shoved his piled plate towards Ecgbert, glanced up from his screen, and for some reason, quite inexplicable, graced them both with an enormous smile. It lit up his face. It was so unexpected, it lit up the entire room. 'Have some!' he said warmly. 'Your butler-man gave me way too much.'

Ecgbert reached across the table and lifted some bacon off the fat man's plate. 'Thank you,' he said. 'Surprisingly kind of you. I appreciate it very much.'

Alyster said: 'So tell me. Who didn't sleep well? And why do I care? As long as my superstars are OK?'

'Your superstars are fine,' Alice replied, 'so far as we know. I presume they're still in bed.'

'Good. So.' *Munch munch.* 'Who didn't sleep well, *Sir* Ecgbert ... ?' The name clearly tickled him, on this sunny morning. He laughed; the mountain of flesh beneath his head juddered with delight. He said it again. 'Who didn't sleep well, *Sir Ecgbert*? Hahaha.'

Ecgbert, swallowing his bacon and looking hopefully at Crowley's plate, in case there might be more, said: 'You're obviously in such a good mood, I'm a bit loath to wreck it ... *However.* The sad new is, somebody got done in last night. Here at the Hall. In the larder, to be exact.' Ecgbert held up a hand, not to be interrupted. '*Before* you go off the deep end, the good news is – it was only Rapunzel. So – I'm not saying anything about the situation is exactly "good" news ...'

129

Unconsciously, he took another piece of bacon. 'No. It's bad. Really ... *awful*. Obviously. But on the bright side, I should think you, along with most of the household, might be a tiny bit relieved she's kicked the bucket. As it were. I should think your superstar Livvie Kellet will be pretty relieved to hear it, too. In fact ... let's be honest. Who isn't?'

Crowley had very much stopped smiling. He'd stopped munching. Stopped moving. Maybe even stopped breathing. He glared at Ecgbert.

'What're you suggesting?' Crowley asked him quietly.

'I'm not suggesting anything,' Ecgbert said. Ecgbert wasn't fazed by much, but spotting the expression on Crowley's face, he paused in his chewing, briefly. 'Should I be?'

'He's not suggesting anything,' Alice said quickly. 'He's simply telling you news ... which you need to know. The police are being informed this morning ... Ecgbert found her with a knife in her back. She was hanging off a meat hook in the larder.'

Ecgbert nodded. 'So it was definitely murder. Unfortunately.'

'I've understood that,' Alyster Crowley said. 'I'm asking Ecgbert what he meant when he suggested I would be relieved to hear it.'

Ecgbert stared at Crowley. He sat down in one of the beautiful chairs, crossed his long legs, and over the plate of food, so recently shared, and the glassy polish of the mahogany table, he assessed the American, as if seeing him for the first time.

Alice thought it was quite cool.

Ecgbert said: 'Well I would have thought that was obvious.'

'Not at all,' Crowley said.

Ecgbert said: 'Trudy, you heard Rapunzel didn't you? Got the bit between her teeth about Crowley and co turning her mother's novel into "homo-propaganda", or something . . . She was quite drunk, I think, and *stupendously* angry, *n'est ce pas*, Alyster? Threatening everyone and everything. Trudy, had you already gone to bed by then? I think you had.'

'I think I'd already gone to bed,' Alice said.

'I have absolutely no memory of this,' Crowley said.

'Well, I heard it, loud and clear,' piped up Lady Tode, from nowhere. A mild smell of methane. A wisp of noxious green gas. 'And I would keep a close eye on this gentleman, if I were you. Maybe we're judging Norman too quickly.'

Ecgbert and Crowley glowered at each other.

'It doesn't much matter now, anyway,' Ecgbert said at last. 'She's dead, isn't she?' He stood up. 'Come on Trudy, let's go . . . By the way, when the police come, they'll probably want to talk to you. But my feeling is . . . ' He couldn't help himself. He leaned over and took the last piece of bacon from Alyster's plate. '*My feeling is* . . . the less we say to the coppers, the sooner we can get this unfortunate business out of the way. And you can crack on with your homo-propaganda or whatever it is. And we can crack on with our lives. And then everyone gets their money, and we all live happily ever after. What do you think?'

Slowly, with the smallest hint of newborn respect, Alyster Crowley nodded. The idiot aristocrat with the silly name was perhaps not such an idiot after all. He said, 'I think we're probably on the same side.' He picked up his iPad. The conversation was over. 'By the way,' he said, 'If you see your butler-man, could you ask him to bring me some more of that bacon? Thank you so much.'

131

'I still don't know what Rapunzel said to him,' Alice whispered to Ecgbert(Sir), as they strode along the corridor, beneath baroque arches, past busts of Roman soldiers, and onward. Ecgbert's long legs propelled him faster than Alice could keep up. She hated running at the best of times.

'Slow down!' she panted as they arrived in the Great Hall. 'It's too hot.'

He stopped.

'Shhh!' he said.

'*But what did she say?*' Her words echoed and bounced between marble floor and domed ceiling, seventy-foot above. They were standing on the very spot where, only ten or so months ago ... But that was then. This was now. Another day, another death. She dropped her voice a notch. 'I heard her reminding him of something about the contract ... Was it that?'

He nodded. 'Sort of,' he said. 'It got much more vicious, later on.' He glanced up, to see if anyone was listening. There was no one about, or not that he could see. He motioned to her to follow him into the garden.

Every external door was locked and double locked and triple alarmed in that monumental house. It was not a simple task, stepping outside at Tode Hall, especially from the Great Hall. After a length of fuss and some low-key swearing, Ecgbert cranked back the Great North Door.

Sunlight flooded in.

The frescos behind the stone stairway looked worn in the fresh daylight, but neither Alice nor Ecgbert were concerned with that just now. They stepped outside.

'*What happened?*' Alice asked.

132

THE QUEEN CHARLOTTE SUITE

ivvie Kellet was on the phone to her mother when Alyster Crowley came knocking. Her mother was the only person in the world Livvie, as a single, beautiful, rich, world-famous woman, felt she could trust, and she called her every day, usually in tears. Her mother had two other children and a husband with early-stage dementia, although she hadn't told this to Livvie yet. Her mother loved Livvie very much. She was also the sort of mother who was always as unhappy as her unhappiest child, and Livvie was generally miserable. So.

Here was Livvie at Tode Hall, sprawled across her enormous, ancient bed: the same four-poster that her fellow Oscar winner, Laurence Olivier, had lain in when he performed his famous death scene, in the last-but-one screen adaptation of *Prance*. However this – piece of movie trivia – wasn't what was on her mind at that moment. She was sobbing this morning because, so she told her mother, she felt that no matter how many prizes she won, or how passionately she worked at her art, men would always see her not as an actor, first, but as a woman and not just any woman but as a woman to be desired.

'I'm sick of it, Mummy. You can't imagine how awful it is.'

'I'm sure they take you seriously as an actor, darling,' said her mother. 'You worry too much.' She was trying to open a sachet of cat food, but it needed both hands, and she had to keep the phone up to her ear, so it was tricky. Plus, she'd heard this lament many times before.

Livvie could sense her mother's lack of focus, and it made her feel even lonelier. If her mother wasn't there for her, couldn't help her to carry the pain, then who in the world *was*? No one. 'Mummy,' she sobbed, '*It never ends!* The torment of being "*Me*" never ends ... I wake up as *me*, Livvie, and that's OK. But then, people don't *see me* as Livvie. They see me as someone else. As Livvie Kellet. *Nobody sees me as Livvie.*'

'Darling – I'm sure they do ...'

'You're not listening, Mummy! I'm staying in this crazy, *massive* house. I'm on my own. I'm just so *on my own.*'

'There must be other people in the house? What about ...' The mother couldn't remember the other Oscar winner's name. The one Livvie was starring with. 'Whatsisname? Isn't he there?'

'Yes! But, Mummy, he's gay! It doesn't count! He sees me as an actor.'

'Well then—'

'But that's only because he doesn't desire me. *Why can't you see?*'

The mother really couldn't. Plus, now she'd got cat-food juice all over her hands, and her husband was calling for her upstairs. She said: 'Sweetheart, I'm ever so sorry, but can I call you back?'

'NO! Mummy, no you can't!' Livvie needed her mother's attention so badly right now. She had to say something to keep her on the line. Anything, just to keep her there. Livvie dug deep. 'Last night I had to run away from a disgusting little Professor who was groping me. *Groping me*, Mummy! It was so disgusting. And *it's not fair. How am I supposed to live with that, day in and day out?*'

The mother said: 'Did you tell him to stop?'

'Of course I told him to stop! I kicked him very hard in the face!'

'Did you, Livvie?'

'YES!'

The mother sighed. She wished her daughter wasn't so crazy. The mother blamed Hollywood. She blamed fame. In the meantime, she played along with Livvie, because she could see that Livvie needed her. She allowed Livvie to keep her on the phone. 'Well, good for you darling. As long as you're sticking up for yourself, you can't go wrong, can you?'

Livvie's misery-drenched reply was stopped in her throat by three thunderous knocks on the big bedroom door. Alyster Crowley's voice boomed from the other side. 'Livvie? Baby, you gotta open the door! *Right now.*'

Livvie pulled herself together. It took just under three seconds. She hung up on her mother without even saying goodbye. Breathed in, breathed out. Said '*Ahhhh.*' Checked her reflection. Pulled a single lock of hair over her beautiful face. And trotted across the vast room to let him in.

Crowley had Teddy MacIntosh with him, which was a bit of a shock. He too was still in his pyjamas.

'Let us in,' said Alyster Crowley. No smile. No preamble. But then that was Alyster.

'Hello Alyster. Teddy ... What's happened?'

Alyster barged past her.

'Close the door,' Alyster ordered.

She looked from one to the other, and closed the door. Teddy's face was very white. He looked terrified. 'What's going on?'

Alyster said: 'Where's Thistlestrupp. We need him in here.'

'Well he's—'

'Second thoughts. No we don't. He wasn't there. Any case,' Alyster Crowley winked, to no one in particular. To himself, perhaps. 'Thistlestrupp needs this as much as everyone else. He'll do as he's told.'

'*What's happened?*' Livvie asked again.

'He won't tell me, either,' Teddy said. 'He dragged me out of bed, and brought me in here. Like I'm a kid. I was actually fast asleep.'

The Oscar winners sat side-by-side on Lord Olivier's four-poster, looking truly at a loss. Teddy, in his striped pyjamas, looked like a little boy on his first day at prep school. Even more so than he normally did. Livvie, in tousled satin, looked like Livvie Kellet: a woman to be desired.

At that instant, Alyster Crowley had more important things on his mind than the appearance or desirability of either. He described to them the grisly fate of Rapunzel, and told them the police were on their way.

'*What?*' cried the actors. 'Murdered? Rapunzel Piece?'

But why?

How?

Where?

This is too terrible!

Rapunzel?

I can't believe it!

Poor, *poor* lady!

Alyster said. 'Yup. Stabbed in the larder—'

The actors struck up again: '*It's too awful. It's*—'

But this time he talked over them. And when they didn't fall silent immediately he snapped: 'Shut up and listen.' So they did.

'Like I said, they've got the police coming.'

'Well *of course* . . .'

'Shut up. The police are on their way. OK. So – once we've got over the shock and the grief and all that –' he waved it aside, 'we need to be clear about a few things. First of all: if we have police poking their noses all over the place, they'll be trying to shut down production. We don't want that.'

'Absolutely not!'

'Right.' He looked sternly at his two actors. 'There's plenty riding on this show for all of us, Livvie – we both know you haven't had a hit for some time. Plus, let's face it, you're not getting any younger.'

Livvie puffed. He didn't give her a chance to reply.

'Teddy – you're a great actor. You both are. But this is big for you, huh? You know it.'

Teddy clutched his ticking ticker, too emotional, at that moment, to speak. Of course it was a big deal. Everything was a big deal. Every moment in Teddy's life was a big deal, and he needed to work. Teddy only breathed when he worked. If shooting stopped – what would he do with himself tomorrow? What would he do with himself next week? *What if he never found work ever again?* Teddy felt his lungs tightening up. His heart was doing its beaty-thing. This was stress. 'What . . .' he said, looking down at his pyjama-clad knees. 'Tell me what we have to do . . .'

Alyster Crowley nodded. 'Livvie?' he said.

'Absolutely,' she said. 'Whatever I can do to help. That poor, poor woman. I must say, last night, she had a very direct way of communicating with people. But as a woman I still felt a connection with her. A very real mother–child, child–mother connection . . .'

'Excellent,' said Alyster. 'I just need you both to remember how much you liked her. All right?'

'Of course!' said Livvie. 'Of course we liked her!'

Alyster held his hands in the air, hesitating before he said the final thing. It had to be said. 'Right. So the conversation we had – do you remember? Rapunzel, you, me, Teddy – after dinner, in the lounge – whatever they call it, when she came over to pick the fight . . . you remember?'

Teddy and Livvie hesitated, not sure if they were meant to nod or to shake their heads. Of course they remembered it! She'd threatened to withdraw permission for the entire production!

'The conversation when she—' Alyster leaned in, dropped his voice, 'when she said what she said – about your character not being homosexual, Teddy – *Teddy?*'

'Yah. Mm-hmm. Yes, I remember . . .'

'When she said she was going to halt the whole fucking series – hahaha. We knew she was just fuckin' around, but even so. She said it – and nobody else heard, except Sir Fartlipool, whatever he calls himself, and he's not talking, and this is what I'm saying, guys. *Nobody needs to know.* All right? Nobody needs to know she was threatening to fuck everything up for us. So. Are we clear? When the cops ask us what we think about Rapunzel, or they want to know what we all talked about last night – we tell them the truth. Yeah?'

138

'The truth?' Livvie was now genuinely confused.

'We tell them,' Alyster said slowly, 'that we liked the old lady very much. That she was a quiet character, didn't say too much. Was thrilled with what we were doing with the production. Thrilled to meet the famous actors. All that crap … That we are *devastated* … Is that clear?' He glared down at his idiots, seated obediently before him. A driblet of sweat rolled off his cheek and landed *splat* on the silk Chinese (three-hundred-year-old) carpet at his feet. 'All righty?' he smiled at them. But it wasn't like the smile he'd given to Ecgbert(Sir) when he was sharing his breakfast bacon. This was a different kind of smile. Kinda scary. 'We stick together on this. OK? … After all, who knows – maybe it was one of you who did the old bitch in. Maybe you did. Honestly, I don't give a fuck. And I don't blame you. We just gotta keep the cameras rolling.'

'I didn't kill her!' cried Livvie.

'Good,' said Alyster. 'Neither did I.'

'Neither did I!' said Teddy. 'This is ridiculous.'

'Well – somebody killed her,' Alyster said. 'And I don't want you guys talking to *anyone* – without lawyers being present.' He straightened up. Slapped his short, hot thighs. 'Oh-kay!' he smiled. 'You got the rest of the day off, as you know. Shooting starts tomorrow. There's breakfast in the … one of the dining rooms, I forget what it's called. And we've got drivers coming over to take you to the hotel in a couple of hours. Have a restful day. See you later.'

LORD MUNCHIE'S DRESSING ROOM

Noah Thistlestrupp was on the phone to KitKat when Alyster Crowley came knocking. He was in his dinner jacket still, wondering if the butler guy brought him breakfast in bed, and if that was part of the service, or if he'd have to venture out into the long dark corridors in search of coffee for himself. The line kept bleeping, because his high-earning wife was trying to talk to him about a broken fridge. But Thistlestrupp had been dialling KitKat's number every two minutes for the past hour. She'd finally taken the call, and at that particular instant, Noah, whose head was thumping with the sort of hangover he'd not experienced since his early twenties, had a lot more he wanted to say to KitKat than he ever did, or ever would again, to his amazingly successful, pregnant spouse.

'What happened to you last night?' he began. Without even a 'good morning'. The second she said *Hi Noah* (sounding weary), he launched into his complaint. Not very tactical. But his head was hurting; and he'd been so drunk when he went to bed he'd not even bothered to change into his sleep gear. This happened every now and then. Usually he self-lubricated with kale smoothies and eco-friendly purified water and avoided alcohol altogether, but sometimes his Nordic roots led him into the darkest of tunnels, his iron will abandoned him, and he drank himself into oblivion.

It had been a stressful day, after all, with Alyster Crowley prowling around, threatening to withdraw the finance because he objected to the colour of the lawn. And then that appalling, homophobic old woman, threatening to withdraw copyright permission because she didn't ... *how the hell had it come to that?*

'What happened to you KitKat?' he moaned. 'What the fuck? I thought we were lovers.'

'We were, Noah,' she said. She sounded regretful, and sad, and slightly resentful. 'But we can't do it anymore. I can't. I'm sorry Noah. It just doesn't feel right.'

'*What* doesn't feel right? Since when?'

'Since yesterday.'

'*Yesterday?* Why are you saying this? It feels perfect ... What's happened to you ... Are you *stupid* KitKat?'

It was a little hint. Thistlestrupp's reminder to her that he was the boss. He held the power. But in fact KitKat was not stupid, and Thistlestrupp was mistaken. He did not hold the power. Also, as she now reminded him, his high-earning wife was pregnant.

'You should be ashamed of yourself, Noah,' KitKat said.

'*What?*'

'Don't call me again. Call your wife—'

Bleep – Bleep.

'Fuck off!' cried Thistlestrupp. 'Since when did you give a damn about my wife?'

'Since now,' KitKat said.

'Never you mind about my wife. You keep her out of it.'

'No, Noah. I won't.'

Bleep – Bleep.

'This has got nothing to do with my wife! We both know that – you think I'm an idiot? You think I don't know that shit-fuck Yorkshire peasant hasn't been *sticking it to you* all night?'

'You don't know what you're talking about.'

'Yes, I do. You're a slut. You're a fucking slut bitch slut fucking . . . I'll kill him. I'll kill you both.'

KitKat hung up.

'KitKat? KitKat! Don't you dare . . .' Thistlestrupp groaned and clutched his head. And that was when Alyster Crowley came knocking.

THE LADY LAVERTY SUITE

N orman and his mother had been given connecting bedrooms with a shared bathroom adjoining the two. India
couldn't remember which guest had been put in which of the
rooms, so she spent a few moments knocking politely on the
wrong door. When no answer came she shunted along the
corridor, and knocked politely on the next door along. No
answer there either.

'Hello . . . ? Norman? Are you awake?' she called.

Nothing. No movement at all. Obviously a very sound
sleeper, she thought, and felt loath to persevere, given she was
only waking him to tell him bad news. On the other hand – this
was an emergency. 'Norman?' she raised her voice. 'Norman,
I'm really sorry, but you have to wake up . . .'

Still, nothing.

She felt she had no choice but to push open the door.

The curtains were drawn closed. But the bed was made.
There was no sign of him: no suitcase, no coat or shoes.

Nothing. Perhaps she was confused? Had she not put them in these rooms? Perhaps Mr Carfizzi had changed the plan without informing her? All of this was possible. She walked through the empty bedroom and on through to the bathroom. A single toothbrush lay on its side by the basin. On the floor, by the bathtub, was a pair of sturdy walking shoes – size, very small. Folded very neatly on the chest beneath the window, a petticoat; some denture cream toothpaste, some talcum powder, and a tube of medicine for athlete's foot.

At the other end of the bathroom, the connecting door to the second bedroom hung open. She knew very well that Rapunzel wasn't in there. Even so, it felt strange to be creeping around.

'Helloo?' she called, quite softly. 'Norman? Are you there?'
Silence.

She tiptoed closer to the open door.

'Hellooo?'

She poked her head around it.

Another bed that clearly hadn't been slept in. Another set of curtains drawn. The difference was – there was a suitcase lying open, and a scattering of clothes on the armchair, a copy of *The Putin Kleptocracy: Murder, Mafia & Money* lying face down, open, on the chaise longue. Someone – Rapunzel, judging by the hideous flowery dressing gown beside it – had been intending to return here, even if she never made it back.

India called out Norman's name, more forcefully this time. But he obviously wasn't in either room. Nor was his suitcase. Nor anything belonging to him. Aside from the drawn curtains, his room was as pristine as if he'd never been there at all. He must have packed his bags and left, last night, before the house was locked up – and without a word to anyone.

Very suspicious, India concluded. Also, bloody rude.

She had one more look through both rooms; checked in the cupboards and under the beds – but there was no doubt about it. He and his bags were gone.

Well then, she thought, closing Norman's door and heading back to the Red Dining Room to report back. That pretty much clears up *that*.

THE RED DINING ROOM

'Murder mystery solved!' she announced, quite cheerfully. But nobody was in there except Nicola, eating Coco Pops. 'Oh,' India said, disappointed. 'It's you. Where's everyone else?'

Nicola shrugged.

'Where's Eggie? Where are they all? Have you seen Alice yet this morning?'

Nicola said, but the words were slightly muffled through the Coco Pops, 'Haven't seen anyone. Thought I was the first up.'

'Well—' India stared at her. 'So you don't know?'

'Don't know what?'

India's gaze turned to the Coco Pops. 'Where did you find them? Where did you find those Coco Pops, Nicola?'

Nicola said: 'Oh sorry,' but it didn't sound *at all* sorry. 'Are these for Ludo and Passion? Am I not allowed the Coco Pops now?'

'What? No! Of course you can have the Coco Pops. Just – did you go into the larder, Nicola?'

'Huh?'

India said: 'Never mind. It doesn't matter. Just – whatever you do, don't go in the larder. You'll probably puke. And for God's sake, *whatever you do*, don't let the children in there. All right?' India had forgotten the children – or, she had forgotten them in the context of the larder, and there being a dead body inside, as well as chocolate cake. She rushed off to tell the nanny to keep them away.

'What's going on?' Nicola shouted after her, but she got no reply.

THE LIBRARY

The police had come. Men in plastic body suits were scooping up body and evidence from the larder, and Egbert(Mr) was making polite conversation with two detectives in the Library. It wasn't a room the Todes used often, but with so many rooms taken over by the film crew, their options were a bit limited. Also Egbert(Mr) was keen to draw as little attention as possible to the police presence. He didn't want the children upset. Nor, frankly, did he want to get another earful from the repellent Alyster Crowley. The Library was at the end of the house which was furthest from Estate Wing, where much of the film unit was based; and in another wing entirely to the Red Dining Room, family kitchen, Chinese Drawing Room, and of course the larder, where the murder had taken place. Actually it was a good five-minute walk from the scene of the crime. The detectives asked to be based somewhere nearer. Egbert had been polite, but adamant. If the detectives wanted to cross-question the household – and of course he appreciated that this might be necessary – they could do it from the Library or not at all. In the meantime, could he ask Mr Carfizzi to fetch the officers some coffee?

Yes.

Jolly good.

'Do, by all means, feel free to question us all,' Egbert(Mr) told them generously. 'It's a dreadful tragedy, and we must all do our bit to capture the culprit ... However ... as my wife has already told you, the victim's son, Mr Norman Wright, is probably the individual you should be going after. He did a flit in the middle of the night, so far as we can understand. And I tell you what, there wasn't much love lost between those two! So – if you take my advice, you're probably better off whipping that poor, dear lady off to the morgue asap, and—' Egbert(Mr) made a fist, to emphasise the point, 'really going *all out*, with what resources you have, and I know it's not easy, tracking down Mr Wright. Don't you agree?'

It happened they did agree. But nobody likes being told how to do their job, least of all by a man with a posh voice and a strong jaw, and a house the size of Todeister. Neither detective deigned to reply.

'... Or Mr Wrong, perhaps I should say ...' Egbert(Mr) joked, because their silence was disconcerting.

'This isn't the time for joking, Mr Tode,' one of the detectives snapped.

'You're absolutely right. Not funny at all. I apologise. To be honest with you we're all a bit shocked ... It's all rather horrid. With the children here and everything. How long do you think it'll be before we can get rid of the body?'

'An hour or two, yet.'

'Yes. Of course. Well. I'll leave you to it. The sooner the better, that's all I really wanted to say ... You probably saw all the trailers and trucks and everything, by the Estate Wing? We have a wonderful television series starting their filming schedule tomorrow ... As you know ... '

'Aye.' They were aware of it.

' ... Only ... we were definitely hoping to, er ... to get everything shipshape, as it were, before the, er, "cameras roll" as they say in the biz! Got to keep the show on the road! No need to frighten the horses! What do you think ... Will you all be out of the way before too long? *Is that likely?*'

Egbert's wheedling tone was beginning to get on his own nerves, never mind anyone else's. It was time to call a halt to the meeting. Get out of the room before he said anything else. It occurred to him it might be a good idea to put in a quick call to Chief Constable Barraclough. Just to keep him in the loop, as it were .... Chief Constable Barraclough had been a brick over the previous incident. He'd been wonderfully discreet. He and India had invited him over for dinner a couple of times since, to show their appreciation. And darling India had worked her magic on him, as usual. *No surprises there!* She'd had the Chief Constable eating out of her hand by the end of the first course ... Perhaps he should get India to make the call?

Egbert(Mr), who was normally so calm and effective and stable, was experiencing a moment of turbulence. Nothing more. Only a few days now before the family would be jetting off to Paxos. He couldn't wait.

THE ATLAS FOUNTAIN

t was hot. Ecgbert(Sir) complained of this bitterly as he and Alice walked across the controversially yellow lawn. At the Atlas Fountain, they stopped and sat. The Atlas was not just any fountain, it should be noted. It was more like a medium-size lake. In its centre, water pumping at him from four sides, through trumpet-shaped shells, held aloft by mythical Greeks – there was a vast sculpture of Atlas holding up the world. It was dramatic and beautiful, and after the tawdry larder scene he and Alice had witnessed this morning, it made a welcome contrast. The film crew hadn't colonised it yet either; so it was a good place to speak privately, even if – with so much water pumping between so many Greek mythical sources – it was occasionally quite hard to hear what was being said.

They discussed the murder, first. Ecgbert, still sweltering in thick corduroy jacket and polo neck, was worried Rapunzel's body might start decomposing before the police took it off to the morgue. How quickly did a body begin to decompose? He paused to look it up on his phone:

'Lngth of tme time for body deposing in hotel weathe' (No reading glasses).

There was something from the BBC: 'How to Keep Cool and Carry On in a Heatwave', and something from the NHS advising on the risk of overheating in summer.

'*Useless*,' he declared, putting his phone away. 'Do you sometimes wonder if the internet isn't a massive scam?'

'In what way?'

' . . . Cobbled together by sinister government forces . . . ' He lost interest. 'Anyway, the point is, I wanted to say something, Trudy. Not about the murder, which I'd rather hadn't happened. Obviously. But I've been wanting to say something else. And you can't just not say things, because other things come along. You can't. Not really, can you? Not when they have to be said. Do you mind?'

Alice said: 'Depends what it is, Ecgbert.'

He'd been rehearsing it all night. He wanted to say something like this:

You, Alice, are the first thing I think about when I wake up, and the last thing I think about when I go to sleep. Since you came back to Tode Hall, everything has changed! My life has been transformed. Just knowing you are nearby makes me happy. You are beautiful and interesting and clever and wise. You are the only person in the world I want to be with. I love you. I have always loved you. I would go to the ends of the earth for you. I would die for you. Trudy – Alice – my darling – tell me you feel even just the tiniest bit the same way.

152

Who knows how many gallons of water cascaded over Atlas's globe as he tried to form the words?

Alice thought he looked very handsome, sitting there at the water's edge. Also, she'd liked the way he hadn't been fazed by Alyster Crowley. She liked the way he never seemed to be fazed by anything, very much: not by dead bodies in larders, nor even by being disinherited in favour of younger cousins. She liked the way he called her Trudy. She liked the way she had known him all her life, and that, although she'd not laid eyes on him between the ages of fourteen and fifty-one, it was as if, when they were reunited last year, there had never been a break. She liked him. She loved him. There was no one in the world she felt more comfortable with. All this floated around inside her without ever being examined, let alone acknowledged. But her triplets sensed it. India sensed it. Geraldine, Lady Tode (1907–1971) sensed it. So Alice was smiling at him, dangling her hand in the Atlas Fountain water, waiting for Ecgbert to say whatever it was he wanted to say, not thinking of anything much. Just enjoying the sunshine, and the water cascading, and this moment of pleasure, after the horrors of before.

'Trudy – Alice,' he said. He looked uncertain. 'Do you mind me calling you Trudy?'

'Not at all,' she said. 'It reminds me of when we were children ... What were you going to say?'

He lost his nerve. He said: 'I think a corpse probably begins to stink only after a couple of days. So it should be OK. But I tell you what – I certainly won't want to eat the rest of that chocolate cake, will you?' He laughed. It was a silly, noisy laugh, due to nerves. His large head wobbled, his shoulders rocked. And the moment was lost.

Never mind. Alice hardly noticed. She'd not been expecting

him to say anything much in any case. She might have been horrified if he had. And there would be other moments. These two had kissed up by the Africa Folly in 1982. One of these days they would kiss again, by the Atlas Fountain or somewhere else. They were made to be together.

THE GARDENER'S HOUSE KITCHEN

THURSDAY

Two days later, and Rapunzel's body was safely locked away in the morgue; Norman was still AWOL; Alyster Crowley, having postponed his return to LA, not to mention his final payment to Tode Hall Estates, was still hanging around the set making everyone miserable. But he was preparing to leave tonight, much to everyone's relief. They were one-and-a-half days into what was due to be a three-week shoot, and, astonishingly, given everything that had happened, filming was on schedule. Nobody (except for Alyster) had yet thrown any tantrums or walked off the set.

Alice's kitchen at the Gardener's House had quickly evolved into the central social hub for all-comers: a de facto green room for the actors, most of whom hated to be alone; and, because of the triplets, a welcoming hangout zone for much of the crew. India dropped in about ten times a day, and the triplets tended to wait here, walkie-talkies on standby, until their presence was needed elsewhere. Everybody loved the triplets. On a set where the mood was not great, what with the murder, the Mellors–Thistlestrupp–KitKat shag triangle, the Oscar-winning egos, the brown lawn, the bullying executive producer and the suspect-still-at-large, the triplets' warm kitchen and laid-back mother formed an oasis of good cheer.

The situation made Lady Tode a little tetchy, sometimes. But it kept her in the loop. She complained about what she termed, 'this appalling invasion', but in truth she was having the best time she could remember since December 1971, when she died of an amphetamine-induced heart attack, shortly after having it off with Oliver Mellors's great-grandfather, in what was then an empty stable, now a shop selling shockingly expensive teddy bears, blankets and picnic hampers embossed with the Tode family crest.

On that Thursday, at about noon, Alice, Ecgbert(Sir) (and Lady Tode) were sitting around the kitchen with Nicola Tode, on a break from her frantic writing, one triplet (Jacko), and one Oscar winner (Teddy). Teddy was telling Ecgbert(Sir) about his beaty-heart concerns, wondering if Ecgbert had any advice, which he didn't. He let slip that his heart had been even more beaty than usual, since the murder. He confided to the table that he kept imagining Norman, the killer, returning to Tode Hall to kill *him*, Teddy. He knew this was silly, but it was keeping him up at night.

'It's impacting on my performance. That's what's really troubling me,' he was saying.

Nicola said: 'We don't actually *know* it was Norman who killed her. Just because he left without saying goodbye. He may have been suffering from anxiety or stress or ...'

('Nonsense!' Lady Tode exclaimed. 'Will that girl ever stop talking nonsense?')

'Good point, Nicola,' Ecgbert said. 'I agree with you. We're leaping to conclusions. It could have been all sorts of people. Everybody hated her.'

'No they didn't,' Nicola said automatically. 'That's ridiculous. I'm just saying, although I think Norman probably did do it, we should also be tolerant about having open minds to the possibility it was someone else. E.g. – well . . . I don't know. I don't think Mellors liked her much. Ditto Alyster Crowley. Ditto, you, Teddy. No offence. She was very insensitive to you with regard to identifying as LGBTQ+, which I must say I thought was disgusting . . . '

Teddy breathed. And it packed a punch. He fiddled with a smudge of marmalade, the remains of Alice's breakfast, and he left a pause so dense, so perfectly pitched, so exquisitely controlled that nobody dared move; nobody took their eyes off him. He said: 'I admire your openness, Nicola. I wish more people were like you. And of course you are right. I don't like to speak ill of the dead—'

'Rapunzel doesn't count,' Ecgbert said. 'No one can think of anything nice to say about her, and we can't just not talk about her. Given, you know . . . that somebody murdered her, and her killer is still roaming about.'

Teddy looked emotional. He wiped his marmalade finger onto his 1930s shooting jacket (he was in costume, waiting to be called to set). 'You know he assaulted Livvie, on the night of the, erm – of the terrible thing that happened. He assaulted Livvie, in the larder.'

'In the larder?' repeated Alice. '*Really?*'

'Yes, really,' he said. 'She was cutting herself some cake, standing on the ladder – and he came up behind her and put his hand on her – buttock? Or leg? I don't remember. Anyway whatever it was, Livvie was too upset to go into details.'

157

'That is the most disgusting … *thing*,' said Nicola, her face red.

A hooting-snorting-choking noise, very ostentatious, came from Lady Tode's corner; purple wisps of smoke escaped from the neckline of her leopard-skin bathing suit, and a smell of jasmine filled the room. She was laughing.

Ecgbert scowled at her empty chair and said: 'It's not funny.'

Nicola said: 'Nobody suggested it was, Ecgbert. What is *wrong* with you?'

Jacko nodded solemnly. 'Nothing funny about assault, bro,' he said.

'What?' snapped Ecgbert. '*I know there isn't.*'

Alice said: 'He didn't say there was. He said there wasn't.'

Lady Tode continued her hooting and snorting. Alice shot her a look, to no effect.

They all turned back to Teddy. Nicola, a look of delirious compassion on her face, leaned in. 'Of course Norman did that. It makes perfect sense, doesn't it? He was, like, ogling and staring and behaving disgustingly towards her all through dinner. I noticed that. It was, like, I was on the point of saying something at the time. Poor, poor Livvie. Is she OK? Did she tell the police?'

Teddy held on to his heart, which was beating, and breathed, before replying. 'She's fine,' he said. 'Poor, darling girl. She was terribly shaken up. But yes, to answer your question, she *did* tell the police, and the police, I believe, are taking it very seriously.'

Nicola nodded. 'Good,' she said. And then, in a burst of impatience and rage: 'Just … the *fact* … that women like Livvie have to put up with this shit. Day in and day out, in this day and age …. I swear, it makes me so angry …' There was foam – a tiny bit of foam – at the corner of her mouth. 'Fucking *men*. This world would be a better place if *men* never existed . . .'

Jacko nodded.

More hoots from the purple cloud.

Alice chuckled. 'Maybe that's a bit extreme, Nicola.'

Ecgbert said, 'Also super-dumb. If you didn't have men, you wouldn't have women. You wouldn't have a world for them not to exist in.'

'That is such typical bullshit!' Nicola looked set to continue. She inhaled, and banged the table, putting her fist into another stray splodge of marmalade.

Alice said: 'How's the book going, anyway? I can't wait to read it. Where have you got to?'

Nicola turned her eyes to Alice. Only someone who had never attempted to write a self-help memoir could ask such a stupid question. *Where had she got to* indeed! What did that even mean? But Nicola forced herself to smile and reminded herself not to be so elitist. Alice couldn't be expected to know any better. She was an Organisational Coordinator, after all; and her grandmother, embarrassing though this was, had literally been a housemaid. Nicola said: 'It's hard to explain, Alice, but an author doesn't *get to* places exactly, when they're writing stuff. It's not a shopping list! It's more like an . . . explorational journey. The "getting to" is an organic process. And the author/writer of said memoir feels her way through to her own me-place, the heartbeat of the hu-person. If that makes sense?'

More hoots.

Ecgbert groaned.

Teddy MacIntosh looked alert. 'Gosh,' he said. 'Perhaps that's what *I* should be doing. I would call it: *Exploring Me . . .*

maybe. Or maybe something a bit more generic: *Because we are Universe . . .*' His eyes shone. 'Wow. That's actually not a bad idea.'

Nicola said: 'I would object to any white male appropriating words like "universe", Teddy. Under the circumstances. Actually it's quite offensive.' And then, without pausing for a response, she turned back to Alice. 'To answer your question, I'm currently writing about the sexualisation of gender, and how that impacts on the me-place as a woman; gay or otherwise, frankly. Also my belief that where there's sexualisation of the female there *is* pornography and pornography *is* rape per se, inasmuch as "rape" contains any meaning in the modern context, where rape is something that happens every day. It happens every time a female sexualises herself with so called "fun" jewellery and shoes, which is exactly what happens when a woman such as myself, or Livvie Kellet, is exploited by the fashion industry and thereby rendered desirable to male eyes. This is modern rape. And nobody sees it.' Nicola paused. Quite pleased. She actually looked at Alice and smiled. 'That's just a rough outline.'

Alice said: 'Gosh.'

Ecgbert said: 'Seriously Nicola . . .' But he was lost for words.

Lady Tode had evaporated, which usually meant she'd retreated to the sugar pot either in disgust, or for a change of clothes. It was probably a good thing.

And obviously Teddy wasn't listening.

Jacko, rolling himself a cigarette, continued nodding throughout, but he hadn't been listening either. He said: 'A lot of stuff went down in the larder on Monday night, when you think about it . . . First Norman, then – y'know – Rapunzel . . . I was in there with Rapunzel, but I think she went in and out a few times. You saw her in there didn't you, Teddy?'

'Did I?' said Teddy, coming to: sounding twitchy. 'No. I don't think so. I don't remember.'

There followed an extended and confused discussion, regarding which guest went into the larder that night, with whom, when and for how long. The fact is, nobody could entirely remember. Also, which nobody was telling anyone, the triplets had been making themselves popular with the metropolitan faction, by supplying them with weed and any other friendly drugs that they happened to be carrying on their person. It meant there had been quite a lot of coming and going, entering and exiting and, with the weed, a heavy demand for feasting on chocolate cake and jam tarts around midnight. The larder had certainly seen heavy traffic.

'What time did Rapunzel go to bed?' Alice asked. 'Well, of course she never went to bed. But did she stay up late, after I left?'

Jacko, Teddy and Nicola looked at each other blankly. Ecgbert(Sir) had left soon after Alice, who'd left soon after India and Egbert. That much, they could all remember. Beyond that—

'She was still up when I went to bed,' said Nicola.

'Gosh,' Teddy said. 'I mean, she stayed up for ages. I think. Didn't she? Everyone did.'

Later, when the others had all been called to the set, and Nicola had plodded back to her masterpiece, Ecgbert asked Alice, 'Do you think they were all stoned?'

Alice replied: 'I think they may have been.'

LIVVIE KELLET'S TRAILER

FRIDAY

Livvie was meditating. Or trying to. She was due in make-up in thirty minutes, and she intended to use the time productively. She found meditation helped her performance. Stopped the nerves. Made her feel a little less jumpy, especially when she was filming.

The difficulty, on location, was in finding the moments when no one would interrupt. She sometimes wondered if her trailer didn't develop a sort of magnetic field, the moment she put the recording on and closed her eyes. In any case, she'd asked Drez to stand guard outside, and keep the world at bay. Just for twenty minutes. She needed this.

So she arranged herself on the rug. Drew the blinds. Locked the door. Closed her eyes. Let the music *flow through her*. Felt a tiny promise of a little hint of calm returning to her . . .

'Coo-ee! Livvie?'

A tap on the trailer wall. Not even at the door.

She snapped open her eyes. *What the hell?* Where was Drez? Why wasn't he doing what somebody paid him to do?

She closed her eyes and tried again.

A muffled voice against the window. Someone was shouting her name. *What the fuck?* Livvie stood up and pulled back the blind. There was a face: a woman in a red beret, grinning at her. It took Livvie a moment to recognise Nicola Tode. But there she was. Grinning and waving. Nicola Tode, as daughter of the house, or whatever she was, had free range of the Unit Base. Nobody was going to try to tell her where she could or couldn't go. Even so.

Livvie let the blind drop. Now what was she supposed to do?

Outside, she heard Drez, spotting Nicola round the side of the trailer and trying, politely, to send her away. But if Drez and his brothers possessed a single small defect (debatable) it might have been their lack of assertiveness.

He said: 'Really sorry, Nicola. Livvie said—'

And then Nicola said: 'I need to speak to her. On a very important subject. So . . . Excuse me.' Nicola's voice rose a note. 'I'm actually feeling a little bit intimidated, at this moment. Would you mind stepping back from me? Please. Thank you . . . And keeping your hands – *yes*. *Thank you*.' Beat. The next thing, Nicola had sidled around him and was pulling at the locked door latch.

There was a moment, quite unwelcome, when Livvie couldn't help but imagine what it felt like to be Nicola. *Super lonely.* The knowledge gave Livvie goosebumps, also quite unwelcome. She realised she felt sorry for Nicola, and in that instant, had no choice, but to be kind, and to let her in.

'Hey!' Livvie said, opening the door, looking down on her from the highest step, smiling her glittering smile.

'Sorry,' said Drez, standing limply behind her. 'She said it was important.'

Livvie waved the apology away. 'Not at all. Doesn't matter at all. *Lovely to see you, Nicola!*'

But now that Livvie had appeared, Nicola's confidence abandoned her. Livvie was so beautiful and so famous and so brilliant and so successful. Unlike Livvie, Nicola could not imagine what it was like to be anyone else but herself, trapped in her own, unloved skin. She could never imagine what it must be like to be Livvie Kellet, who was a living goddess, not really human at all.

Nicola flushed. Forgot her lines.

Livvie felt all this, in that instant, as if she herself were Nicola. *Pathetic, unhappy woman*, Livvie felt. In any case she was accustomed to helping and encouraging people when her presence rendered them tongue-tied. She said: 'Why don't you come in? Was there something you needed to tell me?'

Nicola shook her head. 'No, no. I don't want to disturb you, I just …' But Nicola's neck was at an unfortunate angle, because Livvie was standing on the top step, way above her. Nicola felt as if she might be about to choke. She cleared her throat. 'I just wanted to say …' Her voice was faint. Not its usual strident *faux-pauvre* self, but something strangulated and childlike. She tried again. 'I just wanted to say … that I heard what Norman did to you. In the larder. And I wanted to tell you how sorry I was for your pain as a woman. And how angry I was, that he would have done that, as a man. And that I hope you're OK, and I just really, really, *really* …' Nicola's voice broke. Tears overflowed and spilled down her cheeks. 'I want you to know that.'

Livvie, moved by so much raw emotion, came down the steps, and gave Nicola a hug.

164

'Thank you,' she said. 'Thank you Nicola, that means so much.'

And for a moment or two, Nicola lost it completely. She rested her beret against Livvie's swanlike neck and sobbed. Livvie squeezed her shoulders. She dropped a kiss on Nicola's beret. And then, before too long, Livvie had gently, sweetly, sent her packing. The encounter lasted less than seven minutes. It meant Livvie still had time to meditate before heading into make-up.

THE GARDENER'S HOUSE

FRIDAY NIGHT

I t was fortunate for India, who was used to getting a lot of help around her big house, that she and her family were due to fly off to Paxos in the morning, because by the Friday night (four long days since the disastrous dinner that ended in murder), Mr and Mrs Carfizzi were still not really pulling their weight, and India was – if not exhausted – certainly fed up.

Mrs Carfizzi had gone to Edinburgh 'to meet a cousin', or so her husband claimed. He was refusing to tell anyone when she would be home.

'Are you sure she's all right?' India asked (again and again).

To which Mr Carfizzi, looking gaunt and less dapper than usual, would only nod his head. Mrs Carfizzi had never been better. She had gone to Edinburgh to meet a cousin because she deserved a rest.

And that was all very well. But so did India. In London, there had been restaurants. At Tode Hall, there had been Mrs Carfizzi. With the best will in the world, as India said to Alice, she couldn't face cooking again, not for the fourth night in a row, especially not on the very evening before schlepping all the way to the airport. It was too much!

India might have dropped in at the Old Stables Farm Shop half way down the drive, and picked up one of Tode Hall's organic beef 'n ale pies, with a Tode Hall crest stamped into the crust. They went for a whopping £45 a pop, and were, not surprisingly, quite good. But honestly, what with the packing and the heat, she couldn't be bothered. She might, on another day, have gone to one of the three Tode Hall restaurant-cafés on the estate, but two were always closed for dinner, and all three were closed for the next few weeks, because of the filming.

'I'm at my wits' end,' she said to Alice. 'Also, I'm a bit worried about Mrs Carfizzi. I think tomorrow, if there's still no sign of her, I'm going to have to – I don't know, insist on at least speaking to her on the phone. Or something. Don't you think? Or is that too bossy? . . .'

Alice thought it wasn't too bossy. In the meantime, since Egbert(Mr) had left for his holiday a day early so he could have lunch with his stockbroker in London, and the children had already eaten with the nanny, Alice took pity. She invited India and Nicola to join her, Ecgbert(Sir), the lovely triplets and the lonely, wifeless Oliver Mellors for dinner at the Gardener's House.

'Oh thank *God* you asked!' sighed India. 'I was so hoping you would.'

It was a very pleasant evening, at least for the first few hours. Alice, as per tradition, rolled herself an evening spliff and smoked it as she pulled together, in her casual manner, some excellent carbonara. She was a good cook. Ecgbert brought some wine, Mellors picked up a crate of raspberries from the Tode nursery garden, and India filched some toffee-flavoured fudge (with the family crest on the lid) from the basement gift shop. Nicola brought nothing but her surly self, and her red beret, which smelled of sweat.

'Your beret smells gross, Nicola. Smells of donkeys,' Ecgbert said, when he bent down to kiss her hello.

She ignored him.

It was four days since Rapunzel's body had been discovered, and the police didn't seem to be making much headway. The hunt was on for Norman Wright, but so far, and despite plenty of publicity, his whereabouts remained a mystery. Detectives had visited his house and his place of work. They had interrogated his students, his adoptive parents and his neighbours (who barely knew him). They had searched in vain for any friends. But the man had left little trace of himself, even when he wasn't in hiding. Now he seemed to have vanished entirely.

In the meantime, Rapunzel's will had been opened, and it transpired that she'd left her son nothing at all. Rights to her mother's literary estate, and everything else Rapunzel possessed – which was a lot, because of course she was a canny investor – had been donated to a little-known research institution based in Idaho, called Eugenics of America.

'I suppose the question *is*,' said Alice, who was, as per tradition for this time in the evening, gently and pleasantly stoned, 'did he *know* she'd left him nothing in her will? And if so, when did he find out?'

'Maybe she broke the news to him that night,' suggested Ecgbert. 'And then he spotted her, all alone with the chocolate cake, standing right there, on top of the ladder, literally *holding* the knife ... And the temptation simply overcame him ... I could understand that.'

India said: 'Hmmm.' She was a bit fed up with the topic, truth be told. She was fed up with the whole *Prance to the Music in Time* filmmaking experiment, and had been ever since the Long Gallery dinner turned so sour. The experience was nothing like she had envisaged it would be: she and Eggie hanging out with the stars, and so on. It only involved having a lot of cables everywhere, and rooms she couldn't go into. And drab-looking people in trainers roaming about the place, muttering into walkie-talkies ... Her mind wandered to the villa awaiting her in Paxos. She couldn't wait. 'You never know,' she said. 'Maybe it was just a terrible accident. If Rapunzel was holding the knife, surely she could have slipped and done it to herself? That's what Eggie says might have happened. I think he's almost definitely right.'

'*Or maybe*,' Ecgbert continued (ignoring India's fatuous interjection. Nobody pushed a knife into their own back by accident), 'maybe she told him she was disinheriting him *while she was up the ladder*. And then she *tipped backwards* in a sadistic manner, to see what he looked like when he heard the news, caught herself on the hook ... and then. Well.' Ecgbert shrugged. 'Seriously. She was already hanging on the hook. She'd just told him she was leaving all her dosh to some weird fanatics in Idaho ... I mean – after all those years putting up with her ... it would have been the final straw. Irresistible, no?'

Nobody replied.

Ecgbert said: 'If it was up to me, I'd let him off. Seriously. I hope they never find him.'

Mellors, who hadn't spoken for some time, said: 'Maybe he didn't do it. Maybe it were someone else.'

'*Hmmm*,' said India, again. 'Or maybe she did it to herself.'

'Yeah, right,' said Nicola (also ignoring India). 'Of course you'd think that, Mellors; because he's a white male, and therefore incapable of wrongdoing—'

'White as they come,' Mellors nodded thoughtfully. 'There were an albino lad like that at my school. Nobody ever said a word to him.'

'Exactly,' Nicola replied.

'Pardon?'

But Nicola had moved on. 'You probably think it was Livvie who did it, because she's beautiful, and beautiful women are considered witches to men. All women are witches to men. Because you can't control us.'

Ecgbert rolled his eyes, but for once resisted arguing back. His sister seemed to be getting madder every day. He wondered, vaguely, if there was something actually wrong with her.

'Yeah, roll your eyes, why not?' she foamed. 'Because of course *you'd* let him off, Ecgbert.' She pointed a finger, waved it between her brother and Oliver Mellors. 'You're all in it together. Meanwhile what about *Livvie*? What about what that disgusting *white male* did to Livvie? I suppose you'd, like, just "let him off", for that, too, would you?'

Mellors laughed. He bellowed with laughter. 'Nicola, you muppet!' he said.

'What?'

'If your brother's about letting the man off for the murder

of his mother, he'll probably be wanting to let him off for touching a girl's bum. Don't you think so?'

Nicola stared at him. 'No,' she said. 'Actually I do not. Those two things are completely incomparable. One is murder. And the other is—'

'Aye! Touching a girl's bum!'

The triplets hadn't caught the beginning of the conversation, and didn't have much idea what anyone was talking about. But Mellors's laughter was infectious; and they were a little bit stoned. They started laughing too.

The laughter rolled on, and gathered momentum. Nicola looked at her hands. Her ears burned red. Alice, Ecgbert and India noted this: she looked very small and angry and lost – and they all, simultaneously, took pity.

Ecgbert thought the best policy was diversion. So – not unusually – he said the first thing that came into his head. He slapped the table: 'Oliver Mellors,' he said. 'Up until now, I never realised what all the fuss was about, but looking at you now – I've just realised how handsome you are.'

His comment stunned everyone to silence. A beat, while they all confirmed to themselves that they had heard him correctly. And then everyone, except poor Nicola, started laughing all over again.

Ecgbert said, slightly irritably: '*What*? What's so funny? He is. Mellors you are very handsome.'

There was a noise outside – footsteps on the gravel by the back door. But nobody heard it, because of the laughter. Alice always left the back door unlocked. It was a habit she had adopted since moving into the Gardener's House, a year ago. After a lifetime spent in London, she delighted in the luxury of going in and out of her own house without using keys. And it was foolish of her, perhaps. Especially in the circumstances, with a suspected killer still at large.

Or maybe not so at large, anymore. At that moment Norman Wright was twisting the back-door handle, and feeling it turn in his grip. While laughter rang out from the kitchen, just a room-and-a-half away, he quietly let himself in to the house.

Norman paused in the hallway and listened to the sounds of happy laughter coming from the kitchen on the other side of the wall. It made him feel very lonely indeed. But that, in the circumstances, was the least of his problems. He recognised Sir Ecgbert's voice, and possibly India's ... so the house was full. *Just my luck*, he thought to himself.

He heard Nicola:

'Ecgbert you are trivialising what Mellors has said, which was in itself a trivialising and diminishing remark celebrating a culture of violence against women, and I can't just "let that pass". Livvie Kellet does not deserve to be objectified, and I feel that, as a man, you should accept some responsibility. It's comments like yours, Mellors, that make rape such a mainstream activity.'

'Mainstream activity?' Mellors repeated, astonished.

Even the triplets dared to voice some resistance. 'That's maybe *a bit* of a generalisation, Nicola,' they tutted. 'Let's be honest.'

'All men are rapists,' she said.

In the corridor, sweating from his exertions and the warmth of that August evening, Norman Wright remembered the existence of the triplets, and once again cursed his rotten luck. He'd been hoping to find Alice alone. But the house was packed with men ready to defend her. It was bitterly unfair, he felt. He only wanted to talk. So. Now what? He needed to be careful.

To the left, there was the kitchen, where they all sat, laughing and squabbling, with the door very slightly ajar. To the right, there was a sitting room: and in front of him, a passage-way leading to the stairs. He would find a place to hide, and wait. If necessary he would hide all night, until the triplets left for the set in the morning.

Norman, chubby, unfit and quite old, had been living rough since late Monday night. He was hungry, and tired – and above all, terrified. Slowly, carefully, wincing with every floorboard creak (and there were many) he crept along the corridor, past the kitchen door and up the stairs. In the kitchen, nobody heard him. Nicola had hit her bull's-eye at last. Everyone was annoyed with her. She had found the fight she'd been looking for all night.

A smell of methane. Lady Tode, resplendent in ermine; wearing a tiara, and the dress she wore at the Queen's coronation in 1953, stood at the kitchen door, looking haughty, waiting for a pause in the argument.

'Darlings,' she said, when no pause was forthcoming. She sounded affectionate, which was unusual, and not quite as languid as she normally did. Ecgbert and Alice both turned. 'I have some bad news.'

'What's up, Granny?' Ecgbert said.

Nicola leapt on it. '*I know what you're doing, Ecgbert,*' she said. '*You think, by suddenly doing your stupid "talking to Granny" thing, you can turn everything into a joke. Do you see me laughing? I am not laughing. And that is because Granny is not relevant to this conversation. And even if she was relevant, and I don't really see how she could be, it would not be funny.*'

Alice had to bite her lips not to giggle. 'I think Nicola's making a good point,' she said. And then she looked across at Ecgbert and winked.

Lady Tode shuddered. 'No, Alice. Really. I beg.' She paused, inhaled through her fine nostrils. 'I'm all for you, as it were . . . I really am. But darling, *winking* . . .'

Ecgbert said: 'I think it's beautiful.'

'*What is beautiful?*' shouted Nicola, exasperated. 'Name one thing that is beautiful about this situation.'

'Alice, winking,' Ecgbert said.

'I am trying to have an important conversation here. And as usual, you're trivialising my efforts with comments that don't make sense.'

Lady Tode cleared her throat. 'Darlings,' she said again. 'I'm sorry to tell you this, but there's a man upstairs, hiding in the linen cupboard.'

'A man?' cried Ecgbert, leaping to his feet. 'In the linen cupboard, Granny?'

'Sit down, Ecgbert,' said his grandmother. 'Stay calm. It's Norman Wright. He's shaved all his hair off. And I think he's crying.'

'Not, "*a* man",' shouted Nicola, banging the table, drunk as a skunk. '*Every* man . . . Every man in every linen cupboard, everywhere.'

Lady Tode considered her granddaughter, and sighed. 'You

need to get that nincompoop girl out of here. Also India, I think. Much as I love her. And I don't think we can trust Mellors, frankly. Only do buck up. In the meantime, fear not.' She tapped her elegant cheekbone. 'I shall keep a beady eye.'

Mellors stared at the threshold, where Lady Tode stood. Took a slug of his beer, shook his head, shook himself, rubbed his eyes, and started to laugh again. 'I think I need to get some sleep,' he said.

THE LINEN CUPBOARD

FRIDAY NIGHT

t was sweltering in there. The door barely closed on his round belly; and there were no windows, just the heat coming off the water pipes, making him drip with sweat. Norman Wright had always been a hygienic man; neurotically so, even. And now, after four nights sleeping in a cow shed, the smell coming off his body and clothes in this enclosed space was making him gag. Or was his terror the root cause? His misery? His regret? Norman couldn't separate them. All he knew was – that he'd come here, to Tode Hall, because he knew he couldn't hide in a cowshed for ever. He needed help. Alice Liddell had been kind to him at Todeister train station; she'd talked to him a little during the dinner. When Livvie Kellet had accused him of staring at her br—

staring at her—

BREASTS. Her *breasts*. Staring at her breasts . . .

(Norman gagged again.)

When Livvie Kellet had accused him, Alice Liddell had sent

him a look, down the dining-room table, he was sure of it, as if she understood how unfair it all was ... And then there was his mother, gloating, drawing out his humiliation. *In your dreams, Norman dear* ... His mother would have been overjoyed to see the state of him just now! Which was funny, in a way. Or it made him smile, at least. *Very ironic*, he thought. In any case, here he was, back at Tode Hall, because he had nowhere else to turn. And he had realised, finally, that the longer he hid away, the worse it would be for him when, finally, he returned. Alice Liddell was a great woman. Grounded and kind. And *womanly*. (He gagged again.) Alice Liddell was the sort of woman he could fall in love with. Definitely. Once all this was settled. She would help him.

Downstairs, he heard voices in the hallway. India, Nicola and Mellors were saying their goodbyes. Hugs and thanks from India. Surly words from Nicola.

'I can't wait to read your book!' Alice was saying. (It was all she ever said to Nicola. Everything else seemed to cause offence.)

Nicola said: 'Unfortunately that's going to be impossible for some time to come. It's a very personal process, finding the authentic voice so—'

'Yeah, all right,' said Ecgbert, slapping her on the back. 'Well whenever you're ready, Nicola. Good night.'

The front door closed.

Norman heard the triplets in the kitchen, clearing plates. But Ecgbert and Alice seemed to be lingering in the hallway. They were whispering.

Lady Tode was with them, not whispering; she didn't need to. She said: 'I think he's harmless. That's my feeling. I mean, whatever he did to his mother, he doesn't look up to much now. Are you ready?'

Alice whispered: 'But don't you think we should call the police?'

'No,' replied Ecgbert and Lady Tode, together.

'What is this obsession with the police?' Ecgbert whispered, genuinely curious.

'It's because she's middle class,' explained Lady Tode.

'Is that it, Trudy?'

'Probably,' replied Alice. 'Or maybe I just don't want to get killed.'

'Well in any case, I think,' said Lady Tode, 'we should find out what he's got to say for himself before we do anything drastic. You have the boys downstairs. He won't get away.'

What, wondered Norman, could they be talking about? Did they know he was here? Impossible! Except now they were coming this way. Walking along the corridor towards the stairs, and getting closer. He heard a foot on the bottom step, and then Alice, whispering:

'Shall we call the boys? What if he has a knife?'

'I don't think he's got a knife,' said Lady Tode. 'Why would he?'

'Well—'

'Don't be feeble,' Lady Tode snapped. 'He's a fat old man, stuck in a linen cupboard. And as I say, I'm pretty sure he's crying.'

Norman, who was not crying but sniffing from a summer cold (the result of four nights in a cow shed), heard the footsteps drawing closer, and realised his mistake. They knew he was here. And he was trapped. The linen cupboard had only one exit, into the bathroom, and the bathroom's only exit was the door that opened into the corridor that Alice and Ecgbert were at this moment walking down.

Why had he come here?

Why hadn't he stayed in the cowshed, where he was safe and nobody could find him?

Cowering against the hot-water pipe, Norman heard the bathroom door creak open. And then Ecgbert, saying: 'Granny are you sure? You're not just doing a practical joke, are you? It's not very funny if you are.'

'Of course I'm sure! Go on, Ecgbert, open it! Open the cupboard. He's in there, I'm telling you.'

Ecgbert hesitated.

Norman started crying.

Ecgbert said: 'Maybe we *should* alert Dregz'n'Co. In case he tries to escape? By the way Alice, I think you should stand back ...'

Another step towards the cupboard. Sweat in Norman's eyes. He thought he couldn't breathe. *This was so unfair.*

Alice's voice, calling into the cupboard: 'Hello? Is anyone in there?'

Norman didn't move, couldn't breathe anyway.

In one swift, surprising move, Ecgbert opened the door. Light from the bathroom flooded into the little cupboard.

There he stood, Yorkshire's most wanted man. Reeking of sweat. Cowering, against the light. Eyes closed, cringing and weeping.

'I didn't do it!' he said. 'I didn't! She's lying!'

'Who's lying?' asked Alice. 'What are you talking about?'

Norman could barely get the name out; the relief of being spoken to by a human being; the cool air on his filthy body, now that the linen cupboard door had been opened; the presence of these two familiar faces, the fear of what they might do to him, all together, made him lose control.

'L-L-Livv-ie *K-K-Kell---et*,' he sobbed. 'I never touched her!' And then, 'Oh Christ, I have to pee.'

He had to pee.

Alice, Ecgbert and Lady Tode discussed whether they should leave him alone in the bathroom and came to the conclusion, so slowly that Norman could feel the pee beginning to seep down his trouser leg, that since his only escape route was the bathroom door they were now blocking, it would be unnecessarily disagreeable for all parties to stand beside him while he emptied his bladder.

'I think,' Alice said, as they waited in the corridor, 'we should call my sons. This is weird. I don't trust him – do you?'

'I think you may be right,' agreed Lady Tode. 'On reconsideration Ecgbert, don't you think so, darling? Imagine if he slipped through one's fingers at this point? One would hardly forgive oneself.'

So after Norman had finished peeing, they brought him downstairs and sat him at the kitchen table. Dregz'n'Co, once they'd recovered their surprise, made him a cup of tea. Morman was goofy enough to suggest taking a selfie with him; but even his brothers saw the folly of that.

Norman said: 'I don't suppose I could have a glass of wine?'

'No, you can't,' snapped Alice. 'What are you doing here, anyway? The police have been looking for you everywhere – as you know. There's a nationwide manhunt going on. And you're sitting here, asking me for wine.'

Norman looked astounded. 'A nationwide *manhunt*? But I didn't do it.'

'Well bro,' said Drez, 'if you didn't do it, why did you run away?'

'Because I was humiliated!' Norman cried. 'Completely, utterly humiliated. Imagine it! In this day and age, who would ever believe me? Livvie Kellet, the most gorgeous actress in the entire world, accuses aged professor in Chinese History of sexual ... sexual ...' He shook his head, unable to finish the sentence. 'I would be ruined. Everything I have worked for would be ruined. And my *mother*—' His face, fat and soft and round, twisted in bitterness. 'I suppose I'll never hear the end of it now! She'll never let it drop.'

Lady Tode said: 'What the bloody hell is he talking about?'

Nobody quite knew.

He started crying again. Wouldn't stop. *'I'm so hungry,'* he wept. He looked at Alice. 'Have you got any food?'

She said not, which wasn't true.

'Mum, we have actually got quite a lot of the pasta left over ...' said Morman.

'He can have some food, when he starts making sense,' Alice snapped. 'He's whining about his career being ruined. Of course it's ruined! That's what happens to people when they murder their mothers and go into hiding.'

'Good point,' agreed Ecgbert. 'Nobody's pretending the old bird was an angel—'

'She was a *pill*,' Lady Tode said. Yet again.

'—But that's no reason to kill her,' he continued. He turned to Norman. 'You must realise that? Pull yourself together, man!' Ecgbert indicated the triplets. 'You're a professor, aren't you? You're supposed to be the sort of person who's an example to these young people. In fact,' he looked at Alice, 'I think you're right, Trudy. I think we should call the police.'

181

At that, Norman lost what little remained of his self-possession. He moaned and wailed and sobbed and cried. It was impossible to get a word of sense out of him. Why were they pretending he had murdered his mother? Of course he hadn't murdered his mother!

'One thing I've realised these past few days,' he said, pulling himself up, 'is that I don't care anymore. And if Livvie Kellet decides to ruin my life with her lies, then so be it.'

Ecgbert rolled his eyes. Crossed his arms. He was running out of patience.

'Trudy—' he said.

She put a hand on his arm. *Wait.*

Norman continued, obliviously. 'And my mother can go to hell. I don't care what happens to me now, I don't need to put up with her. Never again. I don't care about the money. I don't need her stupid money ... *I don't care about her.* She's an evil, hateful, *nasty* woman, and I never want to see or speak to her again.'

'Well that's lucky,' Ecgbert said. 'Because she's dead. As you know, so you can stop pretending. And she didn't leave you any money in her will anyway.'

No fresh tears. Norman fell silent. His soft round face looked ... Afterwards, Alice, Ecgbert and Lady Tode discussed what it looked like, at some length. They agreed that he had looked first stunned, then fearful ... and finally exultant.

He hadn't known. Or so it seemed.

After that, they had given him wine, and the remains of the carbonara; and they had listened to his jittery explanation for what had happened. They wanted to know why on earth, if he hadn't killed his mother, as he claimed, he had run away in the middle of the night, on the very night of her murder?

'You can't say that isn't fishy,' Ecgbert observed.

But Norman seemed to think the answer was obvious. Livvie Kellet had accused him of molesting her in the larder, while they were both seeking out chocolate cake.

'And I didn't *do* it,' he kept saying. 'It's so *unfair*. I came into the larder and there was Miss Kellet, standing on the ladder. She was – she was eating a very large slice of chocolate cake, in a somewhat surreptitious manner. And I *think* – I am no psychologist, but I believe, she was embarrassed to have been caught in that position. Being a movie star and so beautiful and so on. And I stupidly made a comment – *that's all I did*. I made a comment about how the public would be surprised if they could see her now! Which they would have been, by the way. But she jumped out of her skin. She was so angry! I never saw anything like it . . . She was haranguing me, in a disgusting sort of a way. Her fans would have been appalled. As I pointed out to her. She called me all sorts of horrible names, and then – out of nowhere – she said I'd assaulted her! *Me!* That *I* had assaulted *Livvie Kellet!*' He laughed, a most miserable laugh. '*Me!* She said she was going to make a complaint in the morning . . . Why would she do that? *Why?* Maybe she thought I'd taken a photograph, but *of course* I hadn't. I didn't even have my phone with me. Good heavens . . . Why would she say that? *Why?* I went to bed. I felt so ashamed. I went straight up to bed. My mother was holding court in the drawing room, throwing her weight around, as always—'

'She's dead,' interrupted Ecgbert(Sir). 'You might try to be a bit more pleasant.'

'And I packed my bags and left . . . I walked all the way to Todeister. And then I got the first train to – I got a train.' He slurped on his wine, stole a glance, over the rim of his glass, at the haphazard gathering of judges looking down at him, and he had a brainwave.

He said: 'Sorry. It's been a bad few days. I've got an upset tummy and I really need the toilet again.'

'Oh for goodness sake,' groaned Ecgbert(Sir) and his grandmother. Same words, same emphasis. Same everything.

'I'm sorry,' said Norman. 'My digestive system has never been good when I'm away from home, or when I'm feeling stress ... It tends to be one of these all-or-nothing situations for me, with regard to ... passing waste, as it were. And I think being here in this nice warm cosy room, having a glass of wine, I've come a bit loose.'

'*Slap him!*' cried Lady Tode.

Ecgbert said: 'I can't listen to this.'

The mix of adrenalin, weed, Norman's bowel update, and Ecgbert(Sir)'s reaction to it – sent the Dregz'n'Co into domino-effect giggles.

Alice looked at her triplets in dismay. 'Boys,' she said. 'This is serious.' And yet somehow the combination of her sons' helpless laughter, Sir Ecgbert and Lady Tode's identical, aristocratic disgust at the mention of bodily functions – and, no doubt, the spliff she had smoked while cooking dinner – made Alice start laughing, too. No one in the room was at their sharpest – except for Norman, whose freedom depended on it.

He said: 'Look, it's not funny. I need to go to the toilet.'

Slowly, politely, he stood up. His judges were all caught up scowling and giggling at one another. Norman, clumsy and round, slowly, politely, edged towards the kitchen door. 'I'll be two seconds ...'

Click – the kitchen door closed politely behind him.

'Do you know,' Lady Tode announced, 'I'm not sure he *did*

do it. Are you? He's a ghastly little man – no doubt about that. But I mean ... murder is quite a *thing*, you know. I don't think he's quite *man* enough.' She turned to the giggling triplets, who couldn't hear her, anyway. 'Do pull yourselves together,' she snapped. 'And Alice, you're no better. Ecgbert, what do you think?'

Ecgbert said: 'I don't know, Granny. Hard to tell.'

In a burst of hilarity-induced boldness Jacko was spurred, at last, to ask Ecgbert the question he and his brothers had been asking each other all week. 'No offence,' he said, 'but why do you keep talking to your granny?' It set the triplets spiralling into more helpless paroxysms.

Ecgbert said mildly: 'Your sons are being a bit silly, Trudy ... And no, I don't like that man, and I don't trust him either.'

Alice, recovering slightly, said: 'I don't trust him ... In fact, I don't believe he really needs the toilet ... Drez, you're closest – would you just go and check what he's up to, darling?'

'We know what he's up to,' replied Drez. 'He just told us he's on the toilet ... with his bowels ... ' It triggered another round of ecstatic laughter.

But Norman was not on the toilet. He was scuttling across the parched lawn, scrambling through the darkness. Back on the run, all over again.

185

THE TURQUOISE DRAWING ROOM

SATURDAY

Under normal circumstances, nobody would have dreamed of suggesting it so early in the filming schedule. But these were not normal circumstances. Rapunzel's murder – not to mention the brief reappearance of the chief suspect (police had sent out a search party, to no avail) – had left a stain on the mood for everyone, and it was felt that, no matter there was a killer still at large, the crew needed cheering up. There was to be no filming on Sunday. Better still, Alyster Crowley had finally climbed back into his chopper this morning, and flown to London, taking with him the cloud of terror that followed him everywhere, and leaving behind an unspoken sense of gravity-defying relief. This evening, at the end of the day's filming, there was to be a party at the Unit Base, in the field behind the Estate Offices. The catering people were organising a barbecue. The triplets had called a friend in London who'd called a friend in York, who'd come out to shake hands with the stars, and to deliver an array of leisure-enhancing pharmaceuticals.

It was a beautiful, hot day, and it promised to be yet another beautiful, warm evening. Most of the crew were impatient for the party to begin.

But at that point in the afternoon it looked like they'd be in for a long wait.

There must have been a hundred or more people milling around in Tode Hall's Turquoise Drawing Room; the majority under the age of forty, all of them dressed as teenagers. Film crews tend to be a fairly homogenous bunch. Perhaps this is because they spend so much time together in out of the way places, and then have almost nothing to do with themselves when they get there, except wait – for different experts to do very small, very specific things – rejig the lights, adjust the camera angle, reposition the prop, re-polish the floor. In any case, a hum of low-key expertise and Zen-like boredom hangs over most film sets. This one was no exception.

The scene to be shot, which was currently being prepared and discussed in soft monotones in every corner of the room, and in several rooms beyond it, involved the main character, a handsome young aristocrat with a drink problem, named Tintin, played by Teddy MacIntosh, engaging in a wrestling match in front of a burning fire, with his great friend from university, John Greystoke, played by Oliver Mellors.

The scene was meant to end, finally, with Greystoke pinning Tintin to the hearthrug, and kissing him on the lips. It was meant to be an erotic, tender and important moment, since at that point in the plot, the characters hadn't yet confronted their tortured sexual feelings for one another.

But there were problems: namely that Thistlestrupp had yesterday ordered the scene to be rewritten, and was now insisting that both actors play it naked: in *homage*, he claimed,

187

to some film Mellors had never heard of. Teddy MacIntosh wasn't bothered one way or the other. He was very comfortable with his nakedness. Mellors, on the other hand, though he burned the screen with his untortured sexual magnificence, was a gamekeeper by profession and a Yorkshireman to his core, and he was adamant about keeping his trousers on – *despite the fact*, as Thistlestrupp kept informing him, that he had signed a clause agreeing – or rather, not disagreeing – to nudity, in his contract.

Mellors kept saying: 'I don't give a monkeys about any clauses. It weren't in the script. I wouldn't have agreed to it then, and I don't agree to it now.'

What Mellors knew and what Thistlestrupp would die before he ever admitted, was that the scene had been rejigged, not in *homage* to a film that Mellors had never heard of, and Thistlestrupp had never seen and secretly suspected was quite boring, but in revenge against Mellors for having reached parts of KitKat that Thistlestrupp was no longer permitted to go near.

So. Filming had been halted for several hours this morning while the sides battled it out. There were calls to agents and calls to lawyers – but it had become increasingly clear that, legally speaking, Mellors didn't have much of a leg to stand on. He might have done better to have signed with Teddy MacIntosh's agent when he had the chance, because the man now representing him wasn't being any help.

Mellors, in his surly dislike of everything connected to his new life as a movie star, had not played a canny game. He had alienated pretty much everyone except KitKat, but she didn't have any clout. So it was Oliver Mellors, whose expertise until this point had been in pheasants, standing alone against an industry of world-class bullies. They would sue him. They would make him pay back every penny of his fee. They would bill him for all the lost hours of filming. They would fire him and charge him for the cost of reshooting the wasted days – and the figure would run into millions. They would bankrupt him.

Perhaps they were bluffing. Perhaps they didn't have anywhere near that kind of power over him. But how would he know?

At length Mellors succumbed. He'd lose the trousers, he said, but keep the underpants. And the kiss – would be a peck, not a slobber.

Thistlestrupp, retreating to his place beside the camera monitor, nodded to Mellors, patted him on the shoulder as if they were friends, and muttered to his first assistant, 'Yeah right. We'll see about that.'

Three hours later, and unbelievably, infuriatingly, they were still working on the same scene.

'... Nice and quiet now ...'

'... Cameras rolling ...'

Zen-like boredom. Quiet expertise. A hundred or so experts in specific fields stood super-still.

'Slate 136 ... Take 14 ...'

'Action!' called Thistlestrupp.

Greystoke with his shirt off.

Muscular torso catching the light.

Tintin with his shirt off.

Pale skin catching the light.

189

Grunt. Puff. Grunt.

Greystoke on top. Tintin pinned to the rug.

Firelight.

Tenderness.

Greystoke drops the kiss. Not quite a slobber nor yet a peck. Actually, it was perfect.

But Thistlestrupp insisted they do it again. And again, and again, and again. In Morman's words – in everyone's opinion – Thistlestrupp was being a dick. Cue for more Zen-like boredom from the experts. Being a dick, as everyone – except for Mellors and the triplets – knew, was the director's prerogative.

They'd spent three hours on this one scene, and three hours squabbling about it beforehand. Four other scenes planned for today had needed to be dropped. The schedule was wrecked and everyone, except for Thistlestrupp, longed to move on. But Thistlestrupp said he wasn't satisfied. They had to do it again.

More huddles. More waiting around. More quiet words with the actors. The technician in charge of log fires was called in to adjust the size of the flame ... The technician in charge of hearthrugs came in to examine a slight change of light on the corner tassels.

'... Nice and quiet please ...'

'... Cameras rolling ...'

A hundred or so experts in specific fields stood super-still.

'Slate 136 ... Take 33 ...'

'Action!' called Thistlestrupp.

Greystoke with his shirt off.

Tintin with his shirt off.

Grunt. Puff. Grunt.

Tintin pinned to the rug.

Firelight.

Tenderness.

Greystoke drops the kiss.

Not quite a slobber nor yet a peck. Actually, it was perfect. Very tender. Very erotic.

'CUT! Look, I'm sorry guys. I know you're fed up and you want to get to your party, but it's *just not working*. We can keep doing it like this all night, but it's never going to work without . . . Oliver, *we've got to lose the underpants.*'

In a single, swift movement Oliver Mellors had clambered off Teddy, he'd leapt through the air at Thistlestrupp, and sent him crashing to the ground. Bang.

Thistlestrupp lay on his back, pinned to the rug.

Firelight.

Tenderness . . .

'You're a wanker,' Mellors said. 'You know that?'

Thistlestrupp smirked.

Mellors climbed off him: 'You've got what you need, you wanker. You've got it thirty-three times over. I'm going to the pub.'

It was a large room, with many obstacles, and Mellors was only wearing his underpants. A silence fell as he weaved his solitary path towards his trailer. Nobody followed him or came to his aid.

Behind him, Thistlestrupp lay on the floor and continued to smirk, for the benefit of all those around him. But he wasn't feeling it. He had pushed Mellors too far, and he knew it.

OLIVER MELLORS'S TRAILER

SATURDAY

He'd had every intention of stomping off to the Tode Arms but halfway there he realised he couldn't face it, and turned back. People in the pub would tease him about being a movie star. And then he'd get drunk, and ask everyone if they had heard from Kate, and nobody would tell him anything, because when she left they all thought he deserved it. And all in all, it wasn't worth it. Mellors had never felt so miserable. He decided he preferred to be alone, so he headed for his trailer and locked the door.

Oliver Mellors's trailer was a quarter the size of either of the Oscar winners', for obvious reasons. It was more or less the size of an ordinary, old-fashioned caravan. But it had a sofa and wifi and a fridge, and he liked it in there. Unlike the cottage, it didn't remind him of his absent wife.

When they sent someone to wheedle him back onto the set, he kept the door locked and refused to answer. KitKat phoned him three times, but he suspected she'd been told to, and in any case, he didn't want to speak to her. He didn't want to speak to anyone. He missed his wife. He missed his pheasants. He missed his old life.

He switched off the phone. Checked his alcohol supplies (a dozen cans of beer, half a bottle of whisky) and began to drink.

How had he got himself into this mess in the first place, he wondered? What the hell would his dad say, if he could see him now? Here he sat, locked away in a caravan on Eastbreech field, being threatened with bankruptcy for refusing to wrestle naked with a world-famous movie star. Almost, he thought, *almost*, it was funny ...

And slowly, in the coolness of his solitude, it occurred to him that really there was very little any agents or lawyers or directors or producers could threaten him with. They'd talked about suing and bankrupting but, beyond the windfall fee for taking the role in the first place (half of which he had yet to receive), there wasn't much left for them to take. He'd not broken the law by keeping his underpants on – had he? It seemed unlikely. So what could they really do to him? His cottage was owned and paid for by the estate, as were most of his living expenses. His job at Tode Hall was assured – Egbert(Mr) had made that clear. He could simply walk away – and they could sue him as much as they wanted: it wouldn't get them anywhere. Mellors was free because he had nothing to lose.

It was a good moment. He opened his laptop and prepared to relax. He would tell them his decision some other time. Later. When he felt like it.

... On the other hand it was such a miraculous and liberating decision, he realised he couldn't wait to relay it.

They'd emailed him so much crap over the last few weeks. Call sheets, contracts, contact sheets. He dug out Alyster

Crowley's email address from the midst of them all, and before settling in for his private leisure, he wrote this:

> Dear Alyster,
>
> I won't be doing the film anymore. This is for
> personal reazons. If you want to discuss this matter, I
> am not available, so you better talk to Thistlestrupp
> and my agent, name of Richard Dorke. There about
> as useless as each other.
>
> Yours sincerely
>
> Oliver Mellors

And then he pressed Send. And opened another can of beer. And relaxed with his computer.

THE SAVOY HOTEL, LONDON

SATURDAY

Alyster Crowley longed to be back in LA. He disliked Europe, and he disliked England particularly. But – there were tax breaks. No movie mogul could altogether avoid doing business in London. So here he was. In his usual suite, and with somebody coming to give him a massage, shortly. It was better than being in Yorkshire, at least.

A gentle tap on the door of his suite. His masseuse, he assumed.

It was his PA, clutching an iPad, and looking nervous. She had already forwarded Mellors's email to Dave Snare (Series Producer). Dave Snare, on seeing the email, had told the PA to hold fire, while he tried to get Mellors to see sense. But he couldn't make Mellors see sense. Mellors had switched off his phone, and was refusing to come out of his caravan. He called the PA and volunteered to break the news to Alyster himself. And he had tried. But then Alyster had refused to take his call. So here was the PA. Doing what needed to be done. Crowley had to be told. He had $146 million of his and other people's money pledged to this production. He was not going to take the news well.

She said: 'Sorry to disturb you, Mr Crowley.'

He said: 'Uh.'

She cleared her throat, looked miserable, and with humble hands, passed him the iPad. Oliver Mellors's email was open on the screen, expanded to the font size she knew Crowley could manage without his specs.

She said: 'I've spoken to Dave Snare. He says Mr Mellors's problem is with Mr Thistlestrupp specifically. So – he says there's a chance Mr Mellors might be persuaded to change his mind, but not if Mr Thistlestrupp stays on the project ... That's all I know ... Sorry.'

She waited for the eruption. But on this occasion, the eruption did not come. Crowley read the message, handed back the iPad and simply said:

'I need to be in Yorkshire. Right now.'

Another day, another helicopter ride. Another multi-million-dollar production on the brink. Alyster Crowley would rescue the situation, because that's what he always did.

THE PINEAPPLE ROOM

SATURDAY

Party night. Nicola, alone at her large desk, gazing out over the moonlit park, could hear the music thumping from beyond the Unit Base, and every thump sent a shimmer of yearning through her body. She wanted to dance. But she was too shy to join the party. She might have dared, if India and Egbert had been with her, but they'd sugared off to Paxos without her. Nobody wanted her at the party. Why would they?

She thought about Livvie, lucky Livvie, out there mingling with the crowd. Livvie, who was so beautiful and so self-assured. She and Livvie had made a connection. For sure. Livvie probably made a connection with everyone. Maybe. Maybe not. Maybe she and Livvie had something in common: maybe they were soul sisters? Maybe they had known each other in another life? It was possible. More than possible. The soft music buzzed in Nicola's head. The soft evening air, the silver moonlight, and the people outside, beautiful and self-assured, dancing and chatting and laughing and living their lives in a way she never could, never would, never had … it all buzzed so hard in her head, she held on to her ears to block it out, but it only blocked it in.

Nicola wasn't a drinker. She might have felt better if she had been. She might have been bold enough to join the party there and then. But for hours, the music throbbed, and for hours she ordered herself to ignore it. Her work was more important. So she scribbled.

> *Misogyny and Animals:* *Bunny girls. A thing of the past? Maybe they are and yet there is animal-related porn which is much more detrimental to womens self respect as evidenced via any laptop. Women, such as my mother, who was a sexual narsissist, leave a trail of woman-damage with regard to their taste towards perceived fulfillment in the sexual arena, animal-related or otherwise (I do not know) and this nurishes the porn consumer. Sex is Rape until their is a change in the way we do it. And this must stop. People like my mother, who is now deceesed, should THINK before …*

She paused, because the music was really getting to her, and she really needed to dance, at least for a while. She stood up from her large desk and trudged to the middle of her three-hundred-year-old carpet (with embroidered pineapples at each corner). There was plenty of space. She danced to the light of her desk lamp, and though she would never in her wildest dreams have imagined it to be so, she danced well. She danced better than that. She danced beautifully.

But it only made her feel worse.

198

THE FIELD BEHIND UNIT BASE

SATURDAY

I n setting up their off-the-cuff party, the *Prance* film crew had
put their myriad expertise to good use. Between them, they'd
rigged the best lights, the best music, the best layout for any
party yet thrown in Yorkshire that long summer. In the middle
of a nondescript field, the set designers had even conjured specific zones: there was one for dancing, one for chatting, another
for chilling and another for making out. By ten o'clock that
evening, the unhappy day's filming was all but forgotten, and
the crew were living it up in their chosen territories, connecting
intensively, with or without the help of the friendly recreationals provided by the triplets; getting off with each other in
the CooZone; agreeing with each other about social issues in
the ChatZone; feeling good about having chosen to work in
such an exciting, people-orientated industry in the ChillZone,
and so on. No matter who walked off the set, or how many
scenes had been dropped that day – or whose body was found
hanging off a meat hook in the larder – it didn't matter. Not

tonight. This was the best kind of party. Almost everyone was having fun.

But not Oliver Mellors, of course, who was still locked in his trailer, drinking and sulking.

And not Noah Thistlestrupp, who was trying and failing to connect intensively with KitKat.

And not KitKat, who was trying and failing to connect in any way at all with Oliver Mellors.

And not Alyster Crowley, because he was still in his helicopter, just coming in to land, while still wishing to be with a masseuse at the Savoy.

And not Livvie Kellet, because she had forgotten how to have fun long ago.

And not Nicola Tode, because she was hiding in her bedroom, too shy to come down.

But Teddy MacIntosh was having fun! His heart was doing its beaty thing, because he'd taken a lot of cocaine, but on this occasion it didn't worry him one bit. He'd heard through the grapevine that Oliver Mellors had pulled out – not just from the naked scene, but from the entire production. '*Because*,' Teddy said to his agent (now forgiven) on the phone earlier that evening, 'it's all very well having the S-E-X factor, and I'm not saying he doesn't . . . But a pro, is a pro, is a pro. [And I'm a pro.]'

Teddy was lonely. He needed a mate. More than that, he needed a companion. But a mate would do, in the short term. No doubt he would find one as the evening wore on.

Ecgbert(Sir) and Alice were having *great* fun. They were dancing on the grass. A little bit stoned, but not too stoned. They'd taken off their shoes. The moon was out. It had to be only a matter of hours – minutes – now, before they wandered off into the rosebushes.

And of course, in faraway Paxos, sleeping off their excellent dinner, and with the sand still in their hair, India, Egbert(Mr), Passion and Ludo were having the hols of their lives.

Livvie Kellet, a little drunk and a little wired, busy being her delightful self, heard the whirring of the helicopter coming in to land, and felt a little sick. It meant Alyster was back, and the thought of his fat little hands, and the performance that would be required from her in response to them, made her wonder if making herself scarce might be a good plan. Or not? Being alone might be worse. She thought about sexy Oliver Mellors, sulking in his caravan, wrecking everything for everyone: so bewilderingly undelighted by her, no matter how hard she tried; and the thought of him warmed her loins in a way her loins weren't often warmed, these days. He was very sexy.

He really was, *weirdly* sexy.

She'd taken a few loin-enlivening recreationals, thanks to one of the delightful Dregz'n'Co: she never knew which was which. It was probably what spurred her to do it, in any case. She checked her supplies (they'd given her plenty), grabbed an extra plastic cup of wine, and set out across the fields towards his trailer door. Along the way she had another idea. Because what if Mellors was the sort of seriously straight kind of guy who didn't want to get high? How boring would that be? *For shits and giggles*, she chortled to herself, and dropped the three remaining pale blue pills, similar to the one she herself had taken earlier, into the bottom of his cup.

... Shits and giggles ... shits and giggles ... He must be feeling

awfully lonely, she thought, as she trundled along ... *What a beautiful, moonlit night. Hadn't his wife just walked out on him? Well, he wouldn't be lonely for long.*

She tapped softly.

The light was on. He was in there. She could hear him. There were noises – voices. Oh. He was watching something on his laptop. *Bit awkward.* Never mind. She halted at the steps and knocked again.

'Hello, Ollie?'

No reply.

'Oliver?'

The sound stopped. She imagined him in there, head shooting up, on full alert, hurriedly zipping his flies. She bit her cheeks, trying not to laugh. 'Oliver? It's me, Livvie ...' And then, because she was high, and didn't get an immediate response, and because, at that instant, she was experiencing a rush of lust for Oliver Mellors, and because she was an international star, long accustomed to being received, she added: 'You know, Ollie, you don't need the laptop – you've got the real thing out here ... I'm right here, Ollie ... You wanna let me in?'

A long pause. She wasn't sure if he'd heard her.

'Hello, Oliver?'

Silence. Perhaps he was straightening himself out? That was probably it.

She said in a singsong voice: 'O-li-veeer, I'm wai-ting ... Won't wait for ever though!' The step looked inviting. She'd been standing for hours. *His trailer was tiny compared to hers. How did he manage?* She sat down. 'Ollie?'

His trailer moved as she sat. Not much, but he felt it. Her (negligible) weight on his trailer; her body standing guard at his door. After all that happened to him today, and all the alcohol he had swallowed this evening, he felt a fury bubbling up inside him, and it continued to build with every second that he knew she was out there, chortling about having caught him watching porn; chortling because she was so confident he wouldn't turn her away. He waited, not moving, not speaking . . .

Rat-a-tat-a-tat-TAT TAT . . . She drummed out a merry little rhythm on the door.

'Come *on*,' she said. 'Don't be boring.'

He snapped. Shouted through the door: 'Get away from my door, you crazy slut. I'm not interested.'

The moment he said it, he felt ashamed. But it was too late by then. Mellors wasn't the sort to backtrack or apologise. He held his head in his hands in the silence that followed, and waited until he felt his trailer floor lift – not much, just a tiny bit, and he knew she was gone.

OLIVER MELLORS'S TRAILER

SATURDAY

Half an hour later, Oliver Mellors, alone in his trailer again, and really quite drunk now, was considering making a move towards home. He could hear the music pumping from across the field, and wondered if it would be safe for him yet, to make his way back to his cottage, without fear of being accosted. They'd all come knocking at some point tonight: Livvie Kellet, Teddy MacIntosh, Noah Thistlestrupp (with his begging bowl), Alyster Crowley, Dave Snare. A bunch of others – he could hardly remember. Had KitKat come? Probably. Some of them had come more than once. He'd told them all to bugger off.

He checked his phone: a lot of messages, but none from his wife, and none for an hour or so; and nobody had come since the last one, whichever that was. So perhaps they had all forgotten about him for now. Maybe they had accepted that he meant what he said, and they had all given up already . . . There was not a part of him that regretted it. The sooner he could get back to normal, the sooner he could win back his wife. The sooner he could forget what an idiot he'd been to have accepted the job in the first place.

Also, his trailer had run out of alcohol. He wanted to go home. That was all. He just wanted to go home.

He shuffled to his trailer door. He opened it a crack and peered out. There was a plastic cup on the step, full of – he picked it up and sniffed it – wine. One of his callers must have left it there. Good. He slurped it back. Why not?

The music thumped. The moon was bright. For a moment he wished he could be a part of it. Maybe he could track down KitKat, whose calls he'd been avoiding since the morning after the Monday night, when they'd been lying together in his bed, and she'd taken the call from Thistlestrupp and dumped him, there and then, and turned to Mellors with triumph on her pretty face as if . . . as if the two of them had a future! Mellors had realised that their night of delight had meant considerably more to KitKat than it would ever mean to him, and it had been an act of great self-will not to have climbed out of the bedroom window and run away, screaming.

Anyway. At the sound of the thumping music, and the feel of the moonlight, he weakened momentarily. Perhaps a boogie with KitKat wouldn't be such a bad thing after all? Might cheer him up.

He sat down on the step to think about it. Or, he sat down on the step, because it looked comfortable down there and who knew how much time passed? He looked at the moon, which was throbbing in time to the music. *Waxing and waning*, he thought. *The moon is waxing and waning*. The words lingered. They stuck. The moon is waxing and waning. Waving? The moon is waxing and waving. Waving and waning. Waving and waxing and – how did it go? The moon. He should go home. Before somebody spotted him. Time to stand up. Definitely. Time to go home.

The light from his own caravan reflected onto the wall of Livvie's trailer. But he didn't want to think about Livvie. The words he'd said to her made him ashamed. The light from his own caravan shone onto the grass beneath Livvie's trailer, and he thought he could see a figure, lying there, just metres away. He could see the whites of the eyes, and light shining off the skin. He could see it! There was a figure, lying under Livvie's trailer and Mellors could feel the eyes gazing directly at him.

'Who's there?' he asked, too drunk to feel alarmed.

The figure jolted to life and at once began to scramble – but its progress was blocked, caught by the trailer's chassis hanging low in the centre. The figure threshed and the figure writhed. Apparently, it was stuck.

Slowly, clumsily, Mellors rose. He crossed the narrow strip of grass between the trailers, stooped down, and on the third or fourth attempt, succeeded in grasping a foot. He grabbed it with both hands, and dragged the body out.

Stocky, pale, panting and terrified. It was Norman.

'*You?*' said Mellors, looking down at him in disbelief. 'You got the whole of Yorkshire police on a manhunt looking for you! What're you doing, hiding out under Livvie's caravan?'

'Don't kill me!' Norman whimpered.

Mellors said (still holding the foot), 'What're you *doing?*' He noticed a light flickering on the grass. Norman's phone. With clumsy care, Mellors rested a knee on his prisoner's chest and stretched to pick it up. A video was playing – grainy, out of focus, badly framed.

Mellors chuckled. 'You dirty bastard,' he said, and kept watching.

'Give it to me,' Norman cried, flailing beneath the knee. 'Give it back!'

Mellors's smile faded. The body was amazing. Plus his vision was blurry. So it took him a while to notice that the body's face belonged to Livvie Kellet. The mirror she was gazing into, the décor, the bundle of narcissi and hyacinth – were all familiar to Mellors. Norman must have been filming her through the window of her trailer.

'. . . It's not what you think . . .' whimpered Norman. 'She accused me of something I didn't do . . . You called her a slut, I *heard* you, so I know you understand. I was getting revenge. Anyway that's all there is. Give it back. There's nothing else.'

But there were dozens of pictures – fifty or more. Livvie in her trailer, naked; Livvie in her trailer, dressed; Livvie in her trailer, crying, reading, plucking her eyebrows, picking her nose.

'Give me back my phone,' Norman whined. 'This is outrageous.'

There were pictures of Livvie in a red velvet dress, standing on a ladder in the larder, eating cake. A video taken up her skirt – that one came to an abrupt end. He must have dropped the phone.

'This is revolting,' Mellors said, in shock. 'You're a disgusting old man. You should be ashamed of yourself.' He slipped the phone into his pocket and delivered a kick to Norman's ribs: partly aimed at Norman; partly at himself for having been so foul to Livvie earlier. 'And I thought *she* were lying, when she accused you,' Mellors said. 'I thought so – we all did . . . Goes to show, don't it? You little bastard.' He gave Norman another kick. 'Well,' he said, patting his pocket. 'We've got evidence now, haven't we? What were you doing in the larder that night, Mr Norman Wright, besides peeping where you had no business? Putting a knife in your mother's back, I don't doubt . . .'

'I didn't,' cried Norman. 'I didn't do it! I didn't even know she was dead.'

'I'm sure. Save it for the police, why don't you,' replied Mellors. 'You're in for it now.'

But Mellors was already drunk, though he didn't know it, and getting higher every moment. And Norman was not. Mellors's concentration wavered. Norman felt it, and seized his chance. He kicked out. Mellors lurched. And Norman was gone, scuttling across the parched lawn, scrambling through the darkness. Back on the run, yet again.

Mellors attempted to follow. He turned this way and that. The music throbbed and the moonlight shimmered. Shimmied. The moonlight shimmied, and waxed and waned. Mellors held his spinning head. He didn't feel well. His head was spinning. It was – waxing and waving. His head was waving, and the man was getting away. He should call the police.

He needed his phone. Mellors patted his pockets. All of them. Pulled out Norman's phone, and for a moment, couldn't remember how it had got there. His own phone was smaller, wasn't it? He pressed the home button and an upskirt image of Livvie in her red dress, buttocks, pants, horrified face looking down at the camera, illuminated the screen. It took him a moment – *Why was his phone showing pictures of Livvie's pants?*

Had he left his phone in the trailer? He turned back towards it. Turned several times, trying to remember where it was and which direction he'd come from.

He'd not been this drunk since he was a teenager. It was horrible.

THE CARETAKER'S FLAT

SUNDAY

Nicola's night, though probably more comfortable than Norman's, had not passed much more easily. Neither had slept a wink. While Norman cowered and scurried between hedges and other hiding places, Nicola had spent most of the night roaming the house and grounds, hating the world and everyone in it, above all herself. She was not in a good way.

Apart from a brief chat with Alice, and a two-word exchange with Kveta regarding the whereabouts of a cheese grater, she'd not had an actual conversation with anyone since Egbert(Mr) and India left for Greece early on Saturday morning. She felt battered by the thoughts that banged and echoed in her head; empty with the lack of company. It was 7.30 a.m. A long day stretched before her. She swallowed her pride and called her brother, Ecgbert(Sir), but he didn't pick up. Probably still asleep. She would have called Alice, but it was Sunday and she was aware that Alice was an employee of the Hall, not a personal friend. She would have called her – or maybe she could have dropped in. Everyone else seemed to do that; and the triplets might be there, making breakfast.

But what if they didn't want to see her? She couldn't call on Alice, not if the triplets were there. She wasn't brave enough.

Then came the brainwave.

Mrs Carfizzi was unwell. Or that's what India had been saying, before she sugared off to Paxos. And if Mrs Carfizzi was unwell, she would probably be delighted to get a visit! Nicola would be doing her a favour! She could bring some chocolates or something: whatever she could find in the basement gift shop. It was a perfect opportunity, Nicola confirmed to herself. Mrs Carfizzi's illness had been sent by the universe, so that she and Mrs Carfizzi might actually bond, at long last. Mrs Carfizzi would be delighted.

It had been a long time since they'd spoken: not since 1984, when Nicola announced she was vegetarian. But they could reconnect now, with no distractions. Perhaps they could play cards together, or perhaps Mrs Carfizzi might even teach her a few words of Italian? It was such a good idea, Nicola wondered why she'd never thought of it before.

Feeling better already, she set off for the gift shop. Was outraged to discover she couldn't get in, due to its being closed, and padded on to Mrs Carfizzi's door, empty handed.

Mr Carfizzi answered the doorbell in his dressing gown, looking old and thin and greyer than Nicola would have imagined him. He was dismayed to see her standing there at all, let alone so early on a Sunday morning. He held the door close, and told her Mrs Carfizzi was in Edinburgh, visiting a friend. But Nicola had got this far, there was no way she was going to retreat. She insisted on coming in.

'It is very early. I am afraid I am not dressed,' he said, stating the obvious.

'Not to worry,' she reassured him, settling herself on his pale leather sofa. 'You go and get dressed. I don't mind at all. It's no inconvenience, honestly! I'll just wait here ...'

'But – you understand, *Mrs Carfizzi isn't at home*,' he said again, and quite slowly this time. 'You can't see her, Nicola, as she is not at home. She is in Edinburgh, visiting a friend.'

'Is she? That's a big shame, I was looking forward to seeing her. She can't be very ill then, if she's "in Edinburgh, visiting a friend". I thought she was ill? No worries!' She grinned at him. 'I'm happy hanging out here with you. Feels like *ages* since you and I had a good natter, Mr Car Fizzy.' She'd seen India do this to great effect. Nicola, emboldened by her desperation not to be alone, gave it a try: she beamed at Mr Carfizzi and said: 'I've *missed* you!'

So Mr Carfizzi wandered off to get dressed, and Nicola waited.

'Would you like me to make the coffee while I'm waiting?' she shouted through to him.

He shouted back: 'No!'

But maybe she didn't hear him.

She was unfamiliar with the layout of the flat, having never been down here before, and was unsure where to locate the kitchen. There was the door which Mr Carfizzi had just stepped through. She thought better than to try that; and a door which she now discovered led to the bathroom. Nicola was shocked to discover a life-size, black-and-white photograph of the actor Dominic Rathbone (late of this parish) gazing back at her. The same Dominic Rathbone whom, it so happened, had tumbled to his death from the gallery in the Great Hall, only nine months previously.

212

St-rr-a-nn-ge, she thought, before backing out of the bathroom and trying the next door along.

But there was nothing in there. No pictures, no photographs, just a single, stripped bed and the lingering – unmistakable – scent of cooking fat, and stale sweat, and Revlon Charlie (Eau de Toilette) which had accompanied Mrs Carfizzi everywhere since the day she arrived to live at Tode Hall, thirty-nine years ago.

Confronted by this, Nicola found herself asking some uncomfortable questions. Was this, for example, Mrs Carfizzi's bedroom? If so, where were her belongings? Had she left the flat for good? Had she disappeared? Had she been murdered, perhaps? No one had seen her for days. Nicola stepped back into the hallway and closed the door behind her (least said, soonest mended), and felt herself bumping up against the dense upper thighs of Mr Carfizzi. He was standing right behind her, still in his dressing gown.

'Oh! Hello. You're here. I was looking for the kitchen,' she said nervously. 'Sorry. I didn't realise you had a spare room down here. How nice. Have you thought of doing Airbnb? It's such a gorgeous flat. You could probably make a bit of cash on the side. I'm sure India wouldn't mind.'

'I don't think so,' he said.

'OK.'

Silence.

Carfizzi glowered at her.

'Shall we have coffee?' she suggested brightly. But by now she was regretting the whole situation. She wished she'd never come. She thought maybe she would have done better to have headed back to Edinburgh instead. In fact – *yes*. Why hadn't she thought of it before? Even Edinburgh was better than Tode

Hall. 'On second thoughts,' she said, 'maybe shall we *not*? I actually came to say goodbye, Mr Car Fizzy. In case you want to know. Because I've decided to head back to Edinburgh.'

To her astonishment – he shook his head. 'Absolutely not!' he said. 'You're here now. And so am I. Of course you must stay for coffee, Miss Nicola.' He took her arm and shepherded her along a short corridor, to a kitchen. And in that small moment Nicola felt a bolt of something remarkable. She'd not been touched for so long, that just the sense of his human hand on her sleeve made her eyes smart with a feeling she couldn't identify: it was part sorrow, and part joy.

He said: 'We are both lonely. Am I not right?'

'No.'

He nodded and smiled. 'Yes we are. In our own ways. Your girlfriend has left you, I understand. My wife has left me.' His eyes slid to the bathroom door. 'And Mr Rathbone is gone, now, too, of course ...'

'Mr Rathbone died,' agreed Nicola, pointlessly.

'My wife has found a gentleman from the internet, a Russian gentleman, who appreciates her in a way I was never able, Mrs Nicola. Or so she says. In any case, she won't speak to me. She says she hates me. She says she has hated me *all these years* ...'

'Gosh,' said Nicola. She didn't know what else to say. She realised she was hungry, and wondered if Mr Carfizzi had any biscuits to spare.

He shook his head. 'He is a champion in archery, Mrs Carfizzi says.'

Nicola said: 'Who? *I* can do archery. I learned it at the Archery School when it opened. So did Esmé. We did it together. But he was really hopeless.'

'And he took his bow,' Carfizzi continued, ignoring the

214

interruption. 'And then he took his arrow.' With a flourish Carfizzi mimed the action, 'And he struck her! In the heart. With his Russian bow and arrow.'

'He had a Russian bow and arrow?' Nicola said, feeling quite confused.

Carfizzi glanced at her. 'And now Mrs Carfizzi has found love.'

Nicola looked alert, briefly. 'Mrs Car *Fizzy*?' It sounded indignant.

He smiled at her, his white teeth shining. 'For everybody, there is somebody,' and once again his eyes slid to the back of the bathroom door. He sighed. 'And here we are, Miss Nicola,' he said. 'On a Sunday morning. We are grieving our somebodies.'

'Actually no,' she said. 'I'm not doing that. I just came to say goodbye. As I explained.'

Again, he nodded and smiled. 'It was courageous for you to come calling this morning,' he said. 'Because of course you don't find friendship easy ... Also, we have never liked each other.'

Nicola's mouth dropped open. She stared at him. *What was he talking about?*

'Nevertheless, we can perhaps help to make each other feel better,' he continued. 'Don't you agree? Sit down. I will make you some good Italian coffee. We can chat.'

Mr Carfizzi was right. They both needed someone to talk to, they were both lonely. And on another day, this might have been the beginning of a new friendship. But this morning, the universe had other plans for them.

The Carfizzi kitchen looked onto a wall, and above the wall, on weekdays, onto the wheel hubs of the Estate Secretary's

Ford Fiesta, which for twenty-one years had always been parked in the same spot. This morning it looked out onto empty tarmac, and a fashionable pair of wedge-heel women's trainers.

'Help me! Somebody help me! I think he's dead!'

'Oh my *goodness*,' said Mr Carfizzi, peering out. 'Isn't that the girl Mr Mellors brought with him to dinner the other evening?'

OLIVER MELLORS'S TRAILER

SUNDAY

KitKat fancied Mellors more than she'd ever fancied anyone; more than she knew was possible. And the colder he was, the hotter she felt for him. He'd barely spoken to her since the Tuesday morning she'd climbed/been pushed out of his bed. And of course she wasn't stupid. She got the message. He wasn't interested.

But this wasn't about that. She was worried.

He'd locked himself in his trailer and refused to speak to anyone since yesterday afternoon. Last night, after he walked off the set, she must have called him ten times. She must have called him another ten times this morning. His wife had left him. He'd just walked away from a starring role in a major TV series. Everyone knew he was miserable. Something didn't feel right ...

As a junior crew member she was staying not at the luxury hotel in York but at a pub in the village. While her colleagues slumbered on, recovering from the night's excesses, KitKat

217

slipped out of her single bed and drove the couple of miles to Oliver Mellors's cottage. When she found no sign of him there, she headed over to the Unit Base. She realised at once that her hunch had been correct. Mellors's trailer door was hanging open.

She found him slumped over the laptop keyboard, head lolling. His blood had spilled over the edge of the table. It had spilled down his neck and across his magnificent shoulders. And beneath the smears of blood, scrawled across his back in bold green letters, was a single word:

SLUTT

KitKat might have called the ambulance and the police: instead, she called Thistlestrupp at the luxury hotel in York. She woke him up. Thistlestrupp thanked her for calling him first.

He said: 'Don't do anything more KitKat. I'll take it from here.'

He called Dave Snare (Series Producer, staying in a room on the floor below) who called Alyster Crowley (staying in the room next door), who called Stephanie Misletop (the on-set medic, staying, like KitKat, in the less luxurious Tode Arms two miles down the road from the Hall) ... Alyster Crowley ordered Stephanie out of bed and to Mellors's trailer. He said he would sue her if she called emergency services before first checking out the situation and reporting it back to him.

KitKat, meanwhile, young and out of her depth, rushed up

to the Estate Offices courtyard in her wedge-heel trainers, and started screaming.

Alyster called her on the phone. He got her number off Thistlestrupp and he called her personally. *Personally*.

He congratulated her for her presence of mind in contacting Thistlestrupp before anyone else, and asked her to confirm that she hadn't and wouldn't do anything else.

'We have it all under control,' he said. 'You've been super-helpful.'

He said she would be rewarded for it, but he hung up without saying quite how. After that, her concern for Mellors, which was genuine, became a little confused, what with the adrenalin. Her mind kept wandering to the question of how said reward might manifest itself – for example, might it manifest in a spectacular job offer in Hollywood? Might he be able to fix her up with that?

But then she thought about Mellors, who was probably dead, and she started crying again.

THE BELLAVISTA SPA HOTEL, YORK

SUNDAY

Alyster Crowley was still in his dressing gown. He looked luxurious and portly in dark purple towelling, but his face, which was red and angry, suggested he might have felt better if he took it off. He couldn't though, because he had nothing on underneath.

The morning was hot; a sticky, disagreeable heat that hinted, at last, of a brewing storm. Here on the fourth floor of the Bellavista Spa Hotel, York, a different storm had already broken. Crowley stood in the corridor outside Dave Snare's bedroom door, his swollen feet sweating into the woolly carpet and his mobile phone clutched tight to his ear. Beside him stood Noah Thistlestrupp, also in a dressing gown – but his was of well-ironed, Nordic oatmeal. Plus he was tall and lean, and though he reeked of alcohol and sleepy confusion, he cut a reasonably attractive figure, at least in comparison to his boss.

'SNARE. Get outta bed!' (Alyster Crowley banged on

220

Snare's bedroom door with such vigour that a guest ten rooms up, not connected to the film, rang the reception to complain.) 'SNARE! We have a problem. Get outta bed you lazy piece of shit and open the fucking door.' Just then, Stephanie the Medic answered her phone. Alyster stopped shouting at Snare.

'STEPHANIE! What's the situation? Are you with him? . . . Huh? Why not? What the fuck is taking you so long – it's like, half a goddamn mile away. Get the fuck over there – *now*.'

She said: 'Well I would do that, but you keep calling me.' It was brave, and she probably wouldn't have said it, if she wasn't still a little drunk from the night before. But in any case he didn't hear her, because he had already hung up.

Crowley turned to Thistlestrupp. 'This,' he said, 'is a fucking nightmare.'

Alyster Crowley wasn't built to do or say nothing, especially in a crisis. So after saying, 'This is a fucking nightmare,' to Thistlestrupp, he thumped on Dave Snare's door again, and said: '*What the fuck?*' The question was aimed at David Snare, who at that moment was splashing water on his face, and slipping on his pyjama bottoms. 'Would you *Please. Open. The. Fucking—*'

Dave Snare opened the door. He wasn't wearing a pyjama top and for a moment, Alyster's revulsion at this minor detail caused him to pause. Dave Snare had a white, hairless, strangely bony chest, and very small shoulders. Not that it's important. 'What the fuck,' Crowley said, staring at the chest. He pushed at the door, forcing Sleepy Dave slightly off balance. He and Thistlestrupp barged into the room.

'They found Oliver Mellors in his trailer. Someone cracked him on the head, and his body's cold, so there's a thought he might be dead.'

221

'Whaaaat?' said Sleepy Dave. 'What? How? When?'

Crowley said: 'Fuck knows. Stop asking questions. Facts are: he's probably dead. Some sick fuck wrote SLUT on his skin. Blood everywhere, apparently. That's all we know so far. We got the medic heading over now. But she's moving like a fucking snail. So. That's where we are.' He turned to Thistlestrupp. 'How many scenes have we got left – what are we missing?'

'W-with Oliver Mellors?'

'No, with Peter Pan. Yes, with Oliver Mellors. Can we shoot around him? I mean. Without him. Can we shoot around him, or is the whole thing ... fucking ...' He sighed. Bored with beating around the bush. 'How fucked are we?'

'Huh?'

'If he's *croaked*?'

'Well but—' Thistlestrupp was confused. 'But we already discussed this last night. Before any of this. Mellors walked off the film – have you forgotten? We've shot eleven scenes already: we have another thirty more, at least ... if there's no Oliver Mellors, at this point, we'll have to recast. We'll need to reshoot everything. Plus we've got to find the actor ...' Thistlestrupp shook his head. 'There's no way round it.'

'However if he *dies*,' interjected David Snare, who as Series Producer, tended to know what he was talking about, 'we are, at least, covered insurance-wise. We can claim it. That is—' David Snare glanced at his terrifying boss, Alyster Crowley, and gave him a weasely smile. 'We're covered for accidental death – assuming it was accidental ...'

'Of course it was accidental,' said Crowley, wiping sweat away. 'What are you trying to say?'

'Insurance will cover us for accidental death ... If our star simply walks off the set in a strop, on the other hand, as discussed yesterday, we are in Major Shit Street Territory.'

'So what are you saying?' snapped Crowley. 'We gotta hope he croaks?'

'That's correct, I'm afraid. I mean – from a business angle, obviously,' David Snare added quickly. 'It's better for us that he, er, *passes*, than that he walks. Assuming, that is, that no one attached to the production played any part in his murder. I mean *death*,' he added quickly. 'In which case – well, then we're in unchartered waters, aren't we?'

'Oh for goodness sake, Dave,' Thistlestrupp snapped. 'Of course he wasn't murdered!'

Both men looked at him.

'You didn't like him very much, did you Thistlefuck?' Alyster Crowley said.

Thistlestrupp spluttered. 'I'm not the one who recoups £10 million in reshoot costs if my star suddenly, inexplicably drops dead.'

Alyster Crowley pushed his red face up close to Thistlestrupp. When he spoke, small specks of his spit landed on the other man's dressing gown. 'And *I* am not the director who *never works again*, because of bullying a star so bad he walks off the fucking set, causing the whole fucking shoot to grind to a halt.'

'Easy does it,' said David Snare. 'No need for all that. Let's see if the poor guy is dead, first, shall we? Then we can start talking about the hows and wheres, and so on ... I tell you what though, if he *was* murdered, and we can demonstrate we had nothing to do with it, that too would be a ...' he made some quote marks, '"good situation" for us ... So.' He shrugged. 'And let's not forget, we still have that strange little fellow Norman on the loose out there somewhere. So if anyone murdered poor Oliver Mellors, we can probably point the finger in that direction ...'

'It's certainly possible,' nodded Thistlestrupp.

Crowley glowered at him 'Why? Why would he want to do that? You have no idea what you're talking about, so stop talking.' Thistlestrupp's oatmeal gown caught his eye. It seemed to irritate him. 'Why aren't you dressed yet?' he snapped. 'Get over to the location, Thistlefuck. Deal with that girlfriend of yours, before she loses it and starts calling the police.'

'She wouldn't do that.'

'How do you know?'

'Also, she's not my girlfriend.'

Alyster Crowley's phone was ringing again. Stephanie the Medic was back on the line. He waved Thistlestrupp aside, put a finger in his ear and continued shouting.

Mr Carfizzi did not like histrionics: though he himself had never mastered the British art for understatement, it was at the heart of his admiration for his adopted country. So when English people made a scene or demonstrated emotion – of any kind, under any circumstance – he would feel the fragile edifice that underpinned his entire life crumbling, just a little bit. He had not moved to live among aristocrats in rainy Yorkshire for this! This, he could get in Calabria, where the sun shone, and the food was good, and there were fewer rules, and the gentlemen were better looking.

So he was quite sharp with KitKat when he found her, screaming and sobbing in the courtyard car park.

'Shh!' he said. 'Be quiet! You'll wake everyone.'

He led her into the caretaker's flat and made her a cup of sweet tea while she described the scene in Mellors's trailer.

Nicola called Alice to break the news.

'Oh *dear*,' said Alice, feeling quite winded. 'That's ... *too bad* ...' (Mr Carfizzi would have approved.) 'That's *terrible news* ... Is he *dead*?'

'We don't know.'

Alice felt a lump in the throat. She swallowed, and swallowed again.

'And someone had written *SLUT* on his skin?'

'Apparently.'

'That's very nasty ...' Alice had noticed Mellors, since he returned from his week of rehearsals in London, struggling with his new unhappiness. His wife had left him – and now this. 'There's no way he could have done it to himself, is there? ... No. Of course not.'

Nicola didn't say anything at once. She was eyeing KitKat's tea, which looked nicer than her coffee. 'Anyway,' she said, after a pause. 'I thought I should let you know. Do you think you might come over?'

'Yes. Of course. I presume someone's called the ambulance?'

'They've got the medic at the scene, apparently,' Nicola said. 'She's reporting back. I've got to go. Will you come over? We're in the Car Fizzys' flat, having tea and/or coffee.'

Before Alice left, she tapped gently on the boys' bedroom door. Unsurprisingly, given what time she presumed they all came

225

in last night, there was no reply. After a moment, she pushed open the door anyway. Two of the triplets lay deeply asleep on their single mattresses, peacefully unconscious to the world.

She whispered to them: 'Hey. Where's Morman?' (She could always tell them apart.)

'. . . Next door . . .' murmured one.

'Is he alone?'

They both grunted.

'Drez!' she whispered, shaking him awake. 'Wake up! I have to tell you something . . .'

Another grunt from Drez.

'*Jacko?*' Nothing.

She sighed.

'Something has happened to Oliver Mellors . . . Something horrible.'

Their eyelashes flickered. She felt they were listening.

'. . . Nobody seems to know . . . Sorry . . . I shouldn't wake you with this. I just – They found him in his trailer. He may be in a coma or he may be dead. I'm worried about him, and I'm worried . . . with Norman Wright on the loose, and everything that's been happening.'

Alice felt stupid. Why had she woken them? She never behaved like this. 'Anyway,' she said, 'sorry – I suppose I was just checking you were alive.'

The boys half opened their eyes: 'Mum, we're fine,' they said. 'We're just, like, *sleeping* . . .'

Alice nodded. 'Good.' She stood up. 'Sorry to wake you. I'll let you know, when there's more news . . . Go back to sleep.'

She headed downstairs. Outside the sitting room the sound of snoring led her to peer inside. Sure enough, there was Ecgbert(Sir), fully dressed, slumbering peacefully on the old sofa, his long legs sticking out several feet at the end. She considered waking him to tell him the news but – after what had passed between them, or not passed between them, last night – after the way she had behaved, she realised she couldn't face talking to him. Or not now. Later.

As she closed the front door, she could have sworn she heard Jacko and Drez shuffling along the upstairs landing, calling through the door to their brother.

Highly unlikely. Alice assumed she was mistaken.

A VERY NICE VILLA ON PAXOS

SUNDAY

In the walk between Gardener's House and Hall, Alice called Egbert(Mr) on Paxos to update him. It was an hour later in Greece, and there were sounds of children splashing in the background. Alice was obliged to spend a few minutes hearing about Ludo's progress, very nearly swimming *sans* water wings, before she could break the bad news.

Egbert(Mr) was distraught. Of all the people working on the estate, Oliver Mellors was 'probably his favourite', he said: definitely the one Egbert felt most relaxed around. Alice held the phone while he put her voice on speaker, and he and India discussed with one another how best to respond:

'I think,' said Egbert(Mr), 'we had better head home. Don't you think, Munch?'

'It might be better,' said Alice, tactfully. 'Sorry to bring you such horrible news ... but I'm not sure I can hold the fort with the film crew, and Norman missing – and now this ... Plus, poor Oliver ...'

India worried the children would be upset. They were having so much fun.

'Also,' Alice added, as an afterthought, mostly: because yesterday Ecgbert(Sir) had been muttering about her general state of mind, 'I think Nicola's – I know she's not your responsibility. Only she seems a bit lonely . . .'

'OMG, OMG, *poor* poor Nicola!' India cried, with a strength of feeling that surprised the others. '*Of course* she's lonely, poor little thing! I do worry about her, you know. I told you, Eggie, didn't I? We should have brought her with us. She's got absolutely nothing to do. Nothing going on. And I don't get the sense she has *any* friends . . .'

She and Egbert had discussed the tragedy that was Nicola at some length, as they lounged by their swimming pool. (Egbert would have preferred to crack on with the excellent biography of Winston Churchill, bought specially to read on his hols, but his darling wife wasn't a big reader: couldn't concentrate for more than three minutes without finding something new to chat about.) India said she was making plans to give Nicola a makeover. 'It's going to be my autumn project, Egg,' she'd said. 'Whether she likes it or not. It's going to be like a course in self love. Radical Self Love, I'm calling it. And if it works I'm going to trademark it, or whatever. We could run courses at the house. Don't you think? A lot more worthwhile than these awful film crews. Plus it'd be me, putting something back. When I'm so lucky and everything.'

'Fabulous idea, Munch,' he said, resting Churchill on the swimming trunks. 'Radical Self Love. I love it! Radically! Ha ha. I radically love it, Munch!'

'Very funny, Egg.'

'You are brilliant . . .'

She nodded. 'I'm going to make Nicola love Nicola. You watch.' Once again Egbert(Mr) was touched by the sweetness of his wife, and the perfection of all thoughts and feelings that issued from her. He squeezed her hand, and turned back to his book:

> *On 28 July 1900, Jennie Churchill married George*
> *Cornwallis-West, a handsome Army officer, born two*
> *weeks before her eldest son, who had little means of*
> *financial support ...*

But that was yesterday.

Today, Alice was calling them home, because Mellors was in trouble/possibly dead, and Nicola was lonely and needed them. It was what India would call either 'a no brainer', or 'a message from the universe', or possibly both.

'Alice, you're so right!' India shouted into her husband's phone as he held it aloft between them. 'Of course we have to come home. Will you send Mellors just *tonnes* of love from us? If he's alive. Tell him to jolly well get better soon!'

'I will,' said Alice. 'Just – fingers crossed . . .'

By which time Alice had arrived at the Estate Wing door, and not being skilled at multi-tasking, she needed to hang up before she could key in the code to let herself in. India and Egbert(Mr) said they would start packing at once, and would be on the first flight home, either this evening, or early tomorrow.

THE GARDENER'S HOUSE

SUNDAY

The triplets shuffled downstairs, hours before they'd been intending to surface on this, their day off. Morman had a girl called Scruff-do in his bed upstairs, who worked as boom-operating assistant, but this wasn't something she needed to get involved in. Scruff-do snoozed on.

They found Ecgbert(Sir) at the kitchen table, crunching on burnt toast and talking in a tetchy voice to his granny, apparently, though she wasn't there. Lady Tode (since Alice hadn't bothered) was updating him on the situation regarding Mellors.

'You all right?' asked Morman. And then, because he was actually quite curious: 'Who were you talking to? Was that your granny again?'

Ecgbert(Sir) waved the question aside, spraying toast crumbs in the process. 'No one,' he said. 'Doesn't matter. You've heard the news, have you? Poor Mellors. He was a great man. Very handsome. You probably didn't notice it – I didn't for years.

231

But he really was. My mother adored him. He's in his trailer now, alive or dead – we don't know. So I think I'm going to head over and see what's happening ... Unbelievable, really. Who in their right mind would want to do in poor old Mellors?'

Lady Tode said: 'I could think of a few people.' Ecgbert(Sir), on the alert not to seem mad, post Morman's impertinent question, took a bite of toast to stop himself from replying.

Lady Tode continued: 'In fact, I can hardly think of anyone who wouldn't have been quite pleased to see him dead. The Swedish chap – Thistlestrupp. Loathed Mellors. For sexual reasons. That little American with the devil worshipper's name – Alyster Crowley. Would save himself a lot of money, if poor Mellors were dead. I heard him say so, into his portable telephone, last night. Something about insurance. Then there are all the women Mellors spurned – and believe me, darling, there have been plenty. Then there's the queer actor – what's his name?'

'Teddy MacIntosh,' Ecgbert replied.

'Pardon?' asked the Drez. 'You think Teddy MacIntosh wanted to do in Oliver Mellors?'

'What? Of course not,' snapped Ecgbert.

'... Eaten up with professional jealousy,' continued Lady Tode. 'Also, frankly, I would guess he was pretty jealous of the Adonis factor. I mean. What man wouldn't be? I bet you are, darling, aren't you? Frightfully jealous of how handsome Mellors was.'

'Absolutely not,' snapped Ecgbert irritably. He was hung-over. Plus he wished Alice was there. 'Don't be ridiculous. You say ridiculous things.'

'Sorry,' said the Drez.

The triplets shuffled about, putting kettles on, making a mess around the toaster, muttering to each other conspiratorially.

Lady Tode said to her grandson: 'Can you hear what they're saying? Do you think there's something wrong with them?' She gasped. 'My goodness, Ecgbert, do you think *they* killed Mellors? That wouldn't make any sense at all . . .'

Ecgbert considered the questions. The triplets looked worried, he realised. They never looked worried. It wasn't normal. He said:

'You all right, guys?'

'Yeah – yeah, fine,' they replied.

'You sure?'

That was all it took. Because no, they weren't sure they were fine, not really. They sat down at the table, looking tousled and goofy and frightened and young. They were concerned about Oliver Mellors. They really liked him. Also – they didn't want to upset their mother . . .

Ecgbert(Sir) said: 'Good for you.'

Lady Tode said: 'First sensible words they've ever uttered.'

'It's probably completely unconnected . . .' Jacko began.

'What's unconnected?' Ecgbert asked.

'Probably just the noids, Ecgbert,' Morman nodded. 'Even so.'

Ecgbert said: 'The noids? What are you talking about?'

'. . . We should say something,' Jacko continued. 'Especially if he's – maybe he's in a coma. Maybe he's not dead.'

'Say what? Please do just spit it out,' said Ecgbert.

Drez spat it out . . . They'd been handing out 'quite a lot' of MDMA at the party last night.

Ecgbert(Sir) said: 'Ah, yes.'

'Don't get us wrong though,' emphasised Drez, 'not with the profit motive.'

'We just wanted to help,' Jacko said. 'Lighten the mood a

233

bit, after the Rapunzel thing, and Norman on the loose and everything ...'

'We were distributing at cost,' Morman said. 'Literally. Probably a bit less, actually. Probably. I haven't really done the math.'

'S,' corrected Lady Tode. 'Math*s*. Can they not speak?'

'It's probably nothing. As we keep saying ... But we didn't keep very close tabs on who was getting what, did we? There didn't seem much point ...'

'We're all adults, right?'

'I mean – I don't think any of us literally *gave* anything, like, to Ollie Mellors his actual self, the individual, did we?' Drez turned to Jacko. 'Did you?'

'No.'

'Did you, Morman?'

'Nope. Definitely not.'

Drez nodded. 'Me neither. But maybe he got hold of some, somehow ... And, like, I don't know if this sounds really far-fetched ... because Ollie – Oliver Mellors. Mr Mellors is a top man. Best guy in the world, probably ... But what if they find drugs inside him. What if that's what killed him?'

'He may not be dead,' Ecgbert reminded them. 'Also – don't forget. He's been bumped on the head. So that's probably going to be the reason. If – *if* – worst case scenario.'

'Great. Yeah. Yeah, yeah. Great.'

Ecgbert tapped his long fingers on the table top and considered the situation. It wasn't ideal. There had been a lot of drugs last night. Everyone knew that. Everyone, except possibly their mother, also knew that the Dregz'n'Co were the chief source; and they had been receiving a lot of love on the strength of it.

The triplets watched the long fingers tapping and waited for the verdict.

Finally, Ecgbert said: 'You shouldn't hand out drugs to people. It's very irresponsible.'

Lady Tode chuckled. 'Bit rich, coming from you.'

Ecgbert said: 'Why? I've never handed out drugs in my life.'

'Lecturing people on responsibility,' chuckled his grandmother. 'Ridiculous!'

'Of course you haven't,' said Drez. 'You're a gentleman!'

'Thank you,' said Ecgbert. He was touched.

'... We feel terrible, Ecgbert. Really bad.' The triplets nodded. 'If something happens to him, and it's our fault ...' Morman sniffed.

'Oh, for *Christ's sake*,' snarled Lady Tode. A curl of green stink seeped from beneath her chignon. Morman had started to cry.

Ecgbert gave him an awkward pat. 'Your mother doesn't need this to worry about, does she?' he said. 'Don't worry lads,' he said. 'I know you mean well. Just get rid of any clobber. That's my advice. And hold tight. I'm going to take care of it.'

Lady Tode gave another of her irritating chuckles. 'And how are you going to do that, darling?'

He glared at her. 'I don't know how,' he said. 'But I will.'

And with that he stood up and, a bit like Superman, straightened his neck, and arranged his long arms by his sides, lifted and hovered, and flew through the kitchen door.

THE CARETAKER'S FLAT

SUNDAY

Alyster Crowley, David Snare and Noah Thistlestrupp arrived at the security-locked Estate Offices door just as Ecgbert(Sir) was keying in the passcode. They barged in behind him, without even saying good morning, and all four men crowded into Mr Carfizzi's once-lonely sitting room together. With Nicola, KitKat, Alice and Mr Carfizzi already there, it made eight people. There was hardly standing space, and they all looked uncomfortable, especially the host himself, who was still in his dressing gown. Alyster Crowley was on his mobile, as ever: red in the face, furious. He was yelling at Stephanie the Medic again. Somehow, in the time it had taken the York faction to dress and drive thirty miles, Stephanie had only just arrived at the trailer. She'd not yet had time to examine the body. 'Well?' Crowley yelled. 'Are you in there? *Are you in? . . . AND? . . .*'

And then his body froze, and such was the strength of his presence, the intensity of this moment, everyone turned to look at him.

236

A moment of acute silence.

Sweat trickled.

'HA! *HA HA HA!* Ohh-KAY! Good news. All right. Well. Thank Christ for that. I'm coming over now. We need to get the word scrubbed off his back. Huh? Yep, *now*. Do it. OK.' He hung up. Looked around the room. Everyone waited. He said:

'He's fine. He's breathing. He's mumbling words. Stupid fucker was just drunk.'

Sir Ecgbert nodded. He already knew this. In the time Stephanie the Medic had heaved herself out of bed, removed last night's contact lenses, brushed her teeth and finished her coffee (*I don't do the day until I've done coffee*, Stephanie liked to say), Ecgbert had already been, seen the light, recoiled, recovered, and gone. He had already examined – and tampered with – the scene.

There was a lot of blood. But on his grandmother's insistence, he had searched for its source and, beneath Mellors's matted hair, found only a small cut. 'Head wounds always bleed profusely,' Lady Tode observed. 'It's nothing. Just a little nick.'

Ecgbert had seen the blood, and seen Mellors's broad back, with SLUTT scrawled across it, and he'd seen Mellors's chest moving slowly, up and down with each breath. He'd noticed the reek of alcohol and concluded – among other things – that the man was fine. Just very drunk.

Nevertheless, as precautionary measures, he did two things before leaving the scene. He pocketed the plastic cup, with the hint of a blue smear inside, lying at Mellors's feet. And, with his shirt cuff and a little spit he rubbed out the spelling mistake in SLUTT.

'What are you *doing*?' demanded Lady Tode.

'Spelt wrong, Granny,' he said. 'We can't have that.'

'Are you mad? This isn't the time ... Get out of here, before someone sees you!'

But Sir Ecgbert knew what he was doing.

At the news of Mellors's survival, a subdued cheer broke out in Mr Carfizzi's sitting room. Everyone hugged each other, despite the heat. The initial relief lasted about seven seconds.

KitKat, for example, having raised a false alarm, was quick to realise that the news wasn't 100 per cent good. Bang went Hollywood. Bang went the dream. And Oliver Mellors *still* didn't fancy her. Alyster turned his beady eye on her, and before he'd said a single word, she began to sob.

'Looks like you got us out of bed for nothing,' he said coldly. 'I assume nobody's bothered the authorities on this? If so, we need to call them off.'

'What about the head wound?' asked Alice. 'And the writing on his back ... Someone has tried to harm him. I don't think we should call anyone off.' She looked around the room, in search of back-up. 'Mr Carfizzi? Don't you think?' Mr Carfizzi looked at the floor. ' ... Nicola? Ecgbert? *Someone?* – You must agree! Of course the police have to be involved. He should go to hospital, get properly examined ... '

'He's fine,' said Ecgbert.

'What do you mean, *fine?*' Alice snapped. There was a lot of unspoken activity going on between these two. A lot of things that needed to be said. Ecgbert touched her on the elbow. She snatched her elbow away. He stooped from his Superman height and muttered into her ear. 'We need to talk.'

'What, *now*?' she said. There was so much they needed to talk to each other about. But this was not the moment, and it was typical of Ecgbert to think that it was. He was infuriating. 'Are you mad?' But he wasn't to be put off. He touched her elbow again, and this time, held it tight.

'Everything's fine,' he reassured her.

'Everything is *not* fine!' she said. She looked around the room. 'Has anyone actually called the police? I presume they have?' Nobody replied. '... Oh my God ... and the ambulance? Tell me someone called an ambulance!'

'Mr Crowley said we shouldn't,' muttered KitKat, at last. 'And look, it turns out he was right.'

Alice said: '... I'm ...' but she was too shocked to say more. What was the matter with them all? She fumbled in her bag for her own phone. She would call the emergency services herself.

'That's right, ma'am,' Alyster said quietly.

Stomachs lurched. Small and sweaty, and ludicrously dressed in shorts and flip-flops and that leather waistcoat again – there was something in his voice that could freeze blood when it wanted. '... Go ahead and call the police,' he continued. 'Most likely, Mr Mellors took a couple too many ecstasy tablets, and then some. This is what I'm thinking ... And I guess we all know where he would've got them. So yeah. Call the cops, why don't you? Seems like the sensible thing for a mother to do.'

A silence. Everyone looked at Alice. 'What are you inferring?' she said. 'How dare you?' She still had a hand in her bag. Swiftly, Ecgbert lurched forward, snatched the bag off her shoulder and swung it away.

'Ecgbert!' Alice said.

'Sorry, Trudy.'

239

'Give me back my bag!' She stretched for it, but Superman moved too fast.

And then, in the distance, they heard the sirens approaching.

'Fuck!' said Alyster. 'Who did that? Who made the call?'

The door opened. Three large, male bodies, smelling of alcohol and sleep, and apologising to everyone, squeezed in with the throng. It was beginning to feel like a tube carriage at rush hour.

'Sorry guys. Sorry ... Scuse. Sorry ...'

'Boys!' Alice cried. 'What the—'

'It was us,' Morman interrupted. 'We called them. Because of the drug thing.'

'You did WHAT?' cried Alyster Crowley and Alice Liddell, in tandem.

'We thought – if it was a drug thing, and then everyone got distracted because of the, like, *SLUT* word, and the blood and everything, they might not realise and know how to save him. So we thought it was important. To, like, fess up, if we have to ... Coz ... what if he died or something, due to them not knowing?'

'... And we probably wouldn't go down for very long, right?' added Jacko. 'Even if the worst happened ...' He glanced at his mother, but his eyes slid away as she gazed back: too ashamed.

Alyster Crowley broke the silence. He began to slow hand clap. 'Fucking genius,' he said, glaring at the boys, who kept their eyes on their feet. 'So now what do you suggest?'

But he was being sarcastic. People didn't much want to hear any more suggestions from the triplets at this point.

The police car screeched to the Great North Door – which, like the Porta Sancta, only ever opened on the rarest and most stupendously important occasions. The Great North Door at Tode Hall was only ever opened for weddings, funerals and the filming of TV drama shows. It was a door the police were now quite familiar with, and which they knew perfectly well would never be opened for the likes of them. Even so, there was a thrill to pulling up in front of the seventh grandest, privately owned house in Britain, tyres screeching and sirens blaring, so they did it anyway.

The paramedics, less familiar with Tode Hall door-opening policies, followed close behind. Together they marched up the wide steps and banged noisily on the door that no one ever answered.

Meanwhile, in Carfizzi's sitting room, everyone looked to Crowley for guidance. But on this occasion it was Mad Sir Ecgbert, the spirit of Superman urging him onward, who grasped the wheel. He ordered everyone in the room to STAY STILL and REMAIN CALM, and strode out, via the Estate Offices exit, across the mustard-grey lawn, to send the unwanted visitors on their way.

'False alarm!' he cried, waving at them from a distance off. 'A million apologies.'

He was unimaginably sorry they had been called out here unnecessarily.

Some of the youngsters had found a friend in an alcoholic slumber and 'quite simply, officers, they *panicked*. Everyone's a bit jumpy, with Norman Wright on the run ... Any luck tracking him down?'

None yet.

Ah. Well. He can't have gone far.

Did someone think they had spotted him, the police wanted to know, reaching for their walkie-talkies.

Ecgbert said not. Unfortunately not. But *other than that* everything was fine at Tode Hall.

Everything was absolutely, outstandingly fine. And wasn't it another beautiful day?

The police weren't satisfied at once. They wanted to check in on the false-alarmers, and remind them about the dangers of giving false alarms.

The paramedics wanted to check in on the alcoholic slumberer, to remind him of the dangers of alcohol.

'Aforementioned alcoholic slumberer is currently in the bath,' Ecgbert said. 'I don't imagine he'll want to let you in. But I can get him to call you, if you like, *from* the bath. Would that be helpful?'

They said it might.

'As for the false-alarmers,' Ecgbert continued, 'rest assured, we have given the lads a piece of our mind. They didn't mean any harm by it, but it's not really the point, is it? They are in absolute disgrace, and they know it. But young people *can be* annoying. Can't they? I find it more and more, the older I get.'

'Nevertheless,' the policemen said, 'we would like to have a word with them. By calling us out on a wasted journey they've wasted valuable police time and public recourses—'

'Absolutely,' agreed Ecgbert, nodding with vigour. 'You're so right. I'll give them a kick in the pants next time I see them. In the meantime, can I offer you a drink? Also,' Ecgbert turned to the ambulance team, 'what about you? It's quite early for a drink. And of course you're driving . . . What can I do to make amends?

Money!' he declared, as soon as the idea occurred to him. 'Can I give you all some money to put towards the Christmas fund? We have a film crew working here ... I think we should make a joint donation as a sort of *apologia* on behalf of the idiots who panicked and called you all the way over here on a Sunday morning, when there was *absolutely nothing* going on ...'

The emergency servicemen didn't immediately object to the suggestion, which Ecgbert read correctly as encouragement. 'If you wait a moment,' he said, raising a long finger, 'I'll be back in half a sec.'

He left them to sun themselves by the Great North Door.

Back in the caretaker's flat, Ecgbert organised a whip-round. There was a safe in the Estate Offices, with £459 in cash: Alyster had another £600 in his wallet. Alice had £15.07. She wanted to give much more, but Ecgbert pooh-poohed the donation altogether. He said £1,059 ought to be more than enough, especially in cash, especially considering it was a sunny day and they hadn't had to come too far. He asked Nicola what she might be willing to donate, only because he was annoyed by her limp silence. She said she objected to bribes, and anyway never carried cash. So. That was it. Ecgbert returned to the front of the house, where the emergency services stood, peacefully sipping lemonade, which had been delivered to them by Kveta, the housekeeper. He handed them the cash in a big messy bundle, and said:

'I really am *so* sorry. I cannot apologise too fully, on behalf of the silly boys. A million apologies for disturbing you on this beautiful morning ... and thank you for all the amazing work you do ... And God bless. And thank you again. Thank you ...' etc.

And so they parted company.

OLIVER MELLORS'S TRAILER

SUNDAY

Once they'd got rid of the police and paramedics there was of course only one place to go. Ollie Mellors's trailer, however, was even smaller than the Carfizzi sitting room, so half of the group had to mill around on the grass outside, waiting for updates to be called down to them.

As she was stepping up into the trailer, Alice turned to the triplets, lingering apologetically at the back of the gaggle. She caught Jacko's eye.

'*Sorry, Mum,*' he mouthed at her, his face full of sadness.

Alice shook her head. She never cried. But this was a tempestuous moment. To the triplets it looked, at that instant, as if she just might.

Jacko's mouth formed on O. Shock and sorrow.

Her three, sweet boys, in a messy line, gazed back at her: O. O. O.

O. She loved them SO. And they were fine. Everything was fine. They weren't going to gaol, and Mellors wasn't dead.

244

She smiled. Shook her head. Blew them a flustered kiss. The moment passed.

Inside the trailer, Stephanie the Medic was administering a B12 shot into Oliver Mellors's upper arm. The blood had been wiped from his neck and head, but he was still shirtless, the word SLUT, spelling amended, still clearly visible across his back. (Stephanie didn't feel it was her job to remove it.) He was sitting up, looking very woozy, obviously not yet quite clear why so many people were squeezed into his trailer – or why, even, he was there himself.

On the table behind him, the blood-splodged laptop had been closed shut. In front of him the angry, sweating Alyster Crowley stood. He was smiling in an avuncular manner, asking Mellors if he felt OK. Behind Crowley, squeezed behind Mellors's chair, stood Ecgbert, Alice, KitKat and Mr Carfizzi, who was in tears, though nobody bothered to ask why. Noah Thistlestrupp had chosen to stay outside on the grass, since he didn't think Mellors would be very pleased to see him; and so had Dave Snare (Series Producer).

Stephanie the Medic said: 'He's still a bit confused, but he'll be fine in a minute. Well, aside from a massive hangover … I've cleaned the head wound … It was nothing really … ' She pushed his hair gently aside to reveal to the group a small gash. 'As you can see … But it's strange – he doesn't remember how he came by it, DO YOU OLIVER?' She addressed him slowly and loudly, not really expecting a response.

'He came up from behind,' Mellors said. It was the first time he'd spoken since they'd all crowded in. 'So I didn't see him …'

A long pause. Nobody spoke.

'Him?' repeated Sir Ecgbert, at last. 'Who's "him"?'

Mellors said, 'Aye,' more to himself than to the group,

apparently. He looked around him. His beautiful green eyes wandered their sockets, as he tried to get to grips with his surroundings. Finally, he scowled. It was very hot in the trailer.

'Can someone open a window?' he asked. 'Why are there so many people in here?'

The door and the window were both already open.

'How do you know it was a he?' Alice asked.

Mellors glanced at her. 'Hello Alice,' he said. 'Nice to see you ...' He threw a more hostile look at his Executive Producer, smiling solicitously down on him. 'Thought I'd seen the last of you, Crowley.'

But Alyster Crowley continued to smile. 'And we thought we'd seen the last of you, Ollie! Good to have you back with us, alive, alive-oh. Your girlfriend here,' he indicated KitKat, 'Miss ...' Alyster had forgotten her name, now that she was no longer useful. 'Madame Totty here, took one look at you and thought you were dead. Had us all "shitting bricks", didn't you dear? To use one of your English expressions.' *Smile*.

Nobody smiled back.

'Who hit you on the head?' asked Alice, once again. 'And who scribbled ...' She hesitated. 'Someone's written something on your back, Oliver ... Are you aware of that? Do you know who it might have been?'

He didn't seem much interested. He made a half-hearted attempt to twist round and look at his own back – an impossible manoeuvre at the best of times – and quickly gave up. Then, as if something important had just come back to him, he glanced at the table top.

'There were a phone,' he said. 'Where is it?'

Stephanie the Medic spun neatly, with limited space, took a phone from the shelf behind her and gave it to him.

'Do you mean this?' she asked smugly.

He looked at it. 'No.'

'No? What do you mean, no?' She was slightly offended.

'That's not the one. That's *my* phone.'

'I thought so. It was on the table when I got here,' Stephanie said. 'I put it up there, so it wasn't mislaid ... How are you feeling, Oliver?' She held a hand up in front of his face. 'Can you see how many fingers I'm holding up?'

'I'm talking about the other phone. There were another phone ...'

Stephanie said: 'Well, I only saw the one ...'

'But there were another one.' He was beginning to sound tetchy. 'Where is it? And why are there so many people in my trailer? Why are you all here? I can't bloody breathe in here, with all you people ogling me ...' Nobody moved. He didn't appear to expect it. 'I'm thinking he must've taken it when he whacked me on the head. Have you seen him yet? Have they got him?'

'Who?' asked Sir Ecgbert. 'Have they got *who*?'

'Whom,' corrected Lady Tode, appearing from nowhere, as usual, although on this occasion, thankfully, without the signature stink. Alice and Ecgbert jumped. She was standing beside Alyster Crowley – towering above him, in fact, in a red satin, floor-length Givenchy evening dress. Alive, she'd been five feet ten. In death, she was, if anything, an inch or two taller. Rubies sparkled in her ears. 'Have they got *whom*, darling,' she said, scowling at her grandson. '*Come on.*'

Mellors said: 'Well it's got all the evidence, hasn't it? And nobody ever said he were stupid ...' He brooded on this awhile, ignoring their pleas to clarify. Then he said: 'Is Livvie all right? Has anyone seen her? Someone should check on her.

She were roaming about last night, poor lass. So God only knows ...'

Ecgbert said: 'For Christ's sake, Mellors, I don't suppose God knows what you're talking about, any more than the rest of us. Can you explain, so we can actually get out of this ridiculous caravan and breathe some fresh air?'

'Norman Wright,' Mellors said at last. 'Who d'you think? He's been skulking and hiding ever since his mum were found dead, hasn't he? Well I found him last night, sure enough. Hiding under Livvie Kellet's trailer, with a phone full of pictures of her in the nude ... Nudie pics,' he said again, unnecessarily. 'Of Livvie Kellet. He's been hiding down there, spying on her. Probably all this time.' He fell silent again.

This was shocking news.

'But I let him get away,' Mellors said. 'God knows, I must have been drunk ... Worse than drunk,' he added. 'Never felt nothing like it. The stupid bastard got away.'

It was Nicola who reacted first. She gasped in – disgust, possibly. Or glee. Or vindication. It was hard to separate the tumult of emotions making merry with the surface of her face, but her cheeks had turned very pink. She said: 'Well, surprise, surprise. Isn't that just *typical*?'

Mellors looked at her, mildly confused. 'Typical of what, Nicola?'

'Seriously?' She shook her head. 'Are you actually asking me that question?'

A pause. 'Aye, I am.'

'With a straight face? No irony. You're asking me what it's typical of?'

A tiny drop of spittle flew from her lips to his lap. He gazed down at it sadly.

'I feel like shit,' he said at last. 'Someone needs to check on Livvie Kellet. Because that man is roaming about, and she's probably not safe until they catch him. Now, please. Can you all fuck off? Thank you very much, and all that … I need to go home.'

Alyster Crowley said: 'Excellent idea, Mr Mellors. I'll give you a lift.'

THE UNIT BASE

SUNDAY

Outside, Crowley said to Thistlestrupp: 'Give me your car keys.'

'How am I going to get back to the hotel?' Thistlestrupp moaned, handing them over.

'Walk,' said Alyster. 'Hop. I don't give a flying fart, as long as you're on set tomorrow morning.' He and Oliver Mellors needed to talk, he said. He didn't add, and to *continue* to talk until either Oliver Mellors dies of exhaustion, or he agrees to return to set.

With Oliver Mellors standing dazed and unhappy beside him, Alyster turned to the assembled crowd. He clapped the pads of his soft hands together to assure everyone's attention, clamped an unwelcome arm around his prisoner, and said: 'Great teamwork, people. You did well. That was a shit-in-the-pants moment we had there, for every single one of us. But we pulled together and between us we made it happen! That's teamwork! I'm proud of you! We are blessed to have Oliver

250

Mellors still with us this morning, alive and well – isn't that right, Mr Mellors? I want you all to *relax* today. You deserve it. And I'll see you all on set 6 a.m. sharp tomorrow. Alright-y? The show must go on!' He gave them a creepy smile and for some sad reason known only to themselves, those that were currently in his employ, namely Thistlestrupp, Snare (Series Producer), Stephanie, KitKat and – most shamingly – the triplets broke into damp applause.

'Hooray for Alyster!' said Stephanie.

'Hooray for what?' Lady Tode asked Ecgbert. 'You're the one who saved the day.'

Sir Ecgbert nodded: 'I'm as confused as you are, Granny.'

Alice, the only person present who could hear the exchange, smiled broadly at both and tried to catch Ecgbert's eye. She wanted to thank him for taking care of the situation with the triplets, but he seemed distracted. Now that the drama was over, he seemed to be in a hurry to get away.

They'd not spoken since last night and, even though she knew this was her fault, it didn't stop her from feeling angry about it. Or was it sad? Alice wasn't a woman who liked to examine her feelings. But after so many breakfasts together, and so little being said, and then – the dance on the grass last night – things had reached a point between them which even she could no longer ignore. She had lost her appetite, which was highly unusual. Also: she missed him. As soon as he left the room, she missed him. Even when he was in the room, she missed him, sometimes, if his mind appeared to be elsewhere. And when he went home and she went to bed, she found herself thinking about him. She thought about him last thing at night, first thing in the morning, and at ten-minute intervals throughout the day.

So.

Alice didn't like relationships. After decades of failed experiments, of inconvenience, hassle, intrusion, messiness, compromise and other disasters, she'd come to the conclusion, about ten years ago, that they simply weren't worth the trouble. Life was complicated and painful enough. So she'd stopped having them. Closed up shop. Refused to play the game. It had been remarkably simple. Alice could barely remember a moment in the last ten years when she had regretted it.

. . . Last night, she and Ecgbert had been dancing, and she'd been lost in the pleasure of the moment: Ecgbert(Sir)'s arms around her waist, the smell of his skin, the soft moonlight and the grass beneath her feet, the hypnotic beat of the music. Everything was perfect. *And then what?* She said she thought she may have left the oven on, which of course she hadn't, and she'd left him standing there, swaying to the chillwave indie-tronica, all on his own in the middle of the party.

He'd followed her back to the Gardener's House and let himself in. He'd stood in the hall and called her name, but Alice had ignored him. She ran herself a bath and went to bed. And in the morning, she'd found him stretched out in the sitting room, too long for the sofa, snoring.

It had been a rough morning. As Alyster had put it, a shit-in-the . . . *he was an awful man.* It had been a very bad morning. She and Ecgbert should have breakfast together and discuss what had happened last night, and discuss other things too, maybe. She probably needed to apologise. It would be a start.

But when she looked across at him and tried to catch his eye, to thank him; to ask him over for breakfast (as if he ever needed to be formally invited), she noticed his gaze slide away.

The sorrow she felt at that moment came as a shock. In

a rare moment of emotional clarity, it occurred to her that her affection for Ecgbert had escalated into something she'd not felt for decades, if ever before: something quite out of control.

'Hey, Ecgbert,' she called out. 'Thank you. For what you did for the boys. *Thank you* . . . Are you coming back for breakfast?' But he was already half a Unit Base away, hands in pockets, head down, muttering to himself about a possible storm.

Mellors sat in Thistlestrupp's car, listening to Crowley's voice as it drilled into his head. He'd never felt so ill. They were parked outside his cottage already, and had been for some time, but the thought of moving his body, and then the thought of being confronted by his empty, wife-less house and his Olympian hangover, all alone, kept him sitting there, pinned to the passenger seat.

When Crowley eventually released him – he helped Mellors to his front door and gave him a little hug which was quite heartfelt – Mellors had agreed to return to the set in the morning. On two conditions. Both conditions having been proposed and accepted by Crowley on Mellors's behalf, without Mellors having to do anything but stare at the windshield, sweat alcohol, and grunt.

On top of his current fee, Mellors would receive a further £150,000. As head keeper at Tode Hall he earned £17,500 a year (with house and car thrown in). So £150,000, though a fraction of what Crowley would be saving by getting him back on the set, was clearly a lot of money. It was also a quarter of what he was paying Oscar-winning Livvie Kellet, and a seventh of what he was paying Oscar-winning Teddy MacIntosh.

The second condition was likely to be more complicated to implement. But Crowley disliked Thistlestrupp in any case. He disliked his smug oatmeal dressing gown, and his smug Nordic manner. So he took some pleasure in assuring Mellors that, as long as Mellors was on set, Thistlestrupp would be forbidden from addressing him directly. When directing a scene, he would have to speak via an intermediary at all times, and with his eyes lowered to the ground.

Crowley and Mellors liked that idea. Even in the depths of his hangover, Mellors managed to chuckle a little bit. They bonded over the prospect of Thistlestrupp's humiliation.

'And no nudity,' Mellors said.

'Absolutely no nudity,' Crowley agreed.

He patted Mellors on the shoulder, climbed out the car and opened the passenger door for him. He settled Mellors into his house, with a promise to send a driver to take him to the set at 6 a.m. the following morning.

'And you take care,' Crowley said. He asked Mellors, before he left, 'Would you like me to send some security to stand outside your door? You think the guy might come back?'

'He won't be back,' said Mellors. 'He's got the phone. So – I expect he's long gone by now. If he's got any sense ... As I say, I think the person you need to look out for is Livvie.'

Crowley nodded. 'Food for thought.'

As he climbed back into Thistlestrupp's car and pointed it back towards the Bellavista Spa Hotel, aforementioned thought nutrition lingered, and developed quite a pleasant aftertaste. Actually, the image of Livvie Kellet, naked in her trailer, being stalked and videoed, and raped and possibly strangled, tickled him enough to keep him tickled for the whole journey. It would be fun to fuck her, he decided. *Why not?* He ran through the movies he had in development at the moment, and wondered which role to dangle in front of her, so that this might be accomplished.

There was *Forgetting Henry*, about an eighteenth-century Syrian-born hermaphrodite with learning difficulties, who – well, who couldn't remember Henry, obviously. She wouldn't want anything to do with that. Crowley didn't either. He wished he hadn't taken it on.

There was *Tea with the Boys*, about Gallipoli or something. But it didn't have any women in it.

There was *Hamlet* . . . They had Will Smith already signed to play Hamlet . . . Could she play Ophelia, perhaps? With good lighting? Fuck it – he drove a little faster. There was no harm in suggesting it, was there? He didn't have to follow through.

THE BELLAVISTA SPA HOTEL
DINING ROOM

SUNDAY

The subdued sounds of English guests, dining in luxury. Too many soft furnishings. Not enough air.

It was much too late for breakfast, and lunch didn't begin for another half hour. The dining room would normally have been closed. But rules in luxury hotels were made to be broken by superstars, and the only two diners in the room were Oscar winners. They were sitting at separate tables, nursing their hangovers, and the misery of fame, wondering which one would buckle first and invite the other to join them.

Livvie Kellet's hands were shaking. She'd spoken to her mother for forty-five minutes already, about the slights that had been piled on in the last twenty-four hours: some vicious insults on Instagram, and a new group on Facebook with 8,086 members already, called LivvieKelletCantAct, and a hideously unflattering picture in the *New York Post*.

She didn't mention her spat with Mellors. It was too humiliating. Thinking about it made her want to cry ... In any case, her mother was kind, and told her she was special. But it hadn't made her feel any better.

They'd brought her egg-white omelette (grilled) and rye bread for breakfast, as ordained by her miserable nutritionist. She pushed it around her plate, and wished ... She wished she could swap lives with the wide-hipped, mumsy-looking waitress who'd brought it over; who had a wedding ring on her fat finger, and badly cut, badly dyed, greasy-looking hair. But a nice face. And a lovely Yorkshire accent, which made everything sound warm and cosy. Livvie had said – burst out – after gushing her thanks for the egg white – 'I expect you wish you were at home with your family, do you, on a Sunday morning like this? Must be a pain, having to work on a Sunday, when you've got family at home.'

The waitress replied, in her lovely Yorkshire accent, that sometimes it was a relief to get away from them.

Livvie nodded, sadly. She said: 'You don't know how lucky you are!'

The waitress thought that was a bit rich, all things considered. But she bit it back. She said: 'Oh, I don't know about that! ... Will there be anything else?'

Livvie said yes, there would. She'd ordered her usual baby spinach and almond milk smoothie. Could she have a little less fresh ginger in it this morning? Because although delicious, yesterday's smoothie had been a bit *too* fresh gingery ...

The waitress said: yes, of course.

Livvie beamed at her again; thanked her from the bottom

of her broken heart; and as the woman bustled away, Livvie wished she'd never become an actress. She wished so many things. She wished she could start all over again.

Instead, she wandered over to Teddy's table and plonked herself down in front of him.

'Hey,' she said.

He said: 'Hey.'

And then they didn't say anything more for a while. Teddy picked up his mobile. The two stars had slept through the dramas of the morning, and had started their days, as they started every day-at-leisure, by googling themselves, and feeling miserable. A message from David Snare just happened to flash up on Teddy's screen as he was refreshing his hashtag on Instagram. (Nobody appeared to have been talking about him much overnight. It was disconcerting.)

David Snare's message read: 'Mellors is fine. Panic off! If u see LK can you ask her to contact asap? Everyone kinda worried she OK. DS'

It was sufficiently intriguing for Teddy to investigate further.

He discovered he had twenty or more messages unread this morning.

'Oh my goodness,' he said, clutching the old ticker, which was ticking normally at that point. 'Liv, darling – have you seen all this?' He was reading the messages backwards. 'Oh my ... Oh me oh my ... They found Mellors in his trailer with SLUT written on his back ... ' Teddy filled the dining room with a peal of laughter. 'Christ alive, Livvie, they actually thought he was dead!'

Livvie's hands were still shaking. When he said that, she was just lifting a wide-brimmed cup of soya-latte-decaf to her lips. The action went wrong, and her drink splashed half onto the linen tablecloth and half onto the egg-white grill, which had just been carried across the room for her by the waitress whose life she had briefly envied.

'My *goodness*,' she said. 'What can you mean?'

'He's fine ... That girl he was shagging in Wardrobe – the one Thistlestrupp was shagging before, who caused all the bad feeling ... she found him in his trailer this morning ... *unconscious* ... Bloody hell ...' He carried on reading. 'This is incredible ...'

He caught her up. Mellors had apparently been bumped on the head with a sharp object. Scribbled on, and left for dead.

She was amazed. Horrified. '*Poor guy!*' she said. 'I mean, he's tricky. He's a tricky guy. His own worst enemy ... but I mean ... SLUT? ... Who would do a thing like that?'

'... Norman Wright, by the sounds of things,' he said. He read on '... Oh dear ... Oh, Livvie ... Oh, darling—' He leaned across the table and clasped her forearm. 'I'm so sorry ... This is *too horrid* ...'

'What?' she said, her voice rising. 'What is too horrid? What's happened?'

He said: 'It's too creepy. I don't want to tell you. Darling, I think you should call Alyster.'

Just then they were interrupted by another wide-hipped serving woman from Yorkshire. This one was dressed in skirt and jacket, and a blouse with feminine yet business-like knotted collar. She bent over the table, polite and apologetic. They were hit with the sweet smell of Burberry for Women. Livvie recognised her as Heather who often worked on reception. Teddy didn't recognise her, and wouldn't next time, either.

Livvie, ever the pro, put on a big smile and said, 'Hello *Heather*! Is everything all right?'

'I'm sorry to intrude, Ms Kellet,' said Heather. 'I just thought I should let you know, there's a lady in reception for you. She says she's Nicola Tode, of the Tode family, of Tode Hall; where I believe you are currently filming? I know you're busy, and that's what I've said to her, but she's a bit upset. She says she just wants to check you're OK. Something about a gentleman who's been following you . . . ?'

Livvie's polite smile stayed fixed to her lovely face. It was hard – impossible – to read what she might have been thinking. She said: 'She wants to see me?'

There came another hyena-like laugh from Teddy. It was disconcerting for him, Livvie getting all the attention. 'Darling,' he said, 'I think she has a teeny crush on you. Try to be kind.'

Heather ignored this. Both the women did. 'I do apologise,' Heather said again. 'I wouldn't trouble you with it. But she seems a bit upset.'

A long pause.

At length Livvie said: 'How sweet. Well, I suppose I can't send her away, can I? You'd better show her in.'

THE GARDENER'S HOUSE

SUNDAY

Alice fretted. Would it be weird to call and ask him over? For dinner, for example? But she never called him – he always called her. Lately, he hardly even did that. He was just always there. Except not today. She'd not seen him since parting company outside Mellors's trailer this morning. He'd marched off across the field towards his own cottage without a backward glance, and Lady Tode had followed him. Alice missed them both, but she missed Ecgbert far more.

She called him.

She said: 'Hey Ecgbert ...' trying to sound casual. Something she usually managed without any trouble. Something she failed to do on this one call. 'Haven't seen you for ages ... I wondered if—'

'What's that?'

'I said—'

'Trudy? Is that you? You never call me! What do you want?'

'I just wanted—'

'HELLO? Trudy? I can't hear you!'

'Can you hear me?'

'No I can't . . . wait a sec, you're breaking up.'

She wasn't breaking up. They were talking on landlines, in houses that were barely two miles apart, and her voice was as clear (and as musical) as a bell. As clear as crystal. As clear and musical as a heavenly crystal ball or bell. The sound of it made Ecgbert's heart soar. He just needed a moment to collect himself. He didn't want to blow it. So he hung up.

She wondered whether she should call back, or whether she should take it as a hint that he didn't want to come to dinner. Not that she'd asked him yet. On the other hand, she didn't usually need to ask. He just came. The fact that he didn't, probably only went to show—

He called her back. 'Ah,' he said, before she had a chance to speak. 'That's much better. What were you saying, Trudy? What did you call me to ask about? I hope I can help.'

She giggled. He sounded mad. She said, 'Ecgbert, I just wondered where you'd got to . . . I wondered if you might come over for supper. It's . . . I'm cooking . . . ' Alice was a very good cook. Not that Ecgbert noticed. 'Well, it's only pasta again. But . . . I wanted to thank you for everything you did this morning. For the boys.'

'Oh, that,' he said. He sounded disappointed. 'It was nothing.'

'It was not nothing.'

'I must admit, Trudy, I'm not very hungry at the moment. So I think I'll just stay at home and, you know, do my own thing. Sorry. What is it you girls say? I'm going to stay in and wash my hair.'

'They don't say that,' Alice said. 'They really don't. Please

262

come to dinner, Ecgbert ...' She took a deep breath. 'Last night. When I disappeared off ... and left you standing there. I'm really sorry about that. I don't know what happened.'

'Perfectly all right,' he said, very loudly, the better to make it believable.

'No it wasn't all right, and I'm sorry. The weed was quite strong, and I thought ... But I can't blame the weed. I know I can't ... Listen, the boys have gone to the pub. They're definitely avoiding me after this morning and I'm not sure I blame them ... *Please* – come over as soon as you can, and we can talk, just us two, before they come in.'

'I'm on my way!' he cried.

It took him five minutes to get there. The long drive that lay between their two houses was all on Tode land, and though Ecgbert hadn't yet passed his driving test, he had a new car parked outside (on which he practised, daily; it was all part of his new life, post the arrival of Alice at the Hall, and the death of his disagreeable mother). Alice was upstairs putting on mascara when his car skidded to its halt.

But it was too much to hope that they might actually get some time alone. Alice and he welcomed each other, without touching, or even locking eyes, and then Alice shuffled off to the fridge to open some wine. By the time she retrieved it, put out two glasses, and Ecgbert was back in his usual place at the kitchen table, Lady Tode had emerged from wherever she'd been hiding. She placed herself at the kitchen table, beside her grandson, and sat there expectantly, with the usual straight back, sparkling earlobes and sweepy chignon, looking only slightly as if she suspected she might not be welcome. When Ecgbert saw her he groaned.

'Granny!' he said. 'Why are you always here?'

'Because,' she said, 'this is my home. Also I wanted to be sure you two patched things up.'

'It's none of your business, Granny,' Ecgbert said.

'And no, it's not the match one had in mind. Of course it isn't. On the other hand ...' She eyeballed Ecgbert in an intense manner. 'On the other hand ... I do think that Alice, despite one's obvious objections ... I do think that Alice [she tried again] ... *despite* one's obvious objections ... is ... really ... She ...' Lady Tode fell silent. In the end, she was too grand to finish what she'd started. But the gap she left was filled with great and unusual warmth.

Ecgbert was unmoved. 'Please,' he said. 'Go away!'

It was a bad tactic. 'Certainly not,' she snapped. 'What a thing to say to your grandmother.'

Alice said: 'Ecgbert has a point ...'

'Nonsense!' she said. She was offended now; evidenced by the usual seepage of green gases from neckline and, on this occasion, armpits. An awkward pause followed. Lady Tode looked extremely unhappy. It was hard for her to make an exit now, without losing dignity. '... I'll go in a moment,' she said after a while. 'I just wanted to be sure you two were "all right". As it were. After this morning ... and those silly, naughty boys. And Ecgbert, being such a hero.' She turned to Alice. 'I don't think you fully appreciate ...'

'Oh, I do!' cried Alice. 'I really do! My boys would probably be in a police cell right now, if it wasn't for you, Ecgbert.'

Ecgbert waved it aside. He was embarrassed.

'What those young men need,' said Lady Tode, '*without wishing to state the obvious*, is a stretch in the army. Somewhere absolutely vile.' With a limp wave, she encompassed ... all the vilest places on the planet. 'Get them marching. A bit of early-morning marching would do them no end of good.'

Alice said: 'I don't think they would agree to it.'

'Of course the army probably wouldn't take them ... You could *beat* them,' suggested Lady Tode, without much conviction. ' ... Or starve them ... Darling girl, you have so many options.'

She was prevented from listing them by the telephone. India was calling to ask after Mellors.

'Oh I just *knew* he'd be OK!' India declared, when Alice caught her up with the news. 'Don't ask me how, but I knew it, didn't I say so Eggie?' Alice heard him mumbling confirmation. 'And how is poor little Nicola, Alice?' India continued. 'I've been hatching plans, by the way! I'm taking her on a daytrip to Leeds and we're literally going to *do* the Leeds Harvey Nics. It's got a spa. I think. Haven't checked. And I'm paying, so she won't be able to say no, will she? By the time I've finished with her that lady's going to look and feel like a superstar! How is she, anyway?'

Alice said: 'Oh, Nicola's fine. She was a bit upset about the stalking thing ... but that's ... you know ... she's fine. More or less.'

Alice didn't want to talk about Nicola. Or Harvey Nichols. Right now, she didn't even want to talk about the triplets. She just wanted some time, alone, with Ecgbert, so they could work a few things out.

The front door opened and slammed shut, making the old house shake. From the hall there came more banging, crashing and youthful laughter, followed by exaggerated shushing sounds and muffled giggles. The triplets were back from the pub.

India chattered on. They'd taken longer than expected getting off Paxos because of a storm, she explained, so they were spending the night at an airport hotel outside Athens which the children absolutely adored because there was an indoor soft-play area in the basement which was ...

By then the triplets had spotted Ecgbert and were deep in conversation. They'd come home early from the pub, hoping to find him, they said. They felt so bad about the troubles they'd caused, they wanted to spend extra time thanking him, and apologising to their mother.

'Your ma is very angry with you,' Ecgbert was saying. 'I don't blame her.'

'We know it,' they chorused. 'We're just so, so, like *so* grateful to you ...'

Ecgbert had a brainwave. He glanced at Alice, still on the phone, wading through the goodbyes. He lowered his voice. 'I tell you what, lads,' he said. 'If you feel like repaying the favour ...'

'Yes! You bet we do. Absolutely. Hundred and ten per cent! We were only saying so just now, in the pub. Weren't we? Ask us anything!'

'It's a bit risky,' Ecgbert said. 'And if you get caught, you must never admit it was me who sent you ... Is that clear?'

'*On Our Death*,' they repeated warmly.

Drez mimed the zipping of his lips.

'Right then,' Ecgbert said. 'Come and see me first thing tomorrow morning, and I'll tell you what I want you to do.'

LIVVIE'S TRAILER

MONDAY

The weather didn't break on the Sunday, as everyone had hoped it would. This morning, the sky was heavy and grey and the air felt like a Turkish bath: the sweatiest it had been all summer. For the first morning in about fifteen years, Livvie had not telephoned her mother. Not even once. And her mother was very worried. Livvie's daily – thrice daily – misery-updates had become something of an albatross around her mother's neck, but it was nothing to the silence she left this morning. Not only had Livvie not checked in, she was ignoring her mother's calls. By 10.30 a.m. her mother was so worried, she'd telephoned Livvie's agent, and left a message begging him to tell Livvie to make contact.

The message presumably hadn't got through, because Livvie was at that moment on the phone to him; doing ab-strengtheners on the thick-carpeted floor of her trailer in pants and T-shirt, telling him the amazing news about Crowley offering her the role of Ophelia.

The Agent (who, like the Mother, need only be known here in terms of What He Does For Livvie) was trying, as tactfully as possible, to get to the heart of this surprise offer. Alyster Crowley had a long and dark record when it came to the casting couch, and – as far as the agent was concerned – it was likely only a matter of time before his career came crashing, as a result of it. And now here was Livvie Kellet, twenty-odd years in the business, jabbering like a schoolgirl about the possibility of being cast for a role that every young actress in Hollywood was vying for.

Livvie was too old to play Ophelia. Who was she kidding?

The agent said: 'That's terrific news, Livvie ... He's just *offered you the part*, has he?'

'I mean,' Livvie said, not listening to him at all, 'there is seriously no reason why this shouldn't be an Oscar opp. God, wouldn't that be great? What I could do with another Oscar at this point. It's actually *exactly* what my career needs right now. Plus, as I said to Alyster, I've always, always wanted to play Ophelia!'

Had she indeed. 'All righty,' said the agent. 'Terrific, Livvie. I'm going to call Alyster now, see what I can find out, and I'll get right back to you—'

A knock on Livvie's trailer door.

Livvie leapt to her feet. Noticed she was sweating.

It was the man himself. Also sweating. Bearing a small box of Baci.

'Yeah sure. Got to go,' said Livvie. 'Don't do anything yet. OK? Nothing's definite yet.'

'But—'

She hung up, fixed her smile and the neckline of her T-shirt, and opened the trailer door.

'Baci?' she said huskily. 'For *moi*? Gosh, Alyster, you of all people know I mustn't eat chocolate.'

'Huh? Oh. Sure you can eat chocolate, baby,' he said, and stepped up into the trailer to join her.

THE ATLAS FOUNTAIN

MONDAY, 3.30 P.M.

A big scene. Lots of emotion. The first for Mellors since he'd walked off the set and walked back on again. Thistlestrupp had to direct, as per the new agreement, without looking at or speaking to him directly. Also required in this scene were the two Oscar winners. And this was especially difficult because in a way the scene didn't belong to either of them. It was Mellors's scene. The Oscar winners were only present to enable it. So.

Add to that the unusually heavy weather and the still-missing murder suspect, and the mood was fraught. The sky was grey; the light was horrible. Also, which had already ruined what Teddy MacIntosh swore was his best take, in the distance there could be heard an occasional rumble of thunder.

So they were going for a retake.

In this scene, with the fountain flowing, and the great Tode Hall looming magnificently in the background:

Livvie (Lady Steph) and Teddy (Lord Tintin), whose

characters are both in love with Mellors, have to listen to Mellors (Lord Greystoke) explain why he's decided to become a nun.

None of this really matters. Rapunzel Piece, were she not held up in the morgue, would be turning in her grave. More to the point, there were technical difficulties for the actors, who needed to make themselves heard over the flowing water. The scene involved a lot of dialogue. A certain amount of tears, kissing and other forms of physical embrace; and throughout (which was important) everyone needed to remain winsome and fetching. In summary, there was a lot of this and a lot of that around the Atlas Fountain, on this day of days: a lot of egos, a lot of history, a lot of wounded feelings within the story and behind the scenes, and a lot of thunder in the air.

Also present, recently arrived from their Greek paradise, were India, Egbert(Mr) and the children. They glowed with good health and happy natures. They had stopped off at the Gardener's House to catch up on the news, and – on learning that such a big scene was to be filmed only 200 yards from the door – had dragged Alice to come with them to watch. Ecgbert(Sir) had spotted them as he crossed the lawn on his way to calling on Alice, and had diverted his route to join them.

He caused a ruckus almost at once by sitting himself in an empty folding chair which had been specifically reserved for Alyster, who wasn't present. As soon as he realised his *faux pas* he summoned his little cousins, Ludo and Passion. 'I'll give you a hundred quid,' he said to them, 'if you toddle to the stick room, where we keep the bows and arrows and the cricket bats and fishing rods and any other long, thin sporting items you can think of, except guns obviously – are you aware of the stick room? It is behind the boot room, as I am sure you know. I want you to bring back as many shooting sticks as you can carry. At least four, or the deal's off. More than eight, and that's too many. Off you go.'

The children, very young and unused to being useful, looked dumbly at their older cousin, and didn't move.

'Go along, you idiots!' he said.

'Crikey,' said Egbert(Mr). 'A hundred quid seems a lot. I'll do it for a hundred quid!'

Laughs all round. The children scampered off, soon to be distracted by something more interesting, and never to return with shooting sticks.

Livvie Kellet was a pro, as previously noted. And when the camera rolled she was as brilliant as ever. But between takes, she was not herself. She was sulky and strangely jumpy. Uncharacteristically unfriendly, too. She had yet to acknowledge Mellors's existence at all.

After the fourth take, and some slow-mo muttering between Thistlestrupp and his various assistant directors, it had been decided that they needed to alter the camera position. This involved moving lights and reconstructing a short length of tracking, and it was going to take some time. Not quite enough time for the stars to return to their trailers, yet long enough for them to feel spare.

Oliver Mellors remembered everything he said and saw on the night someone hit him on the head. He remembered Norman Wright slipping through his fingers, and the nudie pics of Livvie; he remembered how drunk he had become, so quickly, and concluded, quite rightly, that his drink had been spiked, though by whom he was yet to guess.

There were two things about that horrible night that he couldn't get out of his head:

Letting Norman slip through his fingers; and calling Livvie Kellet a slut.

He'd not believed her, when she'd first complained about Norman in the larder. To be fair, nobody had (except for Nicola). Livvie had never been anything but friendly and welcoming to him: perhaps too friendly and too welcoming. But that was hardly the worst offence. He watched her now. She looked so nervous, and so unhappy – and no wonder, with Norman Wright still on the loose. He realised he felt sorry for her. Also – perhaps for the first time in his adult life – he wanted to apologise.

He considered his approach.

She was sitting on the stone ledge by the water's edge, with her back to everyone, her phone in her hand, pretending to read a book.

Oliver Mellors stepped up to her. 'Hey,' he said. She didn't look up. 'What're you reading?'

She closed the book, keeping her thumb on the page, and held up the cover:

Hamlet

By

William Shakespeare

She said, 'You probably haven't heard of it.'

Mellors laughed. 'Haven't heard of *Hamlet*?' he said. 'To be or not to be … Everyone's heard of *Hamlet*, Livvie.'

She continued to pretend to read.

He hovered beside her, very awkward now, glanced around sheepishly, to be sure he wasn't observed, shuffled a half foot closer, dropped his voice. He said, 'Livvie, I'm really sorry . . .'

She continued to read.

'I mean I'm really, really sorry. About everything. That I let that bastard slip through my hands . . . And that I didn't look after the phone, so you could have it safe in your hands now, and you wouldn't have to be worrying.'

She turned over a page. 'Forget it,' she said. 'I have.'

She stared at the page. (*Yet here, Laertes! Aboard, aboard for shame! The wind sits in the* . . . Wait. Who was Laertes again?)

' . . . And I'm sorry . . . about what I called you . . .'

Still, nothing.

'I were in a state. But it's no excuse. I had no business . . .'

'Forget it,' she said again.

Another long pause. Mellors wasn't prepared to give up just yet. He felt sorry for her, sitting there, pretending to read Shakespeare. Livvie struck him, just then, as a sad figure: lonely and insecure. He thought of the looming absence of Norman Wright, and how it must be frightening for her. So he mumbled:

'Can't hide for ever, Livvie, you know that don't you? They must have the scent by now.'

Her head shot up. 'What?'

'I said—'

'I heard what you said. What the hell do you mean?'

'I mean . . . Well. What I said. I hope they catch him soon.'

A pause, while she recalibrated. Her face relaxed, and she laughed.

'Oh! . . . Sorry! I thought . . . I don't know what I thought.

I'm just so tired, you know ...? Never mind! Anyway ...'
She smiled at him, at last. Blinding bright. 'Your apology is
accepted ... And I'm sorry I came barging in on you, when
you obviously needed to be alone.'

Mellors, thoroughly confused, but feeling better, smiled and
shrugged and shuffled away, back to his notepad and the letter
he'd been writing to his wife since yesterday, begging her to
come home.

TODE GALLERY LANDING
(WEST WING)

MONDAY

The ceiling was very high, and the boys' whispered voices were echoing outrageously over the upstairs gallery (West Wing). Or so it seemed to them. They kept telling each other to *Shhh*, and that sound, in particular, seemed to bounce like a cymbal off the ceiling. Nevertheless they had promised Ecgbert they would do this, and they were boys of their word.

Morman said: 'This is scary.'

Drez said: 'Seriously, Morman. Stop using S's!' And his angry words pinged this way and that, making the upstairs gallery sound like a snake pit.

So far as they could tell, everyone was outside by the fountain. Or at any rate, everyone they needed to worry about. Except Carfizzi, Kveta (the housekeeper) and Nicola. The problem was, you never knew where the CCTV was in this house, nor how much of it was ever switched on. Ecgbert(Sir) had assured them that security around the house was much less heavy now that the house and gardens were closed to the public. Even so – how could they be sure?

They stood together, three sweet-natured lads in comfortable clothing, gazed down upon from every wall by portraits of ill-natured Todes. They were out of their depth.

Jacko said: 'I think we should call Ecgbert ... explain that it's basically impossible ...'

A wisp of green smoke appeared beside them. They didn't see it, of course. But they smelled it.

Drez sniffed. They all sniffed.

Morman said: 'Who farted?'

They argued about that for a while. Not for too long. In the meantime Lady Tode sailed on past. There was a limit to what she could achieve, of course (not that she would admit to that). But her grandson Ecgbert(Sir) had made some observations, and while these useless boys stood on the landing, squabbling, she would do some investigating of her own.

Outside, a loud clap of thunder sent a warning to the crew that unless they hurried, they might get caught in a downpour.

And then the good news came through. It was Egbert(Mr) who got the call.

'Oh I must say that's terrific news!' he said loudly.

'Quiet please! We're going for a take. Cameras rolling ...'

'ABSOLUTELY TERRIFIC!' yelled Egbert(Mr), whose voice was loud at the best of times. 'GREAT JOB! CONGRATULATIONS! I'll pass on the good news ...

277

Where did you find him? ... *MY GOODNESS* ... Well, I never! What a nerve! He got that far, did he? Good, good. Fabulous news. Thanks so much for letting us know. There'll be a few characters here at Tode Hall who will be very relieved to hear it!'

Norman had been apprehended at last. He'd been spotted by an off-duty officer, ordering a cup of tea in the buffet bar on the 14:43 train to London. He was wearing a beanie hat and sunglasses and – apparently – he stank. It was the tramp-like stink, according to the reporting officer, which had given him away.

Egbert(Mr) broke the news, and on hearing it, everyone cheered. A few of them went up to Livvie and put their arms around her. She was smiling so wildly her face looked in danger of splitting apart.

Alice muttered to India, who was standing beside her, 'She looks terrified, poor thing. She looks like she's going to cry.'

'She does, doesn't she?' India agreed. 'You'd think she'd be happy.'

After the first round of cheering and hugs had subsided, Egbert(Mr) told the assembled crowd that although they had captured the man, unfortunately his mobile phone was still missing. He looked at Livvie. 'Which of course ... in any case ...' he gave an apologetic, embarrassed grimace, knowing that she knew, he knew, they knew, everyone was thinking about her naked photographs, at that moment. Or at any rate, he certainly was, which was excruciating for both of them. Also, probably not fair on India. 'Fear not!' he shouted. 'The hunt continues! No doubt it'll turn up under a tree or something ... Or possibly never turn up at all. We don't know. Just er ... That's the only unfortunate part, really. All in all, I think we can sleep easier tonight.' And then he smiled at Livvie. 'Especially you, Livvie. If I may say so ...'

She didn't smile back.

THE PINEAPPLE ROOM

MONDAY

Nicola sat at her desk and gazed dolefully over the park. She could see the Atlas Fountain from where she sat; almost perfectly framed. She could hear the claps of thunder, and the soft, drab murmur of the film crew, though they were too far off for any words to be distinct. She'd seen Egbert(Mr) and India join the throng, and the children running off towards the house. She referred to them, in her mind, as 'the sprogs'. She didn't like them and sincerely hoped they wouldn't come to disturb her. They had no respect. They were spoilt. Or loved. Or young. Or something, anyway, which made her feel sad and excluded. She heard the sound of people cheering, and watched jealously as crew members embraced each other. They embraced Livvie. Well, of course they did. Everyone loved Livvie.

Because they didn't know her.

Nicola sighed and turned back to her work.

Her chapter title was a long one but, she felt, a culmination of her work to this point. The most important chapter she had written yet. She gazed at the words, gazing back at her on the page:

Violance Against Women <u>MUST</u> be Counterred with Violance by WOMEN!
When a cis or otherwize 'woman' is lost in the cis or otherwize male situation, 'she' and 'they' immediately forfits her/their right as 'a woman', but becomes property of the male universe, and thereby hostile to the female cause and what the male eye calls a slutt. I have had painful insight into this situation in the recent weeks, at a time when I was feeling extremely vulnerable ...

Nicola's hand ached. Also her heart. She wrote a few more lines, as if possessed, and when she could bear the ache no more, she laid down the pen. She wasn't sure how much more of anything she could take. Of human cruelty, and fickleness, and dishonesty and stupidity. She felt, at that moment, more alone than ever before.

This morning she'd woken early, full of life and laughter, because Livvie could do that to civilians, just by smiling at them, and pretending to be interested in what they were saying. Yesterday, she – and Teddy, too (who was less toxic than most cis or otherwise 'men', despite having gone to Harrow, due to his LGBTQ+ credentials) – had welcomed her to their Sunday breakfast at the Bellavista Hotel. She'd sat down with them and ordered some porridge and the three of them had discussed every subject under the sun: homophobia, misogyny, white privilege, greenhouse gases, unconscious bias. And there was nothing they had disagreed on! And the

281

porridge was so good, and Livvie had told Nicola that she believed one day, everyone, everywhere would be equal, and Nicola had said:

'Yes!'

Nicola had glowed. Livvie could do that to people, and so could Teddy, no matter how empty they felt inside. It was their bread and butter. It was how they won their Oscars.

That feeling – only yesterday – while they breakfasted together, the two Oscar winners and Nicola, may have only lasted ten minutes, but they were the happiest ten minutes of Nicola's adult life. And then along thudded Alyster Crowley in his baggy shorts. Livvie switched her attention to Alyster, who barely acknowledged Nicola's presence, and the three of them talked about the schedule tomorrow, and about Mellors agreeing to come back to finish the movie.

'I'm just so relieved,' Teddy said, though he wasn't. 'Poor, darling Mellors! What a thing to happen! I do believe that guy has a truly *great* career ahead of him. Don't you?'

Nicola finished her porridge and plodded back to her car soon afterwards.

But not before Alyster Crowley said to Livvie that he wanted to have dinner with her to discuss a very exciting new project. Nicola asked: 'Why do you have to discuss it over dinner?' because even then, she was suspicious; and jealous, too. *She* wanted to discuss exciting projects over dinner with Livvie. Of course she did. In any case, nobody seemed to hear the question, because nobody replied.

As Lady Tode seeped through Nicola's bedroom door, her accompanying smell masked, in this room, by the unscrubbed smell of Nicola herself, and the piles of her dirty leggings strewn across the floor, Nicola turned to her laptop. It was open beside the handwritten masterpiece, and as she touched it, the sleeping screen sprung back to light.

It opened onto her photo album, and a video in freeze-frame, freshly uploaded.

'Oh, good *Lord*,' exclaimed Lady Tode, looking over Nicola's shoulder.

Nicola tapped the screen and the video started moving.

'Oh my Lord. Oh *dear*. ... *Oh really* ... Too disgusting!' Lady Tode sighed a gust of otherworldly despair. Nicola felt a welcome chill course through the room, and shivered. 'Poor Nicola,' said Lady Tode – to herself, of course: no one else could hear her. She didn't much like her granddaughter. She didn't like the way she dressed or spoke or thought or moved. On the other hand, she was family. She was a Tode, and watching Nicola watch the video filled her with great sadness.

Livvie should have learned to draw her curtains by now. First there was Norman and his camera, and now there was Nicola. The video had been taken through the window of Livvie's trailer: grainy and badly framed – but the gist was clear enough.

There was Livvie, in the pants and T-shirt she had been wearing this morning, the box of Baci on the table beside her. There she was, on her knees, one of the greatest actresses of her generation: delving inside Alyster Crowley's baggy shorts, smiling and licking her lips, as if there was nothing in the world she more wanted to be doing.

Nicola's phone rang. Lady Tode noticed there were two

283

phones on her desk. The nearest was flashing Ecgbert's name. Nicola, with a disagreeable sigh, picked it up.

'What d'you want?' she said. 'I'm busy.'

Out of her window she could see him in the distance, looking up towards her. He waved. She didn't wave back.

'Thought you might like to know, they've got Norman. They found him ordering tea at the buffet on the 14:43 to London . . .'

He waited to hear her response, but she didn't offer one. She was breathing heavily.

'You all right?' he asked. 'Why don't you come down? Everyone else is down here. Come and join us. Stop hiding away, you funny old bat,' he said affectionately. 'Come down and celebrate with us!'

She hung up. Muttered something to herself. (Lady Tode couldn't catch it.) She paced the carpet, bit her nails, swore under her breath, and abruptly left the room.

She stomped along the Gallery Landing, in a world of her own, past the triplets who heard her coming and hid themselves, ineptly, behind an exceptional ivory-inlaid *armoire*, added to the Tode collection by the 3rd Baronet on his Great Shopping Tour of the Northern States in 1786. She didn't notice them. Not the triplets, nor the *armoire*. Nicola had been stomping past it, on and off, for fifty-plus years, and she hadn't noticed it yet.

The triplets waited, breathless, until her footsteps faded.

'She's gone downstairs,' Morman whispered. 'I think we should do it.'

One by one, they crept out from behind the armoire. Morman led the way. The room would be easy to find, Ecgbert(Sir) had assured them. The name was on the door. In any case, they'd just seen Nicola walk out of it. Slowly, silently, they slipped inside.

Lady Tode had to admit that she was pleased to see them.

Or she would have been, if they weren't being so half baked. Ecgbert had explained very clearly what he needed them to do; she had been there when he instructed them: find Nicola's book – the memoir/self-help book she claimed to be writing, and bring it to him. And there it was, lying wide open on the desk. But the three boys were so nervous they couldn't seem to see it. They weren't even looking in the right direction.

They needed to see the book. They needed to see what was on Nicola's computer, too. And yet there they stood, goggling at the four-poster bed, as if they'd never actually seen one before. It was too frustrating. Worse than that. Lady Tode couldn't turn over pages or start computers, or move objects or make herself heard by anyone not predisposed.

But she could read – of course. She had read the page that lay open on her granddaughter's desk – the last few lines she had scribbled, even, as Lady Tode had watched her doing it. And Lady Tode had come to the conclusion that the girl was out of control. She needed to be stopped.

Meanwhile the boys just stood there, gawping. A wisp of green smoke seeped from her ears, and still they gawped. A blast of green smoke puffed from her nostrils. Still nothing. A most noxious smell filled the room. The idiot boys sniffed the air and giggled and squabbled. Lady Tode thought she might explode with the frustration. And so she did – in her own way. Or, rather, implode; which is what tended to happen in her spirit state, at times of intense emotion. Her body began to lose its shape; to twist and stretch, as if caught in the middle of a tornado. Some small reflection of all this supernormal activity caught a breeze in the physical world, in the Pineapple Room. The boys turned to the window at last, just as the green vapour evaporated, the desk shook, the computer sprung to life, and Norman's mobile telephone dropped to the floor.

'Wowser,' said Jacko. 'Did you see that?'

Morman said: 'There's the book!'

They crowded around it and read – the last few lines. In purple ink. In capitals. Underlined.

> *... Slutts are NOT women but any people who WEAKEN the cause of women, and we <u>CANNOT</u> have space for 'them' in our battleground, as they have to be <u>taken out</u>, eg as I did with RAPUNZEL. Sadly I realize I have to return to the 'battle field' again: as I am what I call The Tode with Modern Twist, as it seems I am the 'shining LIGHT' fighting alone for this cause ...*

'Fuuuuck,' murmured Drez. 'Are you reading this? We have a *Major* Crazy Alert, my men. Ecgbert was right.'

'Of course he was right!' snapped Lady Tode, back in one piece again. 'Now take the book, and the computer, and the mobile *and get out of here*!'

But they couldn't hear her.

'She's nuts ...' said Jacko. He flicked back the pages – pages and pages of purple ink and capitals, and angry scribbled drawings. 'Holy cow ... This is *serious* ...'

'Let's just get it and get the hell out of here,' said Morman.

Too late. Footsteps in the gallery. Trudge, trudge, trudge. The triplets scrambled for cover. As the door opened, the last of their limbs tucked under the bed, and the valance fell back into place.

She plodded through the room, looking neither left nor right. In her arms she carried a longbow, longer than she was, and a single arrow. She plodded across the carpet to the open window, squeezed herself and the longbow around the side of the desk, balanced her elbows on the window ledge and took aim.

A clap of thunder filled the room.

THE ATLAS FOUNTAIN

MONDAY, 4.01 P.M.

*C*ut!

The take would have been perfect, but for the thunderclap. Rain was imminent now: it would be the first to fall on this corner of Yorkshire in more than two months. People could already feel drops on their skin.

Livvie did some breathing; some limb loosening. It was tough for an actor, to drum up the same emotional energy over and over again. But she didn't complain. This was her job, after all. She stood, waiting for the retake, one hand trailing in the fountain, as the director wanted, the other hand fanning her hot face. To one side stood Mellors, also acting well, and to the other, Teddy MacIntosh, quite fed up, because the scene wasn't about him.

The camera was set fifteen or so yards in front of Livvie, between the Hall and the fountain. Alice and India stood to one side of the camera, Ecgbert(Sir) and Egbert(Mr) on the other, all four growing a little bored by now, waiting for something to happen. When Alice felt the first rain on her skin, she grimaced. Maybe after the next take, it would be time to go in.

'Nice and quiet please. We're going for a take.'

'... Cameras rolling ...'

'Speed ...'

'Slate 161 ... Take 6 ...'

'Action!'

There came a low rumble from the ground: not thunder – it was nothing like thunder. The earth beneath them shook. Everyone felt it. Lady Tode's voice filled the space, but only Ecgbert and Alice heard it. It was a roar so loud, so urgent, it made their hair stand on end; it shot through their eardrums, and simultaneously both grabbed to cover their ears. They looked up at the house; saw the open window, heard Lady Tode's unearthly roar:

'NOOOOOOOO!'

They saw Nicola at the window, her red beret bobbing, and a glint of metal, as the arrow left the bow. They saw it together; and they knew where it was headed; and they leapt towards it, simultaneously. They flew through the air towards each other, leaping and stretching towards that flying arrow.

There was Livvie, centre frame, aghast. She saw the arrow soaring through the air, heading straight for her heart. And time ... stood still.

Alice landed first. *Thump*. Onto the grey grass at Livvie's feet. Ecgbert landed on top of her. There was a final clap of thunder as he landed and at long last, the rain broke. The rain poured. Ecgbert had caught the arrow in his teeth.

Alice looked at Ecgbert through the torrent, and Ecgbert looked at Alice. She reached up, and took the arrow from his mouth.

'You saved her!' he said.

'No, *you* did!' she said.

He said: 'I love you Trudy. I've been trying to say it for ages.'

She said: 'I know you have. And I love you too.'

And *he* said: 'Is it still raining? I hadn't noticed.'

And Noah Thistlestrupp shouted, 'CUT!'

From: India Tode

To: AlgieB, Antonia (family), Arabella, Alex,
Alexandra, Archie R, Archie C-S, Archie D, Aiden McR,
Avery S, Bella, Boo, and 419 more . . .

Subject: Happy Christmas!!!!

Hello all you special people!

Well it's been QUITE a year here at Tode Hall! I think
'good and bad' might be one way to sum it up! On
the 'good' side, Ludo finally learnt to swim without
his armbands. Superproud Mum here! And Passion is
doing her level best to catch up. She says she wants
to be the youngest young lady in the universe to
grow lettuces on Mars! So — Eggie and I are just so
proud of her pioneering spirit. Next stop, Number 10
Downing Street, I should think!

Meanwhile Eggie's completed his Paraguay triathlon,
and he was really pleased because he actually
beat his personal record in the biking section.

So we were all very pleased about that. Loads of celebrating!

Also we have a new member of the family, a gorgeous little Labrador puppy! After much discussion, Ludo and Passion insisted on naming him Pepper, after their least favourite food flavouring! (Don't ask!!!!)

Another good piece of news is that cousin Nicola has come home from Green Springs Rehab in Arizona literally feeling SO positive and determined to 'get on' with things, now that everything has calmed down. Luckily there was no evidence to show any 'wrongdoing' as it were, as tragically her brilliant self-help memoir which they kept banging on about in the newspapers was never found! Also, though you might have read some *very* nasty articles, she was never anywhere near the larder at the time of the accident involving the tragical Rapunzel Piece, who we all miss so much, and whose death remains one of life's 'great unsolved mysteries'. Also despite a 'near miss' dreadful tragedy and accident involving a bow and arrow, which you probably *also* read about in the papers, the courts proved very clearly that her arm slipped and she didn't mean any harm. Therefore, all's well that ends well! Nicola has decided she wants to live with us here at Tode Hall, although we are hoping she might take up the offer of a house on the estate, as we all feel it would be better for her health and well-being, to live in a house of her own.

And finally the other piece of good news is that you can soon have a good goggle at our fab house on the box, as the TV show of *Prance to the Music in Time* is due to be released on our screens this summer.

Watch this space!

So in fact now that I think about it, there isn't any bad news! Except obviously we are all super-sad about Rapunzel.

Happy Christmas everyone!

Love from

Eggie, India, Passion, Ludo — and not forgetting Pepper the puppy! XXXXX

ACKNOWLEDGEMENTS

A million thanks to Anna Boatman and to all the team at Piatkus; to Clare Alexander, Ned Cranborne, Peter La Terriere, Nick and Vicky Howard, Zebedee and Bashie. And special thanks, as always, to Panda the Great.